DEATH ON C[illegible]

Also By Jo Allen

Death on Dark Waters
Death at Eden's End

DEATH ON COFFIN LANE

A DCI Satterthwaite Mystery

Jo Allen

An Aria Book

This edition first published in the United Kingdom in 2020 by Aria, an imprint of Head of Zeus Ltd

A CIP catalogue record for this book is available from the British Library.

ISBN 9781035903634

Typeset by Siliconchips Services Ltd UK

Cover design: Debbie Clement

Aria
c/o Head of Zeus
First Floor East
5–8 Hardwick Street
London EC1R 4RG

www.ariafiction.com

To Alan, Ian and Elen.

AUTHOR'S NOTE

All of the characters in this book—barring, of course, the Wordsworths and other historical figures—are figments of my imagination and bear no resemblance to anyone alive or dead.

The same can't be said for the locations. Many are real but others are not. I've taken several liberties with geography, sometimes where the plot required it, and sometimes because I have a superstitious dread of setting a murder in a real building without the express permission of the homeowner. So, for example, you won't find Jude's home village of Wasby on the map; you will find the village of Grasmere, but you won't be able to locate many of the individual locations within it, such as Cody's cottage, the New Age camp and the hotel where Cody delivered her talk.

I hope the many fans of the Lake District will understand, and can find it in their hearts to forgive me!

Prologue

The first thing Cody saw was the noose.

She'd thought the kitchen empty, but as she flicked the switch on the wall the light illuminated the rope Owen held coiled loosely around his outstretched hand. The rest of him, hanging back, betrayed his cowardice. Even before she'd finished processing the scene she knew she had him on the run, ramming home her advantage with the speed of a prairie rattlesnake. 'What the goddamned hell do you think you're doing?'

She was quick but not quite quick enough and he jumped away from her in shock, thrusting the rope behind his back as she snatched at it. Owen was a pasty youth, too much in thrall to his books to fritter away precious hours in daylight. There was barely any colour in his face on the best of days and what there was had drained away the second they both understood that whatever he'd planned for her was doomed to fail.

But he tried. Give him his due, he tried.

'Bitch.' He forced the word out but his voice shook when he must have intended it to intimidate. Then, to her surprise, he launched himself, not towards her as she'd expected, but at the table in the centre of the room. A modern light fitting hung from the heavy oak beam which, black with age, supported the old slate roof of the single-storey cottage. His movement set the cord leaping as if in alarm, so that shadows danced around the edges of the kitchen where under-unit lights normally kept them at bay. In its spotlight, Owen clutched at the table's edge, his knuckles the whitest part of his pale poet's fingers. 'Come here. I've had enough. You've bullied me long enough…'

Cody laughed. If there was one thing she'd learned growing up in Wyoming it was how to tell when a man was capable of handling a rope and Owen, running the rough hemp loosely between his twitching fingers as if it were woven from poison ivy, wouldn't last half an hour out on the range. 'Honey, spare me. I don't have time for this. I have two hundred people coming to listen to me tomorrow morning and we need to be ready. If you want to talk to me about your employment conditions, fine. We'll do it later.'

As the light stilled, the kitchen lost its air of menace. Sure of his impotence, she turned her back and crossed to the granite-topped unit to pick up the folder she'd come in for, though she kept a precautionary eye on his reflection in the plate glass window. The darkness outside hid the view of Grasmere lake and village in their daylight greys and greens, and the rearing Lakeland Fells beyond them. The only sign of life was the flickering fire from the hippy camp at the lakeside and the attendant shadows of its occupants, like a coven of witches casting their spells.

'I'm going to kill you.' He regrouped, though his voice still shook. 'You're a bitch.'

'And you're a child.'

'I'm twenty-five!' he shouted at her, like a teenager rowing with his mother.

'Then act twenty-five. Get on with the job I'm paying you to do. Or is the pay part of your problem?' She turned back to face him, ready to defend herself if she had to, to run as a last resort, yet certain that she'd have to do neither.

Owen was damned by his reasonableness. The pay was the one thing he couldn't complain about. 'Not the pay. But the conditions…'

'Take it up with your union. If you dare.' Which he wouldn't. She softened her tone, but only in mockery, tapping her slipper-shod foot so that he knew she had better things to do. 'Maybe you need a break, Owen. Maybe you've been working too hard. After tomorrow is over, we can both have a holiday.'

'I'm going to hang you. I'm going to string you up from that beam and watch you die.' Sweat gathered under his long black fringe, giving him the look of a vampire caught out by the dawn. '*Full soon thy soul shall have her Earthly—*'

She slammed the folder down on the table and had the satisfaction of seeing him jump a foot backwards, the quotation left incomplete. 'All right. Let's get serious. Who put you up to this?' Because Owen sure as hell wasn't capable of thinking it up for himself.

'No one. You. You're a bitch. You're a bully. You've pushed me too far and you're going to pay for it.'

For a man working towards a PhD in English literature, Owen's vocabulary was sadly limited. No doubt there were plenty of words running through his head, rehearsed and ready to come out as the last thing she'd ever hear, but the way his mouth flapped open and shut as he fought to control his breathing merely increased her contempt for him. Even the Wordsworth quotation he'd chosen had been a poor one. 'It isn't your idea. I doubt you have the brains to plan it and you sure don't have the balls. Who put the idea into your head? And why?'

In the silence generated by his abject humiliation, she glanced at the clock. 'Tell whoever it is that they don't frighten me.'

'I'm going to tell everyone. I'll tell the papers.' His feet stuttered on the grey flagged floor as if he was urging himself on, but he made no movement forward.

'I'm always happy to talk to the papers about my work.'

'Not your work. I'm going to tell them about you. The truth. That you're a liar and a fraud. And a murderer.'

'Owen. I think you've just demonstrated why I don't trust you with certain of my sources. You're emotionally unstable and entirely unreliable. Tell whoever you like whatever you like. If you dare.' She glanced at the clock again. There was still plenty of time. 'You're clearly upset so I won't ask you to help me finish setting up for tomorrow. But I damn well expect you to be there in the morning, doing the job I pay you for.'

She walked past him slowly, closer than she needed to in a way that was intended both to show him how little she cared and to dare him to take her on because to show fear, even to admit it to herself, would be fatal weakness. Her heart hammered as she passed and his fingers tightened around the rope, but it was the limit of his fantasies and he stepped back in defeat.

'*Our best conceits do prove the greatest liars*,' he called as she left the room, but the words were barely audible and entirely bereft of threat. 'You're a liar, Cody Wilder. And a fraud.'

'And a murderer,' she mocked him before closing the kitchen door behind her.

I

The first light was beginning to illuminate the sky above Beacon Hill to the east when Jude Satterthwaite opened the front door of his house in Wordsworth Street and stepped out onto the pavement. Waiting while his girlfriend checked that she hadn't left anything behind, he glanced at his watch. Eight-fifteen. That gave him plenty of time to drop Ashleigh at work before heading on to pick up his mother and take her through to Grasmere for Cody Wilder's much-publicised lecture on Dorothy Wordsworth. Reading was a luxury for which Jude could rarely find the time and he didn't regard himself as an intellectual, but he was looking forward to hearing the controversial American academic, even if only to see if the reality measured up to the hype. At the very least, it would be an interesting experience. 'Come on, Ash. We don't have all day.'

'Yes, sir.' She gave him a smart salute and followed it up with a wink; Jude couldn't resist the temptation and leaned in to kiss her. A disapproving twitch of a curtain over the road didn't bother him. The folly of love was a lesson he'd learned the hard way and wasn't keen to repeat, but he was confident enough to allow himself to be besotted with Ashleigh O'Halloran, even if was largely at a physical level. There could be no risk to his heart in that.

'Okay. That's the fun over. Let's get to work.' They lingered for a moment on the pavement before he opened the driver's door of his Mercedes, clipped his seatbelt shut and started the engine. Time with Ashleigh was hard to come by even though they worked together. He couldn't resist a sly look at her profile before he pulled out of the parking space.

'You're such a hard taskmaster.' Ashleigh pulled the vanity mirror down, fished in her bag for a tube of un-detective-like scarlet lipstick and recreated the subtle but perfect makeup he'd so spontaneously disarranged. 'Look at me. It took me half an hour to get this look and you had to go and ruin it.'

'It's your own fault for being irresistible.' He grinned as he negotiated the roundabout onto the one-way system, thinking about the day that lay ahead. It was no wonder he never had time to read poetry, even if he was so inclined. His work was all-consuming. He flicked a sideways glance and a smile at Ashleigh, thanking his stars he'd finally found someone who understood how much his job mattered to him. It was a bonus that the sparks flew when they were alone. And how they flew. 'Are you about this evening?'

'Wasn't last night enough for you?' She flicked long eyelashes at him. 'You could come up to the house and tell Lisa and me all about your day.'

He shook his head, amused, and they drove the short distance through Penrith to the police headquarters in a companionable, early-morning silence. 'I'll call you when I'm done.'

'Do you have any plans for later?'

Technically, he was on a day off. 'I might pop into the office.'

'You probably shouldn't, but I don't imagine that'll stop you. Either way, I'll see you later.'

As he drove into the car park, he switched into business mode. 'Is there anything I need to know? Anything you need to ask me?'

'Nothing I can't ask or tell Doddsy. Now go away and enjoy your day off.'

He stopped the car outside the front of the building with unfortunate timing, picking the exact moment at which his immediate superior, Detective Superintendent Groves, emerged from the grey dawn and paused for a second beside the car as Ashleigh got out, eyeing the two of them with interest.

'Been debriefing your colleague at home, have you, Satterthwaite?' Groves's wink added unnecessary emphasis on the double entendre.

'Jude gave me a lift in.' Ashleigh smoothed her skirt down, avoiding his gaze.

'Day and night. Can't fault your commitment to your job, either of you.'

Jude disliked his boss, as did everybody else he knew, and the feeling was mutual. Fortunately, Ashleigh had the knack of getting out of a car without losing control of her clothing. He sensed her hesitate for a second next to the car as she calculated how far she'd have to walk with the man, and opted to spare her the ordeal. 'I might just pop into the office for a second. See how things are.'

'It's okay.' She gave him a grateful smile. It wasn't far from the car park to the office and she regularly handled people who behaved far worse than Groves, whose patter was more akin to that of a sleazy uncle at a wedding than anything directly threatening. 'You'd better get away. You'll be late.'

Groves's presence prevented Jude from giving her the kiss he'd have liked, but he waited, nevertheless, while they covered the few yards to the front desk, noting the way Groves walked close to her and she stepped away, so that their path veered slightly from a straight line until they reached the doors. Restarting the car, he left Ashleigh to fight her own corner, as she could and did so well. She wouldn't thank him for intervening and he was scrupulously professional, always wary of drawing attention to this blossoming workplace relationship. Normally they made a point of arriving and leaving separately, but the previous night they'd both ended up at his place and neither of them had planned that she'd stay.

It took a further twenty minutes to reach his mother's cottage in the village of Wasby, on the edge of the Lake District, and by the time he got there the sun was climbing with confidence above the Pennines. Pulling up outside he checked his watch. As always, he was in plenty of time. For a moment he paused to look down the single street of the village where he'd grown up, and then got out of the car and strode up the front path.

'Morning, Jude.'

'Morning.' He recognised the voice behind him, rang the doorbell and waited a moment before he turned, to show Becca Reid that he didn't care. He might never forgive her the damage she'd once done to his heart but he was over it, over her, and Becca – with her no-nonsense manner, her smile for everyone that turned to a scowl for him, her sensible shoes and minimal makeup – might be a sweet saint of a woman but she'd never set his blood racing round his body the way Ashleigh O'Halloran did. 'All well?' He smiled. After everything that had happened, he liked her and he could afford to be generous.

'Fine. I'm off to work. You?' She turned the car key over on her finger, subjecting him to her cool gaze.

'I'm on a day off.' He looked past her to see if her cat, Holmes, was lurking in the receding shadows of what looked as if it would turn into a pleasant January day but Holmes who, to Becca's obvious irritation, could always be trusted to make a fuss of him, didn't show up. 'I'm taking Mum down to Grasmere to hear Cody Wilder.'

'The American academic?'

'That's the one.' Footsteps inside the cottage heralded his mother's arrival at the front door and gave him the opportunity to turn his back on Becca without formally concluding the conversation. The slam of her car door and the roar of the engine, as if she'd hit the accelerator more quickly that she'd intended, were her goodbye. With a greater measure of relief than he liked, he turned his attention to his mother as she appeared on the doorstep. 'Ready to go?'

'I know there's plenty of time, but I do want to get a decent seat.'

'You're looking very smart.'

Linda touched her hair; she wasn't used to compliments. 'It's only a lecture, I know, but appearances matter.' She had on a black skirt and scarlet jacket and stepped through the door on heels an inch higher than usual, as if she wanted to make an impression. 'I really appreciate you doing this for me, Jude. Thank you.' She turned and called over her shoulder. 'Come on, Mikey!' And then turned back and offered Jude an innocent look. 'Didn't I tell you? I got an extra ticket and Mikey was very keen.'

Mikey, Jude's stubborn, troublesome and vulnerable brother – very much younger and, both needing and resisting Jude's attempts to be a father-figure – was the one person apart from Becca who never failed to bring a cloud with him when he crept into Jude's mind. On reflection he was surprised, not that Mikey, an English student, was jumping at the chance to hear Cody Wilder, but that his brother was prepared to endure his company for it. 'Is he speaking to me, then?'

It was meant as a joke but the finger Linda raised to her lips warned him that he was closer to the truth than he liked. 'Sshh!'

'Shall I wait in the car?'

'It's such an opportunity.' Leaving Mikey to make his own way out, Linda accompanied him down the path, choosing to ignore the uncomfortable relationship between her sons. 'You know I've always loved Wordsworth. I was devastated when they took him off the syllabus and left us teaching the modern poets instead.'

'Yes, but you're a traditionalist.'

In a whirlwind of black boots and faded denim, Mikey clattered down the path and into the back of the car. 'Yo.' Avoiding eye contact, he clamped huge headphones over his ears and subsided into his seat.

'Yes, there's that.' His mother carried on as if he hadn't spoken. 'But the Wordsworth-Dorothy relationship is an intriguing one, and Dorothy is always overlooked. Cody Wilder is the world's leading expert on her, and everything I've read indicates that she has something new to say about it.'

The publicity material had trailed Cody Wilder's conclusions as sensational, but Jude reserved judgement. 'It's a day out.'

'I'm so glad I'm retired. It gives me the chance to follow these things more closely. We were lucky to get tickets. And it's astonishing she chose to reveal it here. She could have gone to any conference on the Romantic poets.'

Cody Wilder, Jude knew from elsewhere, had fallen out spectacularly with every academic institution she'd worked for, so her choice of location didn't surprise him. A paper delivered to an audience of hostile scholars on some campus university wouldn't have the news impact of a public event in a picturesque Lake District village. 'I'm sure she'll go down a storm, but I'm afraid her wisdom will be wasted on me.'

'Oh, don't talk nonsense.' Linda tutted at him as he were a child rather than a man of thirty-five. 'Anyway, tell me your news.'

'What makes you think I have any?'

'About the new girlfriend. Who is she?'

Amused, when another time he would have found that annoying, Jude couldn't suppress a smile. 'Who told you?' It had been bound to get out despite the efforts he'd made to keep Ashleigh out of the clutches of the bush telegraph, though he didn't know why he was so keen on secrecy. To spare Becca, perhaps, though she wasn't showing any sign she cared.

'Nobody. But either there's a new woman in your life or you've taken to wearing Chanel, and I don't think it's that.'

The smile broadened into a grin. 'You're in the wrong job. I could use a detective like you.'

'So I'm right, then? Is it serious?'

'Do you really think I can answer that?'

'It's too early to say, then? Have you told Mikey?'

'Not yet. Let me find the right moment.' Looking in the driver's mirror he caught Mikey, oblivious, staring in fierce concentration at his phone. Too much at ease with the world to allow either the perennial problem of his brother or the implications of a new romance to trouble him, Jude tapped his fingers on the steering wheel as he turned the car up towards Ullswater.

Jude was a man who valued solitude and in his spare time he preferred to seek it, leaving the charms of Grasmere for the most part to the tourists. He stopped the Mercedes in the car park on the edge of the village, locked it and took a look around while Mikey, still protected from conversation by his headphones, distanced himself further with a few steps away. Today Grasmere was busier than he'd expected on a morning in January, so maybe Cody Wilder had more pulling power than he'd thought. As he and his mother walked briskly past the cafes and outdoor shops with Mikey trailing in their wake, doubt assailed him. 'Do you two mind running on down to the venue and grabbing us some seats? There's something I want to check up on.'

His mother turned reproachful eyes on him, as if she'd known he had an ulterior motive. 'Jude. This is your day off.'

'Yes, I'll join you. But there's someone I wanted to catch up with.'

He slowed to let them get ahead. Cody Wilder was trouble, a problem of her own making, and while her academic credentials were flawless and her research, as far as he understood it, regarded as outstanding in her field, her views on current affairs were a different matter. There wasn't a matter of interest that she didn't have an opinion on, regardless of how well qualified she might be to speak on it, and she never passed up an opportunity to share her thoughts. Inevitably, that created a spiral in which commentators were less interested in the trials of Dorothy Wordsworth two and a half centuries before than they were in what Cody thought of gun violence, feminism, immigration or whatever else was the trending topic in the media. Presumably, Jude thought with a sigh, she justified it on the grounds that at least it made her enough of a name to generate some exposure for her work. He hoped she knew what she was doing, because he could tell a deal with the devil when he saw one, and the results of it were all around him.

Just beyond the bridge, the square mediaeval tower of St Oswald's church sat in judgement on the village. His brow crinkled a little as he approached a group of protestors, standing in the churchyard and waving banners calling on Cody Wilder to go back to America. They looked peaceful enough, a fusion of umbrellas and sensible rainwear jostling under the yew trees and trampling the emerging crocuses. One of them was engaged in what looked like good-natured conversation with one of the cohort of uniformed police officers he'd sent down to Grasmere in order to make sure there was no trouble.

There were more protestors than he'd expected though the small but obvious police presence ought to be enough to dampen any thoughts of law-breaking, and hopefully Cody Wilder would remember her priorities and resist the urge to engage with her opposition. Passing them on the other side of the road, he scanned the interested onlookers and was rewarded when a tall, fair young man in jeans and a good-quality walker's raincoat detached himself from the group of them and came across. 'Okay, Jude? It's looking a bit busier than we thought.'

Pausing to rest his hands on the bridge and pretend to inspect the ducks squabbling on the water beneath, Jude relaxed. Chris Marshall, the detective he'd dispatched to keep an unobtrusive eye out for any activity that might be taking place out of sight of their uniformed colleagues, was capable of taking on far more responsibility than his rank of constable demanded of him. Nothing sinister would get past him. Even so, despite the four policeman who represented the compromise between what was available to him and what he'd have liked to deploy, he was glad he'd turned up. 'So I see.' He flicked a look across the road. 'Who are that lot?'

'They're pro-choice.' Cody's views on abortion were open to interpretation, but so colourfully expressed that both sides of the debate viewed her as their implacable enemy, something which she probably considered a good result. 'The gun lobby are at the back of the garden centre. The First Nation rights people are out in force at the Wordsworth Hotel.'

'Seriously?'

'No. That was a joke. The only protests are these guys and a couple of local nutters who've hung a banner out of their windows accusing her of being a murderer. I don't know what that's all about.'

No matter how serious the situation, Chris's flippancy held firm. Amused at the limited extent of civil disorder in village Westmorland, Jude stuck his hands in his pockets. For a moment, Cody's reputation as a troublemaker had concerned him. 'Did you brief Dr Wilder on what we're doing?'

Chris rolled his eyes. 'As much as that's possible.'

'So far I've managed to avoid her.'

'Lucky you. You wouldn't get on. She's the type that knows it all already.'

In fairness, Cody Wilder had far more experience with this sort of protest than any of the police present. 'Do you reckon we can trust her not to court controversy until she's safely off our patch?'

'Who knows? I like to think so.'

According to Jude's mother, Cody had been researching the lives of the Wordsworths for years so she surely wasn't going to risk compromising her serious academic career for the sake of a few cheap headlines, but the one thing Jude knew for certain about her was that she was anything but predictable. 'What do you reckon? Surely there isn't going to be trouble?'

'I don't think so. She's sensible enough – or maybe media-savvy enough – to have brought in some security to check everyone's bags, so there won't be any problems at the talk itself. Not that I think there would have been, looking at this lot. They're harmless. But there's a bit of me thinks it suits her to hype up the threat.'

Jude nodded. He'd reviewed the matter carefully before he'd delegated it to Chris and he couldn't see any harm coming to Cody Wilder in genteel Grasmere. Most of the abuse she received came from behind the anonymity of a computer keyboard and fake social media profiles, but she was such an anti-hero that he didn't dare take the risk. 'Are you going along to the talk?'

'Literature isn't my thing. I'll be floating about in the lobby and making sure no one puts poison in the post-lecture coffee.'

Chris's enthusiasm was infectious. Jude allowed himself a smile, even as he was irritated at himself for having to check up when he was supposed to be taking time off to make up for countless extra hours worked. 'It looks like you've got everything under control. I'd better get down to the venue, before I get in trouble with the boss.'

'The boss?' Chris's eyebrows lifted. 'Old man Groves hasn't found his way down here, has he?'

'Not that boss. My mother. I'm supposed to be keeping her company on a day out.'

'Thank God for that. I'll walk down there with you. I'd hate to miss anything.' Chris's smile was ironic this time.

They strolled past the protestors outside the church and down beyond the garden centre. Cody had chosen to launch her research in the function suite of a hotel overlooking the lake, ten minutes' walk from the village centre, and they joined the steady stream of ticket holders heading towards it. Local accents mixed with London ones, suits and silk scarves mingled with woolly hats and wellies. A TV crew had set up in the car park on Red Bank Road, filming all who went past.

'There is one thing that struck me as unusual.' Chris lowered his voice as they passed the banner he'd mentioned, strung up from the front of a slate cottage, the last few letters crammed together and the red paint on its lettering bleeding from an overnight shower. *Cody Wilder murderer.* 'There's a bunch of hippies down by the lake.'

In the field that sloped down to the water to their left,

a sad collection of damp tents clustered around a smother of smoke from a campfire. 'Oh, yes. They've been there a while. There's nothing sinister about them.'

'Nothing? They seem completely batty to me.'

'I come across them from time to time. They've always been attracted to this place.'

'That's all we need – a bunch of Flat Earthers cluttering up the scene.' Modern-minded, child of a technological age, Chris betrayed his intolerance of older, slower ways.

'They're harmless. I'll be astonished if they've even heard of Cody Wilder, let alone care about her. They reject the modern world, they reject science. They're all about living at one with nature. It's not a particularly connected philosophy as far as I can tell, but I wouldn't worry about them.'

'I'm sure you're right, but I wondered about one of them. He was skulking behind the tents and staring up towards the venue, that's all.'

Confident in his own judgement of the hippy commune, Jude nevertheless followed Chris's analytical gaze. The man he'd pointed out, tall and broad with dreadlocked hair, did, immediately, drop back out of sight. 'Publicity-shy, maybe.'

Chris was right to note anything unusual, so Jude gave the man an extra look as he disappeared and then strolled towards another man who was standing watching the goings-on from a safe distance behind a wall thick with moss. 'Busy here today, isn't it?'

With the utmost show of reluctance, the man came forward. 'Hopefully they'll all be gone by tomorrow.' Probably in his late sixties, he spoke with a cultured accent, stamped with London disillusion.

Jude leaned on the wall, knowing exactly why these people

nursed so much suspicion of the outside world. He had more time to spare for them than was strictly appropriate, finding himself in sympathy with their rejection of the complexities of the twenty-first century. In his experience the man in front of him and his wife, who he knew of old, were among the simplest and best-hearted people around, and it jarred that whenever he came across them it was in the context of someone reporting them for crimes they'd never dream of committing. 'Let's hope so.' He straightened up and brushed a greasy smear of liquid moss from his Gore-Tex sleeve.

'Is there someone important in town, up beyond?' Responding to Jude's smile, the man gestured up the road towards the hotel.

'You could say that.' Certainly, Cody was important in her own opinion. 'We'd better get on. See you round, Storm.'

'Storm?' queried Chris, as the two detectives set off to the hotel where the last of the audience were heading indoors.

'Not his real name, obviously. I have no idea what that is. His wife, if she is his wife, is called Raven.' But his real name would be in the records along with his wife's, filed away with his fingerprints and a sample of his DNA as part of a report into some petty theft that turned out to be someone else's carelessness. 'Okay. It looks like we're already running late. Let's get on in and see the show.'

2

'Ladies and gentlemen. Welcome to Grasmere. My name is Sebastian Mulholland and it's my job today to introduce you to our speaker. Of course, it isn't me you're here to listen to, so I'll keep the introduction brief. But I would like to say a few words before the main event.'

Remembering her manners, that it was acceptable to seem forthright but alienating to appear ungracious, Cody Wilder crossed her ankles demurely and smiled at Seb as he turned and nodded in her direction. He was a bore with a much greater opinion of himself than he deserved, but she hadn't forgotten that she owed him. Without his help she'd still have got where she was going, but it would have taken her a little longer. If all it cost her to repay him was a share in the glory, she was happy to concede it.

'I first met Cody five years ago when she walked into my second-hand bookshop in St Andrews in search of Dorothy Wordsworth's lost journals. Naturally, I rose to the challenge. I've been in the antiquarian trade for many years. My interest was sparked when, as a student, I took a temporary job for a house clearance company…'

God, how tedious. He was going to talk about himself. She nodded sagely, like a mother listening to the headmaster's speech at a school prize-giving, and confined her fidgeting to a twist of the finger through her elevated blonde ponytail as she mentally ran through her presentation for the umpteenth time. As she listened to Seb coming perilously close to stealing her thunder in his description of the moment when she'd found the lost journals in a box in the back room of his shop, a thrill went through her. Life had its high and lows. There was love and there was sex and there was victory, there was rejection and there was disappointment, but nothing in life had ever offered her a buzz as wild as that she'd experienced in the moment when she'd set eyes on the missing portion of poor, repressed, underrated Dorothy Wordsworth's life story.

She glanced down at her notes. *Dorothy Wordsworth is perceived as the sister of a great man*, she'd written. *Were they alive today, we would be calling him the brother of a great woman*. Brandon would laugh out loud if he were to hear that. Even in full view of two hundred strangers she couldn't stop a smile at the thought of him, but the smile was almost immediately displaced by a frown. He'd promised he'd be there to hear the talk, but she'd heard nothing more from him than his usual vague promise to do his best. Cody's life had always been a lonely one and her brother was the one person left whose approval she craved.

Then there was Owen. Her frown intensified. His hissy fit of the night before hadn't passed and he hadn't appeared at breakfast. She wasn't surprised. The boy was the worst kind of wuss and would be cowering in his room in a funk of shame and embarrassment, but his outburst had been uncharacteristic enough to give her cause for concern. Not for herself – verbally she could eviscerate him, and physically she was more than capable of taking care of herself – but she wouldn't put it past him to stage some sort of stunt to undermine her. Failing to turn up for work and leaving her to do his job, including the chore of meeting and greeting, might not be enough to satisfy his pride.

Let him try. If he did, she'd turn it to her advantage. She scanned the room again to see if he was hiding somewhere in the back row, but he wasn't, and when she looked over the crowd again, she found herself being stared at most obviously by a young brunette in the front row. *Journalist*, said Cody to herself, her media antennae twitching, but she wasn't quite sure why that troubled her. She knew of half a dozen journalists in the room and had researched them all so that she could press the right buttons in talking to them and trigger the responses she sought, but she didn't know this woman, who wore no press pass round her neck. That put her on the back foot, as things she couldn't control always did.

'But enough about me. You all know Cody by reputation – a fearless defender of the right to freedom of speech, a woman who rose to academic heights from a background where learning was a luxury thought to be unaffordable.' Seb turned to her with one of his more patronising smiles. 'Her rise has been meteoric. She took on the academic establishment and rose above it, a household name before she has even reached her forties.' He nodded towards her, as if that was meant to be a compliment. 'She taught us that the fearless and unyielding mind can work – and thrive – independently of academia and need not be trammelled by years of routine and irrelevant research.' At that, the smile turned to a smirk. At least some of the audience would know her university tenure had ended in a row over her political views. 'Her critique of the Lucy poems is regarded even by those who dislike her as the definitive evaluation of that particular work that we attribute to Wordsworth, and many find her assertion that Dorothy was their author to be wholly convincing. The poet's own words will do as a tribute to Dr Wilder: *what we need is not the will to believe, but the wish to find out*.'

Seb, floundering in the dictionary of quotations for a vaguely applicable sentence, had missed the point. People like him always did. Cody picked up her pen and made a savage note on the margin of her speech, a reminder to herself not to let that go. *This is about Dorothy, not William*!

Pausing for a sip of water, Seb shuffled his notes, put them down again, tweaked his scarlet silk tie. A door at the back of the room creaked open. It must be Owen, creeping in late. 'And so, to launch her book *Strange Fits of Passion: The Creation of Dorothy Wordsworth*, in the village beloved by both Wordsworth and his sister, let me introduce you to perhaps the most gifted scholar of literature ever to emerge from Wyoming, the Equality State – Dr Cody Constance Wilder.'

As the audience applauded, Cody stood up and crossed to the lectern, making sure she gave Seb a gracious smile. Glancing round the room she saw that it wasn't Owen lurking behind the door, but some latecomer who was taking the opportunity to home in on an empty seat – inevitably in the middle of the room.

Nothing irritated her like lateness, a sin which implied a lack of respect, and in her big moment, lack of respect was intolerable. Cutting the applause short, she forced the criminal, a tall, serious-looking man in his mid-thirties, clad in well-cut chinos and a designer jacket, to complete his walk through the ensuing silence and the disapproving gaze of those around him.

'Is everybody comfortable?' She glared in his direction, but he'd slid into his seat and was whispering something into the ear of the older woman in the red jacket who was sitting next to him. Hopefully it was an apology, but any apology was due to Cody herself. If he hung around long enough afterwards, she'd track him down and make it quite clear what she thought of his behaviour. 'Good. I'm sorry. We must have started early.' But he didn't even look at her, staring thoughtfully at Seb Mulholland instead. 'However, we're all here and it's my pleasure – my absolute pleasure – to introduce my latest book and share with you what I discovered among Dorothy Wordsworth's papers.'

'The journals themselves, then, were a disappointment. Other than completing the canon of Dorothy's work as far as we know it, they served only to reinforce how anodyne her written work was. True, they carried subtle phrasing that later reappears in William's poems, but that was all. They yielded nothing more than an extension, rather than a deepening, of how we understand Dorothy and her relationship with her brother.'

Cody Wilder was a performer. Though he knew little about Wordsworth beyond what he'd absorbed from his mother's enthusiasm, Jude was impressed by her delivery and her energy when the most exciting revelation so far was that her much-vaunted discovery had been all but worthless. But it was obvious there was a lot more to it than that. Seb Mulholland, nodding as Cody talked, clearly knew there was a big reveal coming and was visibly struggling to rein in his glee.

In his pocket, Jude's phone buzzed. He'd had the foresight to put it on silent, and with his mother next to him and Cody having already directed considerable and obvious disappointment towards him he hesitated to get it out and check the message. It would be work. No one who knew him ever tried to call him on a personal matter when he ought to be working. They knew he wouldn't answer.

But of course. He wasn't working. Sometimes he forgot that. Nevertheless, he opted not to look at the phone but swivelled in his seat to see if the creaking of the door at the back of the room was someone even later than he had been, or something else. His instinct proved correct. Chris, an anxious expression on his face, hovered just inside the door, scanning the room.

On stage, Cody Wilder stopped mid-sentence and cleared her throat.

The anxiety on Chris's face gave way to relief as he caught Jude's eye, jerking an almost commanding gesture towards his superior before ducking back out of the room. Without thought, Jude pushed his chair back, turning to his mother. 'I'll see you outside afterwards. Got to go.'

A few feet away from him Mikey cringed into his seat. In turning, Jude caught the expression of fury on Cody Wilder's face. If he hadn't known already, that look would have shown him how little it took to make an enemy of her, but even without knowing what had disturbed Chris so much that he felt he had to seek help from a senior colleague, he sensed it must be to do with Cody herself.

Someone else could explain it to her later. He wasn't

going to make time to deal with a woman as irascible as she so clearly was. He stood up.

'Excuse me.'

Jude kept walking.

'Excuse me,' Cody snapped at him again. 'You. The man leaving. Is there a problem? Am I boring you? Do you feel I'm not giving value for money? Or can't you handle the suggestion that a woman who was belittled because of her gender in another age should be restored and properly credited in the current one?'

He could quite see why so many people fell so swiftly and so completely onto the wrong side of Cody Wilder. Resisting the temptation to engage, he walked on.

'I'm asking you a question.'

He did stop, then, drawn into the debate against his better judgement but still retaining enough autonomy not to turn fully, but throwing the remark over his shoulder. 'I'm sorry. I had a message. I need to go.'

'In future, if you think you may have to leave an event, may I respectfully suggest you don't attend at all and let someone else make use of your ticket? Unless, of course, what you have to do is vitally important.'

This time he did turn around. She'd stepped away from the lectern and was standing at the front of the stage, hands on hips – a slender figure dressed in grey as if to keep attention on her words not her person, and yet displaying a commanding presence. 'I'm a police officer on call.' He could stand on his dignity, too, sound as pompous and entitled as any academic. Out of the corner of his eye as he turned away, he saw his mother lower her head in embarrassment alongside Mikey's.

Striding swiftly through the ripple of excitement and disapproval his exit had engendered, he made the safety of the breakout area and found Chris out there, speaking into his phone. 'Okay, what's up?'

Chris ended the call and shoved the phone back in his pocket. 'Let's get out of earshot, shall we? It's bad, but at least I don't think we need to be concerned about the doctor's personal safety.'

That was one less thing to worry about. Jude followed Chris into a quiet corner. 'So what is it?'

'Her researcher. Name of Owen Armitstead.' Chris looked at his phone and swiped a message off the screen, unacknowledged. 'He's dead. Looks like suicide.'

Think murder, Jude's instinct warned him. Evil sometimes reared up where you expected it, more often where you didn't. 'What happened and where?'

'Dr Wilder has rented a cottage up at the top of Coffin Lane. She and her researcher have been staying there. The landlord came by to check on something and saw him through the kitchen window. Hanged himself, or so it seems.'

'Okay.' Jude took quick stock of the situation. 'What have you done? Called the doctor, obviously?'

'Yes, and I'm expecting him any minute. The landlord has some first-aid training – he's ex-army – and cut him down and tried CPR. He says the body was still warm, but he couldn't save him. I've got one of the uniformed guys from the village to make sure no one goes up to the cottage.'

'The lane's a dead end, is that right?'

'Yes. I called the two guys up from the village to take charge of the scene and get a statement from Steve Hardy

– the landlord. And I called in to the office and Doddsy's coming down to take charge. He's got all the information I have. It isn't much.'

The arrival of Detective Inspector Chris Dodd, Jude's colleague and close friend, would mean that Jude himself could leave the field and get back to mending fences with his mother and enjoying the rest of his so-called day off, but until then he'd stick around and provide Chris with any help he needed. He glanced through the window. A hundred yards away, he could just spot a policeman, arms folded, at the bottom of the lane. 'You've done a good job.'

'Thanks. I've called for additional support.'

'Let's get up there.' They left the building and walked rapidly, side-by-side, up along Coffin Lane and past the uniformed PC who nodded them past as Chris rattled through the information. 'I asked Doddsy to find us some more people, if he can. In case it isn't suicide. In case it's some kind of distraction tactic. Or even if it is suicide, we don't want someone taking advantage of the uniformed boys being busy elsewhere.'

'Smart move. We don't need any opportunists causing us trouble.' Fifteen years in the police, almost all of them as a detective, had taught Jude to be suspicious even though in most cases the explanation was the simple and obvious one. The sooner Cody Wilder left town the happier he'd be, but she'd have to give some background to the case so it looked as if she'd be his problem for a few days to come. 'Do you know how long Doddsy will be?'

'Five or ten minutes, I expect. I called the minute I heard about it, and then I had to get up and deal with the landlord and the body.'

'So it happened when?'

'Pretty much immediately after I'd left you. I went back out of the building to double check on your hippy pals over the road, and the guy came haring down the lane in a hell of a state, shouting at me to call a doctor and an ambulance.'

'He didn't call them himself?'

'The signal's flaky up there.' Chris checked his phone as he spoke and shook his head. 'I have it now. I didn't a couple of minutes ago. That's why I came to fetch you myself.'

Jude followed him into the garden of the single-storey, slate-roofed cottage and paused to look around. The cottage was up on the hill, nestled against a tangle of leafless woodland that sheltered it from the wind funnelling down off the fells. Across the valley the steep slopes of Nab Scar and Heron Pike towered above the road and the village nestled on the lake shore. In the garden a couple of gnarled yew trees, studded with scarlet berries and surely older than the cottage itself, brought a peculiarly festive feel to January, and the grey-green blades of snowdrop leaves presaged the spring. 'What do we know about the researcher?'

'Nothing. I can give you chapter and verse on almost every enemy Cody Wilder's ever made, but I'd never even heard this boy's name. The landlord only knew it because the man was the doc's secretary as well as her research assistant. He was my age, maybe. Younger.'

A shadow passed over Chris's face. You could see many dead bodies and develop a coping mechanism to deal with them all, but it took a tougher man than him not to betray some kind of fellow feeling at the passing of another human being.

'We'll need to ask her.'

Chris turned towards the house. 'Do you want to see the body?'

'No need.' Jude shook his head. There would be photos, and if it was a routine suicide then Doddsy would deal with it. If it wasn't, it would come up the ranks to him soon enough. 'Where did it happen? The kitchen, you said?'

'Yes. It's one of those olde-worlde places, all stone floor and exposed beams. He'd jumped off the table.'

Keeping as detached as he could, Jude reviewed the context. Was Cody impossible to work with, or had something totally separate driven Owen Armitstead to his death? Given the way he'd already managed to get on the wrong side of her without even an introduction, Jude was grateful she'd fall to Doddsy, whose implacable good nature and inherent belief in the goodness of most human beings continued to resist the evidence to the contrary he saw every working day.

A car drove up through the village and turned up Coffin Lane. Jude recognised it as Doddsy's and relaxed. The case was in good hands and his task of supplying reassurance was over before it began. 'Here's your boss. I'll step aside for him.'

'Yeah, sorry. I know you're not supposed to be on duty.'

'It seems to me you have everything covered.' Nevertheless, Jude lingered, in case there was something he could do. 'I'll maybe take a drift down through the village,' he said, as Doddsy levered himself out of his car and stretched in the pale sunlight. 'Just to check everything's okay.'

'You might want to check up on those hippies.'

Perhaps that was a joke, or maybe Chris really did buy into the idea that anyone who chose to reject the modern world's values automatically rejected the morals and rules that went along with them. 'I'll have a word.'

'Jude.' Doddsy was looking particularly world-weary. 'You don't need to hang around here. You spend too much time on the job as it is.'

It was undeniable, and it had cost him but that was with Becca, in the past. Now he had Ashleigh who not only understood but was as guilty as he was of the same sin. 'I was around.' And ultimately if there was anything involving Cody Wilder it would fall under his remit. 'Keep me informed, though.'

'Where's Dr Wilder?' Doddsy, too, seemed reluctant to go to the scene and view the body.

'Still giving her lecture. Someone will have to tell her about it.'

Always thoughtful, Doddsy ran a slow finger round his chin. 'You don't fancy doing that for me?'

Did he? Jude knew he hadn't made a great impression so far, but if it helped, and if it soothed his conscience for sneaking away and leaving the field to someone else, then he was prepared to do that much. 'I'm going back down there. I need to take my mum and Mikey back home. And as I was there before, it won't look quite so obvious if I try and sneak a chat with Dr Wilder.'

'Are the press around?'

'Bound to be. She's not the type to go anywhere without making sure someone knows about it. As far as I can tell, she's a serious player and what she has to say is significant. Do you think we can avoid attracting too much attention?'

'We can try. I'd appreciate it if you could break it to her gently. I'll send Chris along in a bit to rescue you. It looks pretty straightforward to me, so we shouldn't keep her out of the cottage for long.'

Glad to have the chance to disengage himself from the case before he could get too closely into it, Jude made his way back down to the hotel. The security staff had gone, the accusing banner still fluttered in a faint and forlorn breeze a hundred yards up the street, and when he stopped to listen there was nothing but the quacking of ducks on the lake and the rumble of a lorry along the A591. The protestors in the village had either gone quiet or given up and left.

If it wasn't for this unexplained death, this apparent suicide, Jude would have considered the day a success, but his brief acquaintance with Cody Wilder made him wonder if there might be something sinister connecting her unrepentant aggression with the death of Owen Armitstead.

He'd find out. And in the meantime, it was time to go back down and take on the challenge of breaking the news to the woman herself.

The lecture was over by the time Jude got back into the venue, and Cody was mingling with the public in the foyer, a cup of coffee in her hand. Showing them the common touch, he thought, with the cynicism that clicked so well with Doddsy's positivity; he had to admit she was good at it. When, as he assumed, she was talking about her work her passion showed through and he stopped to watch her for a moment, her eyes shining at every question, her free hand jabbing in front of her to illustrate a point, while he waited for the opportunity to approach.

Eventually his mother helped him out, taking her

opportunity to glide into Cody's orbit with Mikey at her elbow, keen to engage. Her voice floated through to him. 'Dr Wilder. What an extraordinary story that was. To think that Dorothy and Mary committed their thoughts to each other that way, so honestly and openly. And how selfless of Dorothy to sacrifice—'

'Sacrifice is of its age. These days I guess I'd like to see her do things differently. I'm sorry ma'am.' Cody was politeness itself. 'I don't think I know your name.'

'I'm Linda Satterthwaite. And this is my younger son, Mikey.'

'Good to meet you, Linda. You're a bit of a Wordsworth aficionado, then?'

'Oh, I wouldn't say that. I'm an English teacher. Was, I should say. I'm retired. But I've always had a fondness for his work, among all the Lakes poets. If it is his, of course. And Dorothy is such an enigmatic character. And so devoted.'

Taking his opportunity, and in direct defiance of Mikey's scowl, Jude edged closer. So, from the other side of the conversation, did a young brunette, wearing her ponytail in a high 1950s style just as Cody did. Jude ignored her, nudged in beside his mother and deflected Cody's brief scowl of recognition with a smile. 'Dr Wilder.'

'This is my other son, Jude. He very kindly brought us along today.' If Linda saw a scowl, either from Mikey or Cody, she gave no sign.

'Jude? The Beatles, then? Or Hardy?'

'Hardy. I love his novels.'

'For my money, he's a Victorian lightweight, but I enjoy reading him for a little relaxation.' Cody dismissed a giant of literature as if he were a gnat, and turned her searching expression on Jude. 'You must be very busy. I hope you were able to resolve whatever pressing business made you late in and sharp out of my lecture.'

Aware of the press of people around them, particularly of the young woman so obviously desperate to snatch a few words with a celebrity, he leaned in and lowered his voice. 'I'm afraid not. Could I have a quick word with you?'

'On police business?' Her sharp gaze was a window onto an even sharper mind.

'Yes. I should have introduced myself properly. I'm Detective Chief Inspector Satterthwaite, Cumbria Police.'

Cody Wilder never missed a beat, keeping the smile for the benefit of any onlookers, but the cup trembled in the saucer she was holding. 'Has something happened?'

'I'm afraid so. Can we speak in private?'

'Sure.' She stepped away from Linda, who turned a troubled look on Jude, and glanced around. 'There's a meeting room over there. We can speak discreetly there.'

'We haven't met. Fi Styles.' Like Jude, the brunette had been circling waiting for her chance and she pounced before it was too late, holding out her hand. 'Journalist. Dr Wilder, I—'

'Not right now, Ms Styles.' Cody wasn't quite that composed. The tension cracked in her voice. 'I've already spoken to the journalists. Did you somehow manage to miss my briefing?'

The woman wasn't to be deflected. Journalists never were. 'I didn't have accreditation. I'm a freelancer. I write articles for print and digital outlets on art and literature and I wondered if I—'

'I'm afraid I don't have time right this moment. If it's

information about my research you need, my researcher can give it to you. Owen Armitstead. He'll answer any questions. Use the contact form on my website.' She headed towards the room she'd pointed out to Jude.

Fi Styles bounced along beside her with the optimism of a seagull tracking a fishing boat, secure in the belief that persistence would pay. 'I was hoping for an interview. I thought we could do a feature that showed your human side—'

'An interview? I'm planning to head back to New York in a couple of days. But contact Owen and let him know a little about yourself, and I can decide whether an interview would be feasible.' She strode away as if shaking herself free, reaching the meeting room and holding the door open for Jude.

'So… Chief Inspector.' She slammed the door behind him and the cold hostility of their earlier encounter returned as she did so. 'This had better be important. You must know what journalists are like when they smell any kind of a scandal. That young woman won't be put off.'

Jude experienced a sense of intense dislike, but if Cody wanted to take him on, she was welcome to try. 'I think you'll find it's very important. It's about your research assistant, Owen Armitstead.'

'What's the spoiled brat done now? I should have guessed he was up to something when he didn't turn up this morning.'

'It's very bad news. I'm afraid he's dead.' He watched her closely as he spoke, used to reading body language, but he'd never seen anything like Cody, aggressive and defensive at the same time, challenging his authority even before it was established.

She allowed herself a short, sharp breath. 'Who did it?'

'I'm not the investigating officer, Dr Wilder, and we don't know what happened. But as far as I can tell, he seems to have done it himself.'

He'd expected an expression of regret, if only for form's sake, but Cody confounded him with a judgemental snort. 'I don't know that I'm surprised. Owen is a moral coward.'

'I'm not a judge of that. And I'm not working in his case. The officer in charge asked me to tell you and that's what I've done.'

She stared at him. 'Then let's hope the officer in charge of the case is on the ball, Chief Inspector. And if that's all you have to say, perhaps you'll let me get back to my job.'

3

By the time the police had taken Owen's body away, interviewed Cody about his health, mental state and personality traits, checked up on her own personal welfare (receiving the shortest shrift for daring to suggest she might need emotional support) and allowed her to return to the cottage, the night had closed in and, after the crisp clarity of the winter's day, a sharp January frost had snapped down like a lock. She let herself out of the cottage, looked up at the black velvet awning of the sky, and smiled as she set off down Coffin Lane.

She loved the night. In her Wyoming childhood, where the silence was absolute but for the occasional howl of a distant wolf and only the huge moon and the haze of the Milky Way leavened the darkness, she'd seized every chance to step from the tumult of the house into solitude. Summer or winter there had been danger, in the heat or the cold, a snake or a bear. Out in the unforgiving wilderness, merely being human made you vulnerable, but here in the Lakes, positively urban by comparison, she feared nothing and no one. She was untouchable.

Frost crunched beneath her feet as she walked along the grass verge. At the bottom of the hill Coffin Lane gave on to

Red Bank Road, and she turned left towards the field where the New Agers camped. She wasn't the only person out enjoying the night. Voices drifted towards her from around a bend in the road and a beam of torchlight followed as a terrier, capering along towards her ahead of its owners, bounced up to meet her with enthusiasm.

'Howdy, li'l dude. How you doing?' She bent down to fuss it. She liked dogs, even dogs as bijou as this one, and if she hadn't chosen so peripatetic a life, she'd have had one. Not for company, because she wasn't a woman who was ever short of that when she wanted it, but because dogs were faithful to you in a way that few humans were. 'What a good boy you are. Good evening.'

The last remark, addressed to the dog's owners, was met by a damning silence. That surprised her. Currently resident in New York, Cody enjoyed the contrast the countryside offered, with everybody exchanging polite greetings no matter whether they were friends, enemies or complete strangers. In a moment of weakness, she tried again. 'It's a chilly night.'

The couple, very obviously, stepped to the opposite side of the road. The light of the torch swung away leaving her stranded in darkness as the man snapped his fingers for the dog.

The way the animal abandoned her at the sound of its master's voice pushed her good mood too far. 'I'm sorry. Did I say something wrong? Do I not sound British enough? Is it something else?'

Caught trying to please everyone, the dog capered back towards her and the couple turned. 'Dr Wilder,' the man said, almost breathless with emotion, 'you certainly did do something wrong.'

'Oh, right. And that was?' She advanced down the lane and still couldn't see their faces, but she didn't care who they were. They'd offered her a challenge and she was never going to walk away from it. If you did that you showed weakness, conceded victory.

'People like you,' the woman said, in a voice that matched the man's in tension, 'don't think about what you say or what the consequences are. You don't understand the influence you have on vulnerable young people. You don't care about the damage you can cause.'

'Oh, is that right, honey? Well, I guess we'll agree to differ. If you look back over everything I've ever said you'll see that I support freedom of speech, women's rights and diversity of thinking. Do you have a problem with that?'

'Come on Eliza. Don't engage.' The man whistled the dog again, this time with success, took the woman's hand and began walking, towing her behind him.

'Guess you're the kind of guy who treats your wife as if you own her, just like you do the dog,' Cody called after them. 'She's got every right to talk to me if she wants to. I'm always open for a discussion.' And he, after all, was the one who'd opened the discussion. But they didn't answer and disappeared in the direction of the village.

She followed them as far as the bend before she let them go, standing with hands on hips and her breath crystallising on the cold air, watching as their shadowy figures turned in to the cottage where the banner had hung earlier in the day. They must be the people who thought she was a murderer. That was a new addition to the plethora of accusations that had been levelled at her over the years, and now she'd heard it twice in two days. She shook her head. These little places always had their collections of weirdos.

When she was sure no one was watching her, she crossed the road and opened the gate into the New Agers' field. The campfires had burned down to their embers and the forlorn-looking place was in near darkness. In the daylight, patches of dead grass showed where summer residents had pitched their tents, but they must have gone somewhere warmer for the winter. A woman of conviction, Cody couldn't help admiring the convictions of others, even when they were so foolish and unworldly as those held by the die-hard campers and their fair-weather friends.

Taking care not to trip over the guy ropes, she tiptoed past the larger of the tents, where Storm and Raven made their home, past the one they used for storage and the one where Raven wove surprisingly fine-quality scarves to sell to pay for the things they could neither manage without nor acquire for themselves. Beyond those, another tent crouched in the long shadows cast by a clump of bare trees that stood between it and the lights of the village.

'Lynx.' Her voice was barely above a whisper.

No answer. She lifted the flap of the tent and peered in. Her nostrils filled with the odours of tobacco and damp canvas, her veins with excitement. In front of her, the unsophisticated chaos of a simple life sprawled in the dimness – clothes folded in a pile, cooking pots, a box of chocolates. Nothing else.

On the far side of it, seated cross-legged on the floor, a man peered up her and grinned. 'Cody, babe. I knew you couldn't keep away. You've come for something that pretty boy of yours can't give you, huh?'

Lynx was well-named, a name he'd no doubt chosen to match the animal attraction he possessed. With a thrill of excitement, she stepped inside and onto the boards from which he'd fashioned some kind of a floor and let the tent flap drop behind her. 'That pretty boy is dead. Don't tell me you didn't know that.'

He leaned back and looked at her through half-closed eyes. 'Is that what all the fuss was about? I saw the cops up at the cottage and thought they might be getting interested in you. After all this time.'

The air was thick with dust and wood smoke. She unzipped her jacket and dropped it on the floor by the tent opening, picking her way across to sit next to him on the mattress. 'No, that wasn't me. I expect the police will come around asking if you saw anything, if they haven't done that already.'

'We never see anything. Do they think someone killed him?'

'No, they think it was suicide. As do I. He was a fragile flower, was Owen. The world was far too much for him to handle.'

'They can ask if they like. I was minding my own business and living a blameless life. Like you do.'

'A blameless life is a bland life.'

'I could tell the world some things about you.'

'But you won't.' She cast a look round her, at the battery-powered heater and the lamp which gave a golden hue to the canvas womb in which he was enclosed. Lynx's threats added a frisson to their relationship, pushed its excitement beyond the physical into the psychological. She wasn't afraid of him but Owen's shadow was too close. She chose not to engage. 'What are these? Chocolates? Have you gone soft?'

'Take them. I won't eat them. They were a gift. But I'm vegan now.'

Cody picked up the box. They looked like decent quality. 'You don't look as if you've sacrificed all the comforts to me. I thought you came here to leave the modern world behind. Surely you should be sitting in the dark or by candlelight?'

He laughed. 'And have the place burn down around my ears? I'm here for the simple life, but not a dangerous one.'

That fitted. She shifted a little closer to him, riding a tidal wave of earthy, pheromonal scent. 'I'm here to ask you for a favour.'

'Ask nicely and give me something I want in return.'

The thrill pulsed again through her blood. 'I think I can manage that.'

Lynx placed a hand on the top of her thigh and laughed, a deep, throaty laugh. 'Tell me what the favour is and I'll tell you how much you need to pay.'

She fought to concentrate. 'I want you to look after something for me.'

For a second he waited, his fingers playing on the denim of her jeans as he pretended to think about it. In reality, she knew, the deal was already concluded, the only thing left open to them being how long to play about before they got down to business. 'What is it?'

'Nothing important. Just some letters.'

'Compromising letters?' He moved closer and his breath was hot on her neck. 'Can I guess? Letters from Brandon, perhaps?'

She shivered with anticipation. Sex was a game, that was all. She was good at it and Lynx was better than almost anyone she'd known. 'Not compromising at all. Brandon's my brother. Your suggestion is most inappropriate.'

'Then what are they?'

'As if you care.' Reaching out, she curled a hand around the back of his neck, up into his hair, and pulled his face down towards her until it almost touched her own. Close up, a faint smell of soap and shampoo indicated just how little he was committed to the lifestyle he pretended to have chosen. That was what she always liked about him. His conscience had the flexibility of an Olympic gymnast and he could be trusted only not to be trusted, but she thought he'd help her this time. 'They're just some letters I don't want anyone else to get hold of.'

'And no one's going to come looking for your precious treasures with the likes of me. Is that it?'

'Something like that.' Their lips touched before she was ready, and she drew away, teasing herself as much as she teased him. 'Cain Harper. You're a gorgeous beast. Did anyone ever tell you that?'

'My name's Lynx.'

'You'll always be Cain to me.'

'You and your brother are very close,' he purred into her ear, his hand moving with confidence up from her thigh and under her sweater. 'Don't people talk?'

'Of course we're close. There were just the two of us when we grew up. There was no one else to be close to.' You got what the devil gave you.

'Just you and big brother and Mom and Pop. Proper little nuclear family, huh?' He kissed her then, employing strength and power and passion without subtlety or restraint, bending her backwards and pressing his lean body on top of her like the beast she'd just likened him to. 'Hell, I've missed you, honey. I'm going to eat you alive tonight, bite by bite, tear the flesh off your bones like a wolf, and you're going to love it.'

She twisted away from him and turned her back, and he came after her, his teeth nipping at her neck. Pain equalled pleasure and pleasure, in its turn, nullified pain. His fingernails dug into her skin as he clawed his way upward. 'Go on then. Do it.'

'What a woman you are. How did you manage not to spontaneously combust, growing up out on that ranch without a man nearby? Except your father and your brother.'

'Are you jealous?' she laughed. Adrenaline rippled through her body. But she controlled herself, for the sake of heightened pleasure in a few moments' time. 'Is that it? You've nothing to be jealous of.'

'I'm jealous as hell. I'm jealous of every man who's ever laid an innocent finger on you, let alone a guilty one. I always will be.' Turning her over, he rolled her off the mattress on which they'd been sitting and onto the bare boards, crawling on all fours above her. His fingers pulled at the buttons of her top.

She might resist him. She might try and fight him off, for the pleasure of feeling exactly how much he wanted her. Or she might try and take control and fight him that way. She didn't know. She only knew that she wanted everything he could give her. 'You've no need to be jealous. I'm all yours.'

The boards were hard and cold under her back as he stripped her down to her panties and knelt above her. 'You sure are. You're mine, Cody Wilder. Mine.'

She belonged to nobody, but it was an argument she'd

have with him another time. He rolled her over onto her stomach again, like a crocodile trying to drown its prey, and crawled up behind her, one hand creeping over her breasts, catching the nipple in a mean-spirited pinch. 'Shall I take you like this? Here on all fours, like the bitch you are?'

Something snapped inside her, some trigger. 'No. Not like this.' Panic rolled up inside her and she fought against him. 'Not like this!'

He let her go, but only for a second, until she'd wriggled round to face him again. 'Ah! Something you don't like.'

She lay down, safe on her back, reaching up towards him. 'Take me now. Like this.'

He leaned down over her, took both hands and stretched them above her head. 'Someone did something to you that you didn't like. Is that it?'

She nodded. Her heart beat faster, faster.

'Who was it?'

Lynx's body came ever closer to hers and, thank God, expunged the memories. 'It doesn't matter. Forget it.'

'Shall I guess, Cody? I think I have an idea.'

'No.' She shook a hand free and pulled him down towards her. Being in his power, which had seemed so deliciously novel, now seemed like a bad idea. She'd almost forgotten how vicious and manipulative he could be, how the things that made him so attractive and appealing made him dangerous as well. 'No. Never guess. I don't want to talk about it.'

'Oh, I see.' That low animal laugh again. 'Well, you know what? I guess I may know who he was. And ain't it just as well for you he's dead?'

4

'I'd like to sit in on this, if you don't mind. Just to keep up with what's going on.' Jude pulled up a chair next to the table where Doddsy had just sat down with his trademark list of things to get through. 'I won't speak until spoken to. You're the boss on this.' He pushed his chair back a foot, for emphasis.

Forewarned by Jude over the phone the night before, Ashleigh had come into the office fully expecting to find herself seconded to help in the investigation of Owen Armitstead's apparent suicide. Taking care not to seem over-familiar, she gave him her best professional nod. Her previous experience of workplace relationships had been salutary but she'd learned from her mistakes and even if she hadn't, Jude, who was professional to a fault, could be counted on to make sure that it wouldn't get awkward for either of them.

Nevertheless, she stole a sideways glance at him before returning her attention to Doddsy's lean face. At least this time she'd embarked on an affair with a man rather than a woman and neither of them already had a partner. She flushed slightly as she remembered how much of a fool she'd made of herself in her previous job, in the wreckage-strewn aftermath of her failed marriage, and how she'd had to hightail it to Cumbria with what was left of her reputation. She looked across the room at the last leaf of winter still clinging to the top of a tree, and a gleam of light where the sun cracked the clouds and a battalion of sunbeams went charging across the roofs of Penrith. Her relationship with Jude might not go the distance but she was confident it would end well. She turned her attention back to the meeting.

'I'll be glad to have you on my team,' Doddsy said to Jude to general laughter. 'You might have something useful to add. Seeing as you got off to such a great start with Dr Wilder.' He must have heard the story of his boss's brush with the academic, and shook his head in what looked like admiration. 'You're a braver man than I am, taking her on.'

'Is she staying on in Grasmere?'

'Yes. I've asked her not to leave until enquiries are complete. She had plans to go back to the States in a couple of days but seemed happy enough to change them. Says there's always more work she can do.'

'That'll have implications for our operations. I suppose I'll need to leave someone keeping half an eye on her. If there was a threat before, it hasn't gone away.' Jude wrinkled his face in vague dissatisfaction.

Dissatisfaction suited him. Ashleigh hid her smile and addressed herself to Doddsy. 'I don't suppose there's any doubt about what happened to Owen Armitstead?'

'I don't think so. There's nothing that stands out as immediately suspicious, though given the threats to Dr Wilder, we need to treat it as something more than a routine suicide.' That was why Doddsy was involved when normally someone junior would have taken on the task, why Jude was keeping that watching brief. 'I had the CSI people down there yesterday, and I'm expecting the results of the PM around lunchtime. But to be honest, I'll be very surprised if it isn't straightforward. It looks as if he waited until Cody Wilder had left in the morning to go to her lecture, and then hanged himself in the kitchen.' Doddsy spilled some printed photographs onto the table. 'Oak beams. Nasty things. I wouldn't have them.'

Picking up a picture of Owen clad in a pair of stars and stripes boxers and lying sprawled where his rescuer had cut him down, Ashleigh once more contemplated the inevitability of fate. She could imagine him, stumbling about in the kitchen like a student with a hangover, pitching over the edge of the table as he took the last clumsy step to his death. The noose was still over the beam and its shadow lay across his scrawny torso. 'He and his boss were both staying there. Is that right? That's very swanky for an academic. I thought they were all poor.'

'Dr Wilder's controversial, and if you handle that right there's money in it. Books, lectures, appearance fees and what have you. She'd rented the cottage in Coffin Lane for a couple of weeks and they were staying while she finalised her presentation and carried out further research in the archives. According to her version he didn't appear for breakfast and when she called him, he said he'd join her in time for the talk. She went down to the venue and he didn't turn up, so obviously she carried on without him.'

'So he waited until she'd gone and hanged himself.' Tired of fanning through endless intrusive shots, all different angles on a simple conundrum, Ashleigh dropped the photos back on the desk.

'Looks like it. The landlord reckoned he was still warm when he found him. The PM will give us a reasonable time of death, but it looks to me as if he took a while to decide to do the deed.' Doddsy's voice softened with sympathy.

Sometimes Ashleigh thought Doddsy was too good a man to be a policeman. You needed a core of steel, a heart of lead and a titanium soul, something to protect you. It was amazing he'd lasted as long in the force as he had. 'Do we know why?'

'No idea. He left no note, or none that we've found so far. The rope came from the shed, so it wasn't as though he'd had to make an effort to go out and get it. That's one of the things we have to look at.'

'Have we spoken to his parents?'

'Not yet. They're travelling up from Berkshire this morning. The local police have allocated them a Family Liaison Officer.' He hesitated. 'I'd like you to go along and talk to them, too. Not in an official FLO role, obviously. But to ask the odd question.'

There was a frisson of doubt in his voice, and Ashleigh waited for Jude to object. Her last flirtation with family liaison had been an unsuccessful one. She was qualified for the role and it had taken her too long to realise that she wasn't emotionally suited for it. But the department was aware of her strengths as well as her weaknesses. People talked to her and Jude, accepting that, shrugged any objections aside and kept silence.

'Of course I'll do it. What can you tell me about him?'

'Chris did a bit of digging yesterday afternoon and this morning. I'll get him to see what more he can find. Owen Armitstead was twenty-five and came from Reading. He had a first-class degree from Reading University and was studying for a PhD there, on the Romantic poets. He took a year out from that to work with Cody Wilder on her project, which tied in closely with his own thesis. He's academically gifted, without being exceptionally so – more of a grafter than the inspired researcher.'

The perfect foil, it appeared for his mercurial boss. 'How long had he been working for Dr Wilder?'

'Since August.'

'And what do we know about his character?' Because this was where the key to suicides – and murders – was inevitably found.

'Very little. That's why I'm keen to find out. His boss, I should add, was scornful of him, although I didn't engage in a formal interview with her.' He cleared his throat. 'That's something else I'd like you to take on.'

Jude, sitting back and spectating, allowed himself a laugh. 'Good luck with that.'

His reward was a reproachful look. 'I'm not dodging the job. Dr Wilder strikes me as someone who doesn't have a lot of time for men in authority. On that basis, she's more likely to talk to Ashleigh than to us.'

'If she talks to anyone.'

'You broke the news to her, didn't you?' Already, Ashleigh's mind was flitting over how she might handle the notorious, antagonistic Cody Wilder. One thing was certain – a gladiatorial approach wouldn't work. 'How did she react?'

Jude pushed his chair back even further and frowned. 'Not well. But she strikes me as the sort who judges people on the instant and whose reaction to them is fixed in stone, and she'd already taken against me because I arrived late for her lecture and left early. It's as well I'm not directly involved, because I don't think I'd get a lot out of her, and I don't think her response to me was necessarily a natural one. Allowing for that, I still wasn't impressed.'

'I can't say I was,' confirmed Doddsy. 'Nor Chris. But we're all men.'

'Women getting all the hard jobs again, eh?' Ashleigh winked at him. Cody Wilder might be difficult but she'd be intriguing. 'Did she seem upset?'

'No. Irritated, perhaps. She described him as a weakling and a moral coward and her only real concern seemed to me that what happened isn't in any way a threat to her.'

'Which may or may not be the case. But for the life of me, I can't see why anyone would hurt him to hurt her, if she held him in such contempt. She certainly didn't go to any great lengths to hide it when I spoke to her, either.' Doddsy pulled out a picture of Owen Armitstead and laid it on the table.

It was the first time Ashleigh had seen an image of him as a living being – foppishly dressed as if for an over-the-top publisher's party, in a three-piece suit with a sapphire-blue cravat. A long fringe flopped down over his thin face and he peered at the camera from beneath it. The smile that hovered on his narrow lips lacked confidence but the dark eyes were full of fascination. 'He was a good-looking boy, wasn't he? In a Victorian poet kind of way. What an interesting face.'

'Very interesting. I'd like to know what kind of relationship she had with him. Whether it went beyond the workplace. Not that there's anything wrong with that.'

Jude dared to flip her a look. Doddsy was his best friend so there were no secrets to be hidden from him, but even that tiny action suggested he might be loosening up a little. She returned the look, garnishing it with a smile. 'Do we know anything about it? She's pretty scandalous, isn't she?'

'Yes. Chris had a scout around the internet and there's plenty to be found. She's written a series of short biographies of women poets for a feminist publisher that sold well – the critics hated them but the punters loved them. She isn't shy of putting controversial opinions out there, and there's nothing that's off topic. She contradicts herself often enough. It'll be interesting to see what she actually believes. If you can get that much out of her, of course.'

'I had a look, too.' People used social media to create a facade, but even doing so they often gave away some of the truth. When she'd met Cody Wilder, Ashleigh sensed she'd find vulnerability beneath the bullish image the woman chose to project, but there was no sign of it anywhere in cyberspace. 'She's put a lot of people's backs up. And there's a lot of stuff out there that's positively slanderous about her work, and her methods, and her personal life. But she's never bothered to deny any of it.' Though whether that meant the allegations had the grain of truth or were so shallow that Cody could afford to ignore them was something that remained to be established. 'Academically she has a lot of enemies, too.'

'She fell out with the established universities and then made a success of working alone, that's why. It's the reason Owen had to take a break from his PhD to work with her on her big project.' Doddsy looked down as a message pinged onto his phone. 'Ah, I knew this would happen. That's the press office. People are hassling them for a statement. I need to get on. Can I leave it with you to get down to Grasmere and keep me informed?'

'Sure.'

'And to think you missed the reveal.' As Doddsy made his way out of the office, Ashleigh got up and gathered up the photos, sliding them back into their envelope, twitching the last one from Jude's fingers as he stared down at it. 'Did you ever find out what her big story was?'

'I'd almost forgotten. Yes, my mum filled me in on it. The story isn't Dorothy Wordsworth's journal. It's her letters. To William Wordsworth's wife, Mary. Apparently they imply that Dorothy conceived and later lost her brother's child.'

Ashleigh lifted a quizzical eyebrow. 'Is that right? I know there's been a lot of research, and some academics believe there was incest between William and Dorothy, but confessing it to Mary?'

'Dr Wilder's hypothesis is that Mary Wordsworth was complaisant and assisted in the end of the pregnancy.'

'That's certainly a new take on things. She must be desperate to get hold of the other half of the correspondence. I think most people assumed that the missing journal wouldn't exactly be dynamite, but this is different.' Ashleigh placed the envelope of photographs in a folder and found that Jude was looking at her with faint surprise. 'Don't look so astonished. I studied the Romantics at uni. I went to study English, but I dropped out to join the police.'

'Right.'

They hadn't known each other long, but Jude was a man who liked to know everything whereas Ashleigh preferred to keep her secrets. Still, there was no harm in this one.

'Write me down as a failed poet. It didn't feel to me at the time as if there was an awful lot of relevance to what I was reading and I was never sure that digging around in people's past was what I wanted to do.'

'And now here you are,' he said with a laugh, 'doing exactly that.'

When Ashleigh had gone and Doddsy had turned back to constructing a suitably neutral statement to put out to the press, Jude made his way down to the canteen to pick up a cup of coffee before heading up to DS Groves's office. Groves had resented the arrival of Cody Wilder and the pressure it had placed on his resources and he wouldn't take kindly to the news that she'd be staying longer, but until Doddsy had established the cause of Owen Armitstead's death, the very real risk she brought with her would remain.

He reviewed what he knew, even as he sat down in the corner of the canteen with his coffee and prepared to check in with Chris, who was still in Grasmere. Cody's antics on Twitter had attracted a catalogue of the vilest threats and, while the majority of them were the work of keyboard warriors who never saw the light of day, she was too high-profile for him to ignore them. Her revelations about the Wordsworth letters had, he'd noted when he'd checked that morning, generated a new firestorm of accusations about her professional approach and allegations about her personal life to add to the internet's bubbling fury about – among other things – her opposition to gun control and her advocacy of unrestricted violence in self-defence. Even without involving himself in the investigation into Owen's death, he would have to make sure someone was monitoring them.

He sighed as he called Chris. 'I'm just checking in with you. Doddsy's sending Ashleigh down to take over on the unexplained death, but as we seem to be stuck with Dr Wilder for a few days yet, I'm still going to need you to keep an eye on the security front.'

'Sure. I can do that.' A rumble of traffic and the clattering shout of a jackdaw at the other end of the line indicated that Chris must be outside. 'I don't think we need much, to be honest. If you can make sure there are a couple of uniforms floating around in the village that should be enough to remind people we're here.'

'Okay.' Jude reviewed his resources. 'I'm going to send Ashleigh down to speak to Cody Wilder. When she gets there, you can come back up. I've told Doddsy he can use you for ferreting out what we can find about Owen Armitstead, if everything's gone quiet at your end.'

'As the grave. I couldn't even find anywhere open for a coffee until ten o'clock. I thought this was meant to be a tourist hotspot.'

Jude grinned. In time, Chris would learn to have a flask of coffee in the boot of his car. 'Have all the demonstrators gone?'

'Yeah. They packed up and left yesterday evening.'

'And the banner? I don't suppose you found anything about that?'

'Everything. Or rather, someone's version of everything. I spoke to the guy who put it up. His name is Graham Gordon, and he and his wife Eliza run a sweet shop and cafe in the village. They make their own chocolate, that sort of thing.

They've got a sad enough story, but it's nothing to do with Cody Wilder. He and his wife lost their daughter and her unborn baby to a violent ex-partner, and the two of them took exception to an interview she gave to a newspaper.'

Jude sighed. There would be a few people who'd done that. 'What did she say?'

'It was about women's refuges. There are some blinding quotes in it. She went on about the snowflake generation and how they should give as good as they get. If you let people push you around you can't complain about what happens to you. Any self-respecting woman will stand up for herself and if she chooses not to, she deserves what comes to her. I paraphrase, but it's the gist of it.'

'That's one approach.'

Unimpressed by Cody's opinions, Chris shrugged. It wasn't as if he hadn't seen the impacts of domestic violence first-hand, too often, picked up too many battered souls and clapped too many violent partners in handcuffs. 'The best protection is strength of purpose, lack of compromise and, if necessary, a shotgun, apparently. I'm not surprised the Gordons got upset about it, but as their daughter was murdered months before the date of the interview it seems a bit of a contortion to accuse the doctor of having been responsible.'

No doubt, in her particular way of thinking, Cody would chalk that reaction up as some kind of a success. 'Okay. We'll leave it at that.'

He rang off, what passed for a coffee break over. Something at the back of his mind suggested that the relationship between Cody and Owen might not have been as simple as that between employee and employer and that even though there was nothing to suggest foul play, it might yet leave some kind of stain on what passed for her conscience.

Cody's insistence on any interview taking place in a cafe in the village, rather than in the cottage where Owen had been found dead was, Ashleigh suspected, a pre-emptive strike to establish her own authority and dictate terms. The academic's opening gambit reinforced the idea.

'So.' Trim in jeans and a brightly coloured fleece, Cody sashayed her way across the cafe to the table where Ashleigh rose to shake her hand. 'They've sent someone else down to talk to me, have they? You're DS O'Halloran? Let's hope you're a more sympathetic interviewer than either that chief inspector or his sidekick. Queer as a three-dollar bill, he is, by the way. Nothing wrong with that, but let's not pretend otherwise.'

No one could reasonably describe Doddsy as unsympathetic and the reference to his sexuality must be designed to provoke a reaction. Refusing to give her the satisfaction, Ashleigh immediately understood that this witness wasn't going to be easily kept to facts. Extraordinary, given her background in research and her reported meticulous attention to detail and evidence. 'It's good to meet you at last, Dr Wilder. Thanks for agreeing to talk to us.' Though she'd had little choice. A refusal would have indicated she had something to hide. 'I'm sure you want to help me find out what happened to Owen.'

'We know what happened to him. He killed himself, and

I've already given my version of what happened. It's done. Do we really need to know any more?'

'We owe Mr Armitstead and his family a thorough investigation into the circumstances.' Ashleigh took her courage in both hands and met Cody's gaze. Pale hazel eyes, direct and demanding, confronted her, evaluating her as if she were the witness rather than the questioner. 'Also, perhaps, yourself.'

'I hope you're not suggesting I'm in any way responsible for his death.' Cody brushed her hair back from her face and glowered.

With a sigh, Ashleigh recognised a born grievance-monger and reminded herself that you should always leave your enemy a golden bridge over which to retreat. Not doing so might be a mistake Cody chose to make, but Ashleigh was smarter than that. 'No. It must obviously have been very upsetting for you, as well as inconvenient. And as you worked so closely with him, it might be that there's some comfort you can offer his parents.'

'Hmm.' Seemingly unconvinced, Cody turned as she sat and delivered herself promptly into the hands of a young woman Ashleigh had noticed hovering outside the window like a teenager waiting for a date and who had entered the cafe hot on Cody's heels.

'Dr Wilder.' The smile was effortless, the confidence supreme. 'Fi Styles. We met very briefly after your talk—'

'A latte for me,' said Cody to the waitress who'd presented herself as if she knew the hassle that would come with being slow. 'And—?' She looked at Ashleigh.

'An Americano.'

'An Americano. And a piece of that iced fruit cake.'

Ashleigh shook her head at the offer of cake, watching Fi Styles bouncing on the balls of her feet as she waited.

'Dr Wilder. About the interview. You told me I had to contact Owen but—'

'It isn't the right moment, Ms Styles. Can we leave it? I've got important business.'

'Perhaps if I could call you.'

'No. I'll decide whether to call you.' Cody sat down and turned her back.

'I'll give you my number. My card.' Fi slid it onto the table.

'I can find your number for myself, honey,' sighed Cody, without turning around. There was a brief silence, after which Fi beat a retreat and Cody folded the card in half and tucked it into her pocket. 'Sorry about this. These people have no subtlety.'

They sat back while the waitress delivered the order and Fi removed herself completely from the cafe. 'Okay.' Cody ripped the top off a paper tube of sugar and shot the contents into her latte. 'You've got questions. Ask them.'

Outside the cafe, Fi loitered on the pavement by a stone wall thick with moss, swinging her handbag. Intrigued, Ashleigh nevertheless didn't dare risk giving Cody less than her full attention, so she turned away from the journalist with her most reassuring smile. 'We know the facts about Owen's life, but not his personality. What sort of man was he?'

'Intelligent. Dedicated. Hardworking.' Cody stirred her coffee, rattling the spoon around inside the mug. 'I take it you want the truth, not the eulogy. Uninspired. A follower, not a leader. A man with a low opinion of himself and no stomach for the tough things in life.' She paused for a moment, the pause that Ashleigh recognised as encapsulating a fractional breath preceding a lie. 'We got on well. I'm astonished that he took his life, even more astonished that something was troubling him and he felt he couldn't tell me.'

'Your relationship was good?'

'Oh, sure. How could it be anything else? We worked together a lot. Some of the time Owen lived in London and carried out research for me in the UK. I'm mainly based in New York, though I have spent a lot of time over here, in the various locations where the Wordsworths lived. One has to immerse oneself in their world. And Jeez, what a world it is.' She glanced out of the window beyond Fi Styles, at the small-windowed grey stone building peeping through a thicket of rhododendrons. 'When we were in the same place, it was full on. I work hard and I expect my students and researchers to do the same. You get nowhere without hard work.' She dismembered the cake, splitting it into its constituent parts of marzipan, icing and cake, and popped the marzipan into her mouth.

'Owen was on a year's internship. Is that right?'

'Yes. My policy is to take researchers on year-long placements, and I choose post-graduate students looking for some experience of high-level research. Owen was working in that field.' Another fractional pause. 'I have a high reputation in academic circles. A year working for me is a valuable entry on a CV.'

She lifted her head from the coffee and stared hard across the table. The pale eyes narrowed, shoulders drawn slightly backward in what Ashleigh, fascinated, judged the classic pose of a liar, or at the very least of someone skilled in not telling the whole truth. In her experience people often did that in the aftermath of a suicide, to protect themselves from real or imagined blame. They wanted to persuade themselves that it wasn't their fault, that if they'd seen any clues to something being wrong it wasn't reasonable to expect them to act upon them. But Cody Wilder's manipulation of the story seemed somehow different.

'Mr Armitstead was—' Ashleigh made a point of checking her notes, though she knew them off by heart '—twenty-five.'

'You brought me here to tell me what I already know?'

'No. I'm hoping you can help me.' It was a struggle to keep her patience. 'How did his state of mind strike you beforehand?'

Cody seemed to relax. 'I can't lie to you, Sergeant. As we approached the launch, Owen was struggling with the pressure. He ran my social media accounts, and I don't think he was able to cope with some of the trolls on there. Of course, I tried to talk to him about it and I offered him reassurance, but he took it personally. He was always going to struggle to make it in academia. We have to learn to be bitches, in our ivory towers.' Her laugh had an unpleasant edge. 'I believe he was on some kind of medication, so I'm even more surprised at what he did. I wasn't aware of anything specific that was troubling him. You'd need to ask around.'

'Would you say your relationship was close?'

'You mean, was I sleeping with him?' This time the doctor gave way to a snort. 'I'm forty this year and he was a very infantile twenty-five. When I go looking for a sexual partner, I don't look for people like Owen Armitstead. It was a purely professional relationship.'

'She lied,' Ashleigh said to Doddsy, calling him as soon as she'd got through a tortuous half an hour with Cody and ordered herself a second coffee with which to recover. 'I don't mean about everything. I don't even mean a lot. But I'd bet my job that she doesn't want us to know something, and after thirty minutes in her company I'm going to suggest that she's a hell of a difficult woman to work with.'

'The sister act didn't work, then?' At the other end of the line Doddsy allowed himself a sardonic laugh. 'Sorry about that. I thought she'd be more receptive to you than to any of the rest of us.'

Ashleigh watched through the steamy cafe window, as out in the street, Cody paused to check her phone. Fi Styles materialised beside her. The two exchanged words and Cody strode off, leaving Fi looking cheerfully after her. Strange, the way Fi aped Cody with the same style of jacket, jeans, boots and that 1950s high-school ponytail. 'She wasn't out and out rude. But she was obstructive and challenging and evasive. Hiding something, for sure. But that doesn't mean she's guilty of anything other than being unpleasant to him and smart enough to realise, with hindsight, that he couldn't handle it and some people might say she could have stopped it.'

'I think you'd have to say she has an abrupt management style.' She could imagine Doddsy shaking his head.

'She must have made a hell of an impact in the village.

You should have seen the way the waitress was looking at her.'

'They get their fair share of brash Americans, I daresay.'

'I've come across a few myself, but never one like Cody Wilder.'

'Yeah, but hopefully she'll be on her way soon. I've had the results of the post-mortem back, and the crime scene assessment. It all points to suicide. The toxicology results show he'd taken a significant dose of his medication – not enough to kill him, but enough to stop him thinking straight. So except for the formalities, I think we can say it's case closed.'

5

Owen Armitstead's family and Louise, the Family Liaison Officer who'd been assigned to them, arrived on their sorry pilgrimage to Grasmere on Friday afternoon. Meeting them at Cody's rented cottage – the only one in the appropriately named Coffin Lane – gave Ashleigh her first chance to view the scene of their son's apparent suicide.

The kitchen wasn't large, and she and Louise stepped out of the room as soon as they could, so as not to crowd the moment Owen's parents spent with their son's ghost. The dim hallway was typical of its type, the old-world set up with heavy wooden furniture, its walls hung with sepia photographs of hikers and fishermen, or Victorian etchings of surrounding fells. Less interested in the permanent furnishings than in the traces of its current occupants, Ashleigh took a careful look around her. There was little or no sign that Owen had ever been there, as if he'd kept his personal items out of sight. The two coats hanging behind the door, a rain jacket and a thick woollen coat, were both very obviously women's clothing. The pair of leather cowboy boots in the corner had a feminine touch to their decoration. A pile of tattered old books contrasted with a stack of copies of Cody's newest work, on a bureau whose top drawer had a key standing proud from its lock.

She strayed into the kitchen while Louise guided the Armitsteads along the corridor to Owen's room. The kitchen faced the village and she looked out onto a brave January day, with a sheen of ice on the surface of the lake and a breath of cloud snagged on the fell top. Sunlight chased shadows across the leafless woods on the lower slopes of the fells opposite and as Owen's parents set about coming to terms with their loss, the village went about its business. A tourist bus passed along the road on the far side of Grasmere and turned into the car park. Figures moved in the New Agers' camp. Life went on undisturbed as it had done since the days of the Wordsworths, as curious and eccentric to the villagers in their day as Cody was in a modern era.

'Perhaps his personal items...?' Owen's mother was asking Louise as they left his room, almost pleading.

'We'll get them to you as soon as we can.'

'Thank you so much.' Mrs Armitstead stood for a second on the doorstep as Louise opened it for her, straightening the faux-fur collar of her black coat in preparation for facing the world. She wiped a tear from her eye and strode out down the path. Her husband followed, then Louise, and finally Ashleigh closed and locked the door behind her and joined them as they stood where the branches of a yew tree overhung the gate. The cottage had been there a long time and the yew tree probably longer. They'd seen many an unhappy person come and go and would see out many more. 'You've been so good to us. You, in particular. And Louise.'

Louise was, indeed, a reassuringly calm woman with the manner of a sympathetic nurse, who seemed able to absorb the bad vibes and emit the positive, much more capable of handling emotions than Ashleigh herself had ever managed. What surprised her most as she walked down Coffin Lane next to Owen's father with his mother and Louise walking behind them, was their extraordinary acceptance of their loss.

'I'm not angry,' his father said to her, as they reached the bottom of the lane. Cody had made a point of being absent when they'd arrived at the cottage and now the visit to the scene of their son's death over, Owen's parents had expressed a wish to walk around the village as he had done. 'Heartbroken, yes. Of course. He was my child and I loved him. But Owen was someone who always found life difficult. He set himself impossibly high standards, personally and professionally, and he struggled to meet them.' He dug in his pocket for a handkerchief, dabbing at his eyes.

'It must be so difficult for you.'

'Yes. And it won't get any easier. But he was always going to be unhappy. Some people are. Even when he got this job – his dream job – we knew it wouldn't make him happy. Even he knew it. He said that Cody Wilder was a challenge he had to take on and if he couldn't work with her for a year, he didn't deserve to make it in life. And it seems as though he couldn't.'

They turned past the field where the New Agers were camped. An enticing smell of cooked meat drifted towards them and a woman swathed in layers of hand-knitted woollens stood next to a campfire, turning something on the embers of a brazier. It looked as if they had a canny lifestyle, one they'd evolved until it worked. Sometimes, Ashleigh thought, there was a lot to be said for a simple life, free of the pressures people created for themselves. 'Have you spoken to Dr Wilder?'

'No.' Mr Armitstead's expression darkened. 'She wrote us a very charming letter of condolence but she didn't offer to see us and my wife and I would prefer not to meet her.'

That must be why Cody had made herself scarce. She'd gone up on the fells, according to Chris, walking in the Wordsworths' footsteps. 'I see.'

'Owen had a high opinion of Cody Wilder, Sergeant. Purely academically, of course. That's something I understand. But personally, she didn't live up to it.'

Mrs Armitstead must have caught the end of the conversation and stepped forward, leaving Louise behind her. 'Say what you mean. Owen had something of a crush on his boss, and while he never told us anything intimate—'

'Obviously, he wouldn't. He wasn't like that.' Her husband snatched at her hand in an agonised moment of shared loss.

'I had a mother's sense.' Mrs Armitstead was talking to her husband now, as if Ashleigh and Louise weren't there, and he was listening to her with the earnestness of a lover. 'That woman is a sexual predator. Read some of the articles about her, some of the interviews she gave. She's never made any pretence to be anything else, although of course she doesn't call it that. She calls it sexual freedom and absence of guilt. She's given interviews on how it's impossible to have a close working relationship without some sexual tension, regardless of gender. It's something she was proud of.'

'Nonsense to most people, of course,' he agreed. 'But she believed it.'

'She did. And of course, poor Owen saw things differently. He was so much gentler, so much more spiritual.'

'And he was right. But a woman like that doesn't understand how different people can work at different levels. If there was anything between them then he would have taken it far more seriously than she did. When he realised the truth, he'd have felt betrayed, and he'd have taken it out on himself.'

'If the woman did want to see us, we'd be right to say no, wouldn't we?'

'Without question. Although it isn't that we're angry. What's the point in being angry? It won't bring Owen back.'

They stopped and stared at one another in the middle of the street and the tears came to them both. Stepping back to join Louise and allow the two of them their moment of quiet grief before they left to head back and learn to endure life without their child, Ashleigh's eye was caught by a high ponytail bobbing out of the churchyard. Fi Styles. That was all they needed. According to Jude's account of his own brief encounter with her and the quick piece of research he must have managed in a spare moment, Fi was a young journalist trying to make a breakthrough. Her interest in Cody Wilder was understandable at one level, even admirable, but Ashleigh hoped Fi would have the decency to back away from the Armitsteads' raw and open grief. Owen's death was suicide and no one could have anything to say that would add to the story without the loss of decency or dignity.

Fi, clearly interested, didn't disappear, but nor did she

approach, shadowing them round the sombre streets of the grey village, past the cafe and the bookshop and the graves of the Wordsworths. When someone came shooting out of one of the gifts shops to check on who they were and offer their condolences, she hung back, picking up again as they moved on. When the visit concluded at the car park she stopped at the outer edge, leaning on the wall and playing with her phone and looking for all the world like a tourist too saturated with a rural experience to appreciate it.

I'll never stop appreciating it, Ashleigh said to herself as she breathed in the sweet scent of leaves after rain. The Lakes for an office and Jude for a boss in work and an equal outside it? What more could she ask for?

'Goodbye,' she said to the Armitsteads. 'I know nothing will ever compensate for your loss, but I hope that seeing the place will have brought you some closure.' A futile, fatuous thing to say, but it was better than silence.

'Thank you so much, Sergeant O'Halloran.' Mrs Armitstead clutched her hand as her husband, still gallant after decades of marriage, opened the door for her. 'You've helped us through a difficult day.'

They got into the car and Louise started the engine and drove off into the gloom that was encroaching on the sun, fog strengthening around the crags of the Lion and the Lamb, ready to slide down and fill the vale. Aware of Fi hovering yards away, Ashleigh gave her the merest fraction of an opportunity to approach, her politely worded rebuff already phrased, but the woman did nothing, so she slid into the car and called work. 'On my way back into the office now, Doddsy. See you in forty-five minutes. In the meantime, you might want to get someone to look up and find out what kind of relationship Dr Wilder had with her other research assistants.' And then, driving past the marked police car that was meant to show everybody that no matter how objectionable she was, Cody Wilder was still entitled to the protection of the law, she headed back through the gathering fog to Penrith.

'Honey. I'm so sorry it took me so long. Life just gets in the way sometimes. I couldn't make the flights work from Denver. Had to go via Chicago and there were cancellations. Hellish place. Fog. Too late, I know, but I made it.' Brandon Wilder III, his lean cowboy's face stained by the disturbed sleep of a multi-leg transatlantic journey, let go of the suitcase he'd hauled from the taxi and stepped over the threshold into his sister's arms.

The relief. Cody clung to him, brushing her cheek against two days' worth of stubble as he clasped her into a bear hug. Two days of hell since Owen's death – no, she corrected herself, remembering not to exaggerate, two days of stress – melted away. In public and in private she disregarded threats but Brandon's arrival meant that even the slight concern, one she hadn't understood she was feeling, disappeared. Her hero since the day he'd taken their father's shotgun and blasted the head off a snake in the back yard when she was barely more than a child, he would look after her here the way he always had done in Wyoming.

'Where the hell have you been?' Her voice was pitched high with excitement as she rehearsed the question that had raced through her brain for hours, even though he'd already answered it. She'd missed him so much. Even in New York she felt his absence and the faint hostility of tame, green Grasmere would surely be banished by his presence.

'Oh, honey. I know. Sorry I missed your big show. I couldn't help it. Feels like I've been travelling for days.' Letting her go, he checked his watch. 'Hell, I have been travelling for days. Didn't you get my messages?' He reached out and tweaked her ponytail, just as he used to do.

She shook her head, ushering him in from the night fog, doing the calculations in her head. It was two days since the lecture she'd been so keen for him to attend and if he'd left in time to make it, he must have experienced horrendous delays. Chicago was notorious for its fog, rolling in off Lake Michigan and settling on the city for days. 'You could have let me know.'

'You know me.' He gave her the extravagant shrug and the smile for which she'd forgive him anything.

Brandon had never been a great communicator, a man who wrote letters only when he had to and never tried too hard to tackle modern technology. And why would he? Out in the middle of nowhere, twenty miles down a rough track, you had to be able to manage without. She didn't comment. It meant more to her than to him, but at least he'd tried to get there. The thought counted. 'Come in. Sit down. The fire's lit. I'll get you a bourbon. And something to eat. You must be starving.'

'I don't know what time my body clock thinks it is.' He followed her into the living room and sat down by the fire.

'It's only ten o'clock, but your body clock must know it's five o'clock somewhere, as they say over here. And I could do with a drink myself.'

'Didn't it go well?'

Her lip curled. 'The lecture went well enough. I got a very positive reception, a couple newspaper articles and some interest in the paper I've written on it. And sold a lot of books.'

'Then what's the problem?'

'All hell broke loose after that.'

'Oh?' He sank down in the armchair, kicked off his boots and stretched his long legs out towards the fire.

'Yes. That milksop son of a bitch I employed decided to hang himself while I was delivering my talk.'

He yawned.

Bristling a little, still stinging from his failure to be there when she delivered her lecture and finding his response less than she'd hoped it would be, she glared at him. 'Don't you think that's serious?'

'Sure. It sounds very serious. Is that the posh English boy you brought out to New York in the fall?'

She nodded. She and Brandon had too much of a shared history, too much of a vested interest in one another's lives and too close a knowledge of each other's secrets for her to be angry with him for long. 'On the night before he did it, he threatened me.'

'Hey!' He sat up at that. 'Is that right?'

'Yes. He threatened to kill me.'

Brandon's expression creased in remorse. He jumped up and folded her hands between his. 'Again?'

'Yes. I told you I thought I'd scared the hell out of him the last time. But he was serious. He'd gotten a rope from somewhere. A noose.' The noose, surely, from which he'd dangled to his own death just hours later. 'He threatened to tell everybody I was a fraud and a murderer.'

'You must have been terrified.'

She bristled. Terrified of Owen? 'It takes more than him to scare me.'

'Then I'm scared on your behalf.' He sat down.

'You needn't be. Owen is dead.'

'So he is.'

Jetlag again, blunting his backwoodsman's sharpness. Cody was overwhelmed with emotion. She could talk freely, and it didn't matter if he was too tired to take it all in. 'Thank God for it. I couldn't stand the little weasel any longer.'

'Did you tell the police about it?'

'Of course not. If I do, they'll think I have an interest in him being dead, and they'll start asking what he was threatening to tell. And we don't want that, do we?' She turned her back on him and crossed to the sideboard, crashing ice in two glasses and splashing a hefty measure of bourbon over it. 'It's my letters. That's what he was talking about.'

She had his interest. Crossing to place the glass in his hand, she looked out through the open curtains towards the lights of the village. The fires from the hippy campsite were dying down in the field at the bottom of the road, their smoke diffusing into the thickening blanket of fog over the lake. 'And are your letters safe?'

'I was going to give them to Lynx to look after.' She'd thought of going down to see Lynx later that evening, but Brandon's unannounced arrival had changed all that. No matter. Lynx could wait.

'Lynx?' Brandon frowned into his drink. 'Who the hell is Lynx?'

'Cain Harper.' She sat down opposite him on the sofa and watched him, his long fingers curled around the glass as he frowned in pursuit of a memory. 'You did meet him, but you won't remember. He was a student with me in Laramie, twenty years ago. He was always a bit of a hippy and he's reappeared in the village in the full-blown incarnation. There are a few of them there.'

'Oh, okay. When I'm a bit less tired I'll remember, I guess. What a coincidence he's here.'

'Indeed.' She was keen to get off the subject of Lynx, who'd taught her things it was better Brandon didn't know. Her brother, just like Cody herself, was prone to jealousy, to preserving the previous relationship they had. They saw each other less these days, but that couldn't weaken the bond between them. 'I can't say how good it is to see you. I get so many threats.'

'You attract attention. Ain't that what you want?'

She bit her lip. 'I'm not afraid for myself. But I'm worried about my letters.' Owen had known how she felt about them. She cursed herself for allowing him to see that, for allowing herself to feel so strongly about them. Cody was a rational woman, for the most part, but when she quivered at the very thought of those letters, she doubted her own sanity.

'Then keep them safe. Give them to me, and I'll look after them.' He swigged at the bourbon. 'And keep yourself safe. Keep in with the police.'

'The less I have to do with them the better.' She hated authority, anyone who tried to impose restrictions on her through a code of right and wrong that had evolved, at best, twenty years behind the times.

'No. Promise me you'll do it for your own safety. For my sake.' His voice softened. 'Think how I'd feel if anything happened to you.'

She leaned over and placed a hand on his free hand as it rested on the arm of the chair. The world was better when Brandon was there. 'If you think that's sensible.'

'It's the only thing. Because I'm not always going to be able to look after you the way I have.'

Puzzled at his tone, she studied him as he stared into the heart of the fire. 'What do you mean?' They spent so much time apart and now she looked after herself. Sure, she relied on him for emotional support but she trusted him when he was present and knew he'd never let her down if she needed him.

'Nothing.' He hesitated as if his courage had failed him, but that was impossible. Brandon's courage never failed. 'Nothing serious. Just... you're everywhere. Not just New York. Not just London. You were in Auckland last time I tried to talk to you. And now you tell me the kid you employ—'

'We can Skype. Jesus, Brandon, there are no excuses these days.' It would have helped if they'd had those communications twenty-five years before. She slapped the memory down.

He relaxed. 'Skype. Yeah, sweetheart. We'll Skype. Even if we don't see each other so much.' He yawned.

'You must be tired. I'll go and make up the bed in the spare room.' As she turned to leave the room, a glance out of the window showed her a figure moving up the lane towards the cottage. Intrigued, she stopped. 'It looks like we have a visitor.'

'Who the hell comes visiting at this time of night?' Brandon stood up, too, and looked out. 'Is that your hippy pal? If it is, tell him to give you back your letters. I can look after them for you.'

In the end, Cody hadn't given Lynx Mary Wordsworth's letters to her sister-in-law. Her first thought, like Brandon's had been, was that it was him at the door, but she was spared the collision between two men who both professed, in their different ways, to care for her. The ponytail – which irritated her, because it was so like her own as to be a sinister copy of it – gave the journalist away. She was tired of the woman, hovering around the edges everywhere she went. 'I'll send her away. I'm sick of this.' And she headed for the front door, wrenching it open and calling out into the darkness just as she'd called out the chief inspector who'd had the temerity to interrupt her lecture and then compounded the sin by having a very good reason for it. 'You. What are you doing out in my garden?'

'Dr Wilder… I didn't want to disturb you. I was about to leave you a note.' The woman bobbed up on the doorstep, agitated. 'Maybe it's good that I've caught you. We did meet at your launch. Fi Styles. Journalist. I wondered about doing the interview that we talked about. Since you're staying in the area a few days longer—'

'Cody. Honey.'

That was why she loved Brandon so much. He understood her. Appearing behind her he placed his hands on her shoulders and the firmness of his touch warned her, as he'd done so often before, that it was in her interests to stay calm.

'Oh, I am sorry, Doctor. I didn't realise you had—' The

woman's face was in darkness but her voice gave away her interest. 'A visitor.'

Brandon's common sense touched Cody where her own did not. 'This is my brother, Brandon Wilder III. He's just arrived from Chicago and is very tired. So if you don't mind—' Cody turned away, gave Brandon the special smile that meant she understood. 'This really isn't a good time.'

'If we could even arrange a time to meet. It would mean so much to me. And after all, I was a friend of Owen's.'

Cody froze. A quick look at Brandon, a quick nod from him, and she turned back. 'He never mentioned you.'

'Well, not exactly a friend. But I bumped into him a couple of times in the village and we had coffee. He talked a lot about you. I thought if I—'

Owen had said he'd tell the newspapers, and Fi was a journalist. 'I don't mind doing an interview.' Cody had to force the words out, fighting against the way this woman, younger than she was and maybe as tough, was forcing her into it. She'd give ground now but she'd win it back later. 'We can discuss research I've been doing. Who will you be writing for?'

'I told you. I'm a freelancer. I'll see who might be interested when I have the interview.'

It got worse. Surely that was a threat. 'Get in touch with me tomorrow. We'll fix a date.'

'It's better if you get in touch with me, Dr Wilder.' Fi Styles stepped forward and pressed a slip of paper into her hand. 'My card. You must have misplaced the last one I gave you. I can be available any time you like. So nice to have met you, Mr Wilder.' And she faded out into the darkness like the last shout of a bad dream.

Restraint failed. Cody slammed the door though she knew Fi Styles must have heard her. 'Talking to Owen? What did the little rat tell her?'

'Does it matter?' But Brandon's eyes, she thought, were anxious.

'No, of course not.' She forced calm upon herself, but it was struggle. Owen would have told Fi everything, in the evening after his last and latest failed threat to kill her. The problem was that she didn't know exactly how much he'd known.

6

'I'm off out,' Lisa called through to the lounge. 'But I can sense a tall dark stranger coming up the path – do you want me to let him in, or should I send him packing?'

Ashleigh flipped over a tarot card, but she looked to the window before she glanced down to see what it was. Her lip curled into a smile at the sight of Jude's tall figure standing on the pavement. 'Mmm. I'll let you decide.'

The doorbell went. She kept her hand hovering over the cards. He was early, and she was caught, unusually, in two minds. To finish the reading she'd started, or to shuffle the cards away before he could laugh at her the way Lisa always did?

She'd finish it. If their relationship was going to persist for any length of time, he was going to have to learn to stop making fun of her hobby. Reading the tarot cards was an unusual pastime for a detective, and if anybody else in the office found about it she'd attract the wrong sort of interest and a lot of disapproval from colleagues, but the cards, as she grew tired of having to tell people, weren't about telling the future, or even about answering questions. A tarot reading was about concentrating your mind, focusing your thoughts, pointing you in a different direction and showing you how to think. The skill came in knowing how to use them, but if you could channel their creativity, they allowed you a fresh look at an old problem. In her career, she'd come across plenty of detectives who would have benefited from that.

'Good morning, Chief Inspector. Are you here for your appointment with our resident psychic?' Lisa greeted Jude with mock seriousness. 'Madame Vera is speaking to the Fates just now, but I'm sure she'll spare you a moment. Cross her palm with silver and she'll give you good news. Satisfaction guaranteed. She's in the living room. Go on through. Ash, I'm off out. Will you be back for dinner?'

Ashleigh smiled at Jude as he opened the living room door. 'No, we're out for dinner tonight.'

'Come and join us in the pub,' Jude said, over his shoulder. 'There's live music on in the Dockray Hall tonight. Celtic rock, if you like that sort of thing.'

'I've heard far too much of that in my life. Too many of my colleagues are into that. No, I'll give it a miss. I'm planning to binge watch *Love Island*. But thanks anyway.' Ashleigh's best friend and housemate snapped the front door closed behind her and bounced off along the street.

In the silence she left behind her, Jude hovered on the threshold of the living room, leaning against the door frame and watching as Ashleigh sat back. 'I'm glad she's not coming. It'll be nice to have you all to myself.'

'Back to your place again afterwards, then?' She hesitated a moment, waiting for him to come and sit next to her, ready to abandon the reading the moment he came close.

'Don't let me interrupt you,' he said, after a moment of delicious silence. 'I'm interested.'

'You'll make fun of me.' Daring him to do so, she allowed her hand to mask the upturned, unseen card.

'No. You know what I think of it, but we'll agree to disagree. What's that card you're hiding?'

She moved her hand aside. 'The Six of Cups.' Aware of his careful scrutiny, she kept her face composed in what she hoped was an expression of complete concentration while she fought to control her irritation. The card came up too often and always reminded her of Scott, a card that could have either positive or negative associations depending on which way it appeared. Today it was reversed, which meant that the memories it talked about were poor ones and its connotations were irresponsibility, indecision and failure. She didn't like it that way, so she tweaked it the right way up, making the past a happier place, brimming with innocence and golden memories, and transforming her former husband Scott into a friend rather than an ex-lover unknowingly driving them to mutual destruction. That single twitch made the whole reading altogether more palatable and although she would know, Jude wouldn't. 'That's a good one. That tells me to work towards happy reunions and positive future relationships.'

She flashed a smile at him and at last he came to sit next to her on the sofa, an arm stretched along the back of it ready for the moment when she would sit back. 'Who with?'

'That's up to me.' She resisted the temptation to lean back against him, for the pleasure of anticipation.

'Okay. I'll suspend my disbelief. What's next up?'

'The Three of Swords.' This was another that came up often when she was thinking of Scott. It was almost as if the cards didn't realise that everything between them was at an end. For the sake of her new relationship, she interpreted it loosely and liberally, making the best of it. 'Yes, here we go. This indicates divorce.'

'And is this card about the past or the future?'

'The present. My decree nisi went through last week. I meant to tell you, but I forgot.'

'You forgot?' His tone was quizzical and she saw from the tarnished mirror above the fireplace that he'd lifted an eyebrow. 'Something as significant as that?'

'Maybe I just want to put the whole thing behind me.' She allowed the pause to draw out as she looked down on the pierced heart of the Three of Swords. 'And we have far more important things to talk about during the week.'

'That's true enough.' He didn't press the matter, and nor should he. The marriage was dead long before she'd met him, and he'd had no part to play in laying it to rest. Nevertheless, she spared a soft thought of the man she'd loved enough to hope he could change. 'Let's get back to the cards. Will they tell you who killed Owen Armitstead?'

'We know who killed him. He killed himself. Didn't he?'

There was a fractional pause as Jude flapped a hand as if in dismissal of his own uncertainty. 'Yes. That's what the evidence says. Forget I said it.'

'Take one,' she said, his closeness prompting her to abandon the coherent set of observations she'd been intending to make. 'But I've told you before that's not how they work, even if there was any doubt. But if it gives you something to think about, there's no harm done.'

With a sidelong look, as though by joining in he was compromising himself, Jude reached out a hand for the pack, tapping the top card a couple of times before lifting most of them and digging out one from close to the bottom. 'If this is the Hanged Man…' He turned it over. 'The Eight of Swords. What does this mean?'

It was the third card in a row that spelt out difficulties with relationships. If she'd been doing the reading seriously, Ashleigh might have worried, but it was Jude's choice of card not hers. 'What do you make of it?'

He held the card in the palm of his hand. A tall woman, bound and blindfold, stood surrounded by eight swords stuck into the ground, a castle in the background. 'It looks like a typical day in the Lakes.' He grinned, touching a bird of prey silhouetted against storm clouds and purple mountains. 'Is this about justice?'

'There's a specific card for Justice. One for Judgement, too. But yes. You can interpret it that way. Anything else?'

'I don't know.' He frowned at it, and the corners of her mouth twitched into a smile in response. So tolerant in many ways, he wouldn't open his mind to anything that couldn't be measured or supported, and even his acknowledgement of the intangible had to have some kind of evidence to offer proof or disproof. Which was completely illogical when so many criminal actions stemmed from passions and emotions that could be neither predicted nor quantified.

If you wanted to read the cards properly, you took time and treated them seriously. That was why she preferred to consider the tarot alone; only some foolish impulse had made her take them out when she knew she'd risk exposing her eccentricities to sceptical minds. That was why the reading hadn't made sense and so, she argued, she was justified in playing about with it.

'It's a beautiful day,' she said to him, optimism rising. 'Let's get outside and make the most of it.'

'Back to my place later, though.'

'Oh God, yes.' It didn't matter anyway. By playing fast and loose with the interpretation of the cards, the only person she was cheating was herself.

'So tell me,' Jude said, as they strode up the final strides to the cairn that topped Skiddaw, 'about Scott.'

'What's there to tell?' Unused to a long and strenuous hill walk, Ashleigh made the most of the pause she needed to get her breath back, choosing her words carefully. 'I kept telling him I wanted a divorce and he finally accepted it. Stage one is done.'

Scott, incapable of fidelity himself and intolerant of any departure from it in his wife, always promised change but in the end Ashleigh's patience had given out. Love had lost out to self-preservation. Thank God she could blame the relentless cold of the north wind for the tears that suddenly streamed down her cheeks.

'Simple as that, eh?' Jude reached out to brush the moisture away.

'Okay, sometimes I thought he never would agree.' She slid her hand into his. Men didn't understand how women felt for other men, always wanting to be the only one. Maybe Jude would be different. 'He's that persistent.'

'Maybe he thought you were worth persisting for.'

'I'm sure he did.' Her hair had whipped free from her ponytail and as she pushed it back, she missed the expression on his face. They'd arrived at the summit alone, clear of the group of walkers behind them. Now their isolation was a sanctuary for shared confidences, where the wind tore up words and cast them up into the clouds, unrecorded. 'But he didn't think I was worth giving up his philandering for. That was the deal breaker.'

'It would be for me, too. Here. Let's get a photo of you for Lisa.' He got out his phone and slid an arm round her, snapping a selfie of the two of them with the land falling away to the north and Scotland, while the bulk of the lakes and mountains jostled for space to the south. Until she'd come to the Lakes, in the dying months of the previous summer, Ashleigh had never been much of a walker, but Jude had little enough time free and liked to spend it in the hills. If she wanted the treasure of his company, she'd no option but to learn to like it. 'She won't believe you've walked this far without proof.'

'Lisa's a lazy toad. She won't appreciate the enormous effort this cost me.' She slid her arm around him for a second selfie, holding on longer than she needed to, and the two of them swayed together for a kiss.

'So Scott's definitely gone.' He let go with some reluctance as another pair of walkers appeared on the skyline.

'Has Becca definitely gone?'

'No, but that's different.' Turning away from her to rummage in his backpack for a thermos flask, he failed to hide his scowl.

His irritation must be with Becca, not Ashleigh herself, or so she hoped. 'I don't see why.'

'Because she lives next door to my mother for a start, and I can't avoid seeing her. And because we were never married. That counts for something.'

Becca, for all the wrong reasons, had ditched Jude and it was taking him longer than he admitted to get over it, whereas Ashleigh was the one who'd broken the chains of a toxic relationship. Taking the Mars bar he held out to her, she dared reflect once more on Scott, who was the only man she'd ever loved and so the only man who could break her heart. She'd have put money on that was how it had been with Jude and Becca, too.

So much the better. It meant neither of them would make the mistake of going back to the old love or rushing naively into the new. Mentally drawing a line under her relationship with Scott to emphasise the one drawn by the official documentation, she turned from the subject with relief as he tipped his finger under her chin, tilted it up, and the kiss he brushed across her lips was so light the wind blew it away. Her shiver came from anticipation, not the January wind. *Jude Satterthwaite, just wait until I get you home.*

When this kiss, too, was done, she accepted the cup of coffee he poured from his flask and turned to enjoy the rest of the view. 'What are we looking at?'

His arm swung from left to right. 'There are too many to name them all, but I'll point out the main ones. That's the Helvellyn range on the left. Great Dodd. Helvellyn itself. Ullswater's behind. There's Coniston Old Man.' The names rippled easily off his tongue. 'Crinkle Crags. Bow Fell. Glaramara. Great End. Scafell, Scafell Pike, Great Gable. That's Derwentwater down there.'

'Have you climbed them all?'

'Most of them. I went walking every weekend when I was younger. School holidays too. Somehow Glaramara has escaped me, so I'll need to pick that one off. We'll do Catbells next time. It's a nice easy walk. You can get the boat across from Keswick.'

The other walkers reached them, exchanged greetings, took the requisite photos, touched the trig point and moved on. Sipping at the tepid coffee, Ashleigh peered after them. She and Jude had started late and the climb had taken a couple of hours, so that the sun had already started dipping to the east and the short winter day was on the run. 'Should we go back?'

'Yes. We'll easily make the car before sundown, but we should probably head down.'

They lingered a moment longer, while he packed the flask away and she felt in her pocket for her gloves to combat the growing chill, turning her windblown head towards the central Lakes. It was a wild and beautiful scene, but it hid some of the worst of human nature. 'Can we see Grasmere from here?' The Wordsworths, she had read, were enthusiastic hillwalkers.

'No. It's down there, beyond Thirlmere.' His raised arm indicated the slashed trough in the fells where a road wound south, a glint of gunmetal grey. 'It sits in that little sheltered dip. There.'

They shared a silence. Ashleigh's thoughts, as his must also do, tripped back to the death of Owen Armitstead, to his grief-ravaged parents and his unrepentant boss. 'What do you make of Cody Wilder?'

'I should be asking you that. There's no way I can make an objective judgement. We didn't get off on the right foot and she's the sort of person who puts my back up.'

Cody, it seemed to Ashleigh, was merely a female version

of Detective Superintendent Groves, someone who bullied those around her mercilessly and played on their weakness to feed her own insecurity. In Cody it was a deliberate stance and in Groves probably a leftover from an old age of male entitlement, but the effect was the same, except that Cody Wilder was judged more harshly for it on the basis of her gender. She slid Jude a sideways look, wondering how far his open-mindedness went and deciding not to test it. 'Yes, mine too. But she does it deliberately. I don't know what she's hiding but there's something she's afraid of. I'd love to know what it is.'

He turned away from the view but took hold of her gloved hand where the path was broad and easy. 'Doddsy reckons Owen's death was an obvious suicide. From the soundings he's taken, the boy appeared mentally frail. Bluntly, he probably couldn't take the heat and Dr Wilder isn't the kind who understands the need for pastoral care. Maybe she's afraid of being held to account for the way she behaved. I would imagine it'll all get wrapped up pretty soon and we can get on with our business.'

'That's what Doddsy thinks. What do you think?'

'It's hard to argue. Though I do wonder. If it were Cody Wilder who'd been found dead in the same circumstances, I might have been looking at it a lot more closely.'

'But it couldn't have been planned?'

'No. Opportunistic. Someone comes up to confront her, finds a rope in a conveniently unlocked shed, and the victim wandering about in a confused state? I can see how you might take that chance. Only it wasn't Cody. It was a young man with emotional issues and under an awful lot of pressure.'

'Cody would never have exposed herself to such a risk.'

'No. And since you ask, I think Dr Wilder's backstory would bear some examination. Because you're right and there has to be something that makes someone behave as aggressively as she did to me on so little provocation.'

Cody had set out to humiliate Fi Styles too, brushing aside her inquiry in the cafe without mercy. 'There does seem something not right about it.'

'And what do you think? What's your—' he hesitated fractionally over the word: '—*instinct*?'

He hated instinct. When she'd first arrived, he'd resisted her sixth sense for things being wrong, her intuitive understanding of people's personalities and the actions that chimed wrongly with their words. Professionally, it was a weakness as much as a strength, but she sensed that he'd ask her about it out of the office when he never would inside.

'I think she's an unhappy woman, though she'd never admit it.'

'She's certainly a very angry one.'

'The two go hand in hand, don't they?'

'Maybe.' But as they walked down the path from the summit of Skiddaw and the light began to fade away and blur the distant haze from pink to grey, she sensed that while Owen Armitstead's misery might be over, Cody Wilder's was just beginning.

7

Raven – whose real name was buried so deeply in the graveyard of a suburban past that she no longer cared to remember what it was – sat in the tent where she kept her loom and sent the shuttle flying back and forth through the longitudinal woollen threads. She'd pinned back the tent flaps to allow as much natural daylight in as possible, not just for the sake of her eyesight but so that she could maintain her much-cherished connection to the natural world, but the downside was the cold that came in with the light. January had never been her favourite month but it seemed to grow more vicious as she grew older, and the chill came through to her bones. She shivered. She was sixty and if she sat working for too long, even in summer, her fingers complained at the oncoming curse of arthritis.

Sometimes Raven thought this was a curse, a punishment. She'd chosen to reject her parents when she was barely more than a teenager and she'd never regretted it, but four decades later the grinding of her joints was loud and harsh, like the echo of her long-dead mother's laughter. You could never escape your past.

The faint and fleeting light tempted her, dancing across the moss-green and lake-blue of the wool she'd chosen and turning them into the elusive shimmer of a bluebell wood. A walk along the lake to the wintry splendour of Deer Bolt Woods would stretch her legs and give her a chance to rest her fingers. That done, she could come back and perhaps finish the scarf before the afternoon light faded too far.

The short days were a curse. She set aside the shuttle, wedging it safely between the grey strands of the warp, and stepped out into the daylight, her boots squelching on the wet grass. The faint sun and long shadows warned her that it was way past midday and time for something to eat. She looked around. There was no rota but Lynx had promised the previous day to take on the task of preparing something for lunch. Normally he'd be pottering about the place, improving or adjusting something, but he was nowhere in sight.

Sighing, she turned towards the lane that would take her up Red Bank Road and onto the path around the lake and her face creased into a smile when she saw Storm leaning on the gate waiting for her. The winter was harsh to him as it was to her – harsher, perhaps, because he was a man who brimmed with natural energy and this cold season, devoid of growth, left little for him to do. In the summer he occupied himself with the vegetable patches they'd made at the side of the field, but in the winter he slowed down into semi-hibernation and cultivated only patience.

'You're looking very smart today,' she greeted him admiringly, an echo of the kind of compliments normal people paid one another. 'Almost like a normal person.' She dimpled a smile at him.

He plucked at his knitted jumper. 'I got muddy. Soaked right through. At my age I can't afford to get too damp. So I changed.'

'Care to join me for a walk, my lover?' Rain wasn't far away. She sniffed the air, slipping a comfortable arm through his. When she'd first joined a hippy commune all those years before, her head had been full of the seductive ideas of free love. She smiled at that, now. Living and letting live was what it was about and she made no judgement on anyone else, but once she'd locked eyes with gentle, dry-witted Storm the idea of sharing her favours had disappeared and never returned.

'No,' he said, too sharply.

'Have you seen Lynx? He was supposed to be getting us something to eat.'

He shook his head. 'He's got other things on his mind.'

Raven nodded. Living so closely, it was impossible to be unaware of what else was going on. Paradoxically, in the summer, when the community swelled to a couple of dozen, they could achieve a degree of privacy, if not anonymity, but the winter forced them into closer proximity and you learned a lot of things you'd rather not know. 'She'll be gone soon.'

'Not soon enough. If that poor boy hadn't killed himself, she'd have been away by now.'

She patted his arm with her free hand, and made soothing noises, as she would to a child. She could always tell when Storm was agitated, and he'd been that way ever since Cody Wilder had arrived in the village and come swanning down to the camp to introduce herself. Lynx had looked at her with interest straight away.

Cody, she supposed, was an attractive woman, if you liked a certain type, and Lynx was never a man who cared for a pushover. If the two of them followed their natures, then what was wrong with that? So there must be something else about Cody that upset her, and upset Storm. Because he was upset, quivering with the kind of nervous anxiety he'd spent a lifetime trying to escape. 'Where do you think he is?'

'Gone up to her cottage, I expect. Couldn't keep away.'

'It'll blow over.' Stroking the back of his gnarled hand with a forefinger, she shushed him. 'She'll leave.'

'He isn't really one of us, is he?' Storm shook her hand free, too troubled even to accept the comfort she offered him.

She considered. What did it mean to be one of them? Were there degrees of belonging? Lynx was dynamic and occasionally confrontational, but perhaps he just operated on a different wavelength from them. There was no single way to be alternative. 'We're used to doing things a different way. That's all. And it takes time to get used to doing it our way. I don't know much about him but he's clearly been too used to living in the modern world.' And it was a toxic world. 'It isn't always easy to step away from it completely.'

'You're such a sweet hippy child.' His smile warmed her chilled bones. 'It isn't him I have the problem with. It's her. There was no problem before she came. I don't know why she can't leave us alone.'

They knew the answer to that. Cody Wilder was a narcissistic attention-seeker and it didn't matter where the attention came from, to the point that she was even prepared to waste her time by leaning over the fence pointing out to them just where the inconsistencies lay in their philosophy. Being a clever woman, she put her arguments in a way that they couldn't answer. It wasn't a problem for Raven, who'd learned through the years that this was a natural enough reaction for anyone who didn't understand what it was to be different, but she could tell that it disturbed Storm's hard-learned serenity, and who could tell what impact that attitude had on Lynx, beyond his obvious infatuation with the woman?

'She'll be gone in a few days. When they've tied up the loose ends. That poor boy.' Owen, at least, had always been pleasant to them, even if his smiles had sometimes been apologetic as he hurried three steps behind his boss like a subservient husband. On the couple of times he'd wandered down alone, he'd been wistfully open-minded in his interest.

'Yes. It's a damn shame, and she drove him to it.'

They paused and looked across the dank, damp field. In the middle of it, the fire flared up but the brazier, on which they cooked, seemed to have died down. Whatever had distracted Lynx had done so for a long time. 'I'll go and see if I can get us some lunch, shall I?' There were the cold potatoes she'd cooked the day before, and Eliza Gordon had brought down some bread they hadn't used up in the cafe. There was soup, too. It would be enough.

Still unaccountably troubled, Storm turned to survey the scene, a glance which took in the grey-green mud of the campsite, the village nestling into the bottom of the village, the chilled lake and the skeletal features of the leafless woods beyond. 'Isn't that him?'

'Is it? Where?'

'Up along the lane.'

Raven turned to look along the narrow lane, but there was no sign of Lynx in the green cleft between moss-covered dry-stone walls. He must have disappeared around the bend. 'I wonder if he'll be back for lunch?'

'I wonder if he's all right. Maybe I'll go and speak to him.

Find out. It's not like him to let us down.' Storm turned away from her and vanished among the trees and she watched until he was out of sight before she walked across the damp grass. The brazier had burned out completely and would need to be relit. When he'd first arrived, Lynx, who seemed to know a few tricks about living in the woods, had built a timber pile against the far wall, constructed in such a way that even when the rain tipped down on them in its traditional Lakeland way and worked its way through the canvas covering, there was always dry wood to be had inside. She crossed the campsite towards it. It would take her a while to get the brazier restarted and the soup heated up for lunch, but there was no hurry. It would probably take Storm a while to catch up with Lynx, if he'd gone so far ahead that she couldn't see him.

Her path to the woodpile took her past Lynx's tent, which was set a little distance away from hers and Storm's to give them a pretence at privacy, although when the place filled up in summer, they'd all be living on top of one another. He'd left the flap pinned open. Curious, and because they had no secrets, she stopped to peer inside and drew in a breath so sudden and sharp that it sent a stab of pain shooting across below her breast.

Someone had ransacked Lynx's tent. It wasn't untidy – untidiness was impossible with so few possessions – but there was something violent about its disarrangement. Someone, surely not Lynx, who was curiously fastidious, had thrown the bedding aside, piled it into a corner of the tent and ripped up the wooden flooring.

Raven stepped back, her brow shrivelling into an expression of concern. 'Lynx!' she called, although there was no one out on the dank January Sunday to hear her. Grasmere's few winter visitors would be grouped around the roaring fires in the pub or trooping past the trivia of the Wordsworths' life at Dove Cottage. Even the walkers who passed the lakeside in a brisk show of respect to the outdoors had gone back inside and the path where Storm had gone in pursuit of Lynx had been deserted. Only the ducks at the waterside responded to her call with a melancholy quack.

Not quite sure what was bothering her, she kept walking towards the woodpile. There had always been something strange and unsettling about Lynx, but the policy of the camp, which had evolved when she and Storm had come to join it a few years before and continued unspoken as people came and went, was one of trust. You asked no questions, because so many people came to get away from their pasts. You did no evil to others and you expected none from them. The idea that someone might have thought that Lynx had something worth stealing was so peculiar that it could only have come from a random stranger.

It was ironic, she thought as she lifted the canvas flap that protected the woodpile, that she was thinking this way when every summer some stranger placed the blame for a lost or stolen purse on them, because they didn't know, or didn't understand, the healing power of trust. At least the police knew that, and their investigations into allegations were usually polite and always ended up cordially. If you did no harm then you could receive no harm and everything would be well.

And it was with that thought in her head that she found Lynx.

*

'It was that American woman. It must have been.'

'Oh God, what did she do to him? Why?'

'She did it because he upset her. She doesn't care for anyone.'

'Oh, Raven, my dear, come and sit in the cafe and I'll get you some tea!'

Once again, the unlucky one who was on call on a Sunday afternoon, Doddsy took one look at the chaos on the edge of the hippies' field and didn't need the mention of Cody Wilder to know that this was something he'd have to pass up a pay grade. When the initial emergency call had reported a fatal stabbing, he'd known better than to expect it would be simple.

Simple. His mouth twisted. Sometimes his own flippancy over the dead disgusted him, but it was the only alternative to getting too closely involved.

He'd stopped his car at the edge of the field and found that the uniformed officers on the scene had already closed Red Bank Road, but the two of them had been too busy taping off the scene to handle the panicked covey of witnesses. These, a mix of villagers and obvious visitors, congregated in a clucking, chattering group on the pavement just beyond the police tape.

'I'm going to make you a nice cup of tea—'

'Tea? The poor girl needs brandy.'

'Did you see the body? It was awful, awful.'

'Excuse me.' When no one took any notice of him, Doddsy shouldered his way through them and ducked under the tape, pausing before he did so to slip on the pair of sterile overshoes he carried with him to every crime scene, then stood with narrowed eyes, assessing the relative capabilities of the uniformed PCs already on the scene. 'Charlie. You carry on.' Charlie Fry was an old hand and would make no mistakes. He could leave him to it. Tyrone Garner, son of the force's best crime scene investigator, was a rookie – a good one, by all accounts, but a rookie nonetheless. He could be deputed to handle the witnesses. 'Tyrone, sort the sheep from the goats for me, would you? You know what to do. Identify anyone who saw what was going on – we need to speak to them as a priority.'

'I've asked them. No one saw anything. The woman called Raven found the body. Charlie and I checked. It's cold.'

Doddsy nodded him back to work. With relief, he saw another set of flashing blue lights as uniformed reinforcements sped up through the village. There was an ambulance on its way, and a doctor, though from what he'd heard, the doctor would be able to do no more than formally pronounce the victim dead and the ambulance would just take up space. The witnesses accounted for, he made his careful way down to where Charlie Fry stood taking photographs halfway down the field. Inevitably, the ground was churned up by too many pairs of feet. It was amazing how many people came out of the woodwork when there was something exciting to see, amazing how much fragile evidence they managed to obscure. Most amazing of all was that the CSI team almost always managed to turn up something useful from the most chaotic scene. 'Charlie. Where's the body?'

'Over there, by the wood pile.' The constable nodded towards a canvas-covered stack against the wall. His expression gave nothing away. 'Poor bloke. Stabbed him so hard they nearly took his head off. Slaughtered like an animal.'

With care, Doddsy picked a way down towards the site. On the side of the woodpile nearest the lake a pair of denim-clad legs sprawled out from beneath the canvas into a puddle of mud and blood. For form's sake, he lifted the canvas, dropping it as soon as he'd satisfied himself that the man was dead. He'd leave the assessment of the body and how it lay, the injuries and the cause of death, to the specialists. It wasn't his job to deduce how the man had died, but to manage the scene until Jude arrived and then help to put together the specialist evidence and decide who'd done it. 'Do we know who he is?'

'He's one of the hippies who hang around here. Goes by the name of Lynx.' Charlie finished with the tape and stepped away.

'Do we know his real name?'

The flicker of an expression that passed over Charlie Fry's face indicated that his view of the hippy community was closer to Chris Marshall's than to Jude's. 'No one seems to know. He kept himself to himself.'

'What do we know about what happened?' Doddsy stifled a sigh. 'Who found him?'

'One of the campers. Raven. Real name Sarah Twist.' Charlie rolled his eyes, as though he didn't believe that, either. 'She came down to get wood for the fire and found him in here. She says his tent's been ransacked.'

A quick look towards the tent indicated by Charlie revealed the signs of a frantic, but organised, search. 'Has anyone touched anything?'

'She didn't. She ran straight up to the nearest cottage in the village. The couple who own the field live there. They were having Sunday lunch and they came straight down here. But they and the people who came down afterwards for a quick look have walked all over it, and I think someone must have moved the body. Ms Twist said it was hidden under the canvas but it's half out now.'

The layman's desire to help, or the murderer's intention to hinder? It must have been obvious there was nothing anyone could do for him. 'Is there a murder weapon?'

'There's nothing obvious, unless it's under the body.'

Doddsy ran through a mental checklist of things to do. The CSI team would be with him soon and in the meantime the priority was to make sure the scene was roped off. Find out who the victim was. Find out who'd been seen around. Find out who might have a motive.

Tyrone had marshalled the onlookers a few yards down the street and corralled them on the pavements while he took their names and addresses. As Doddsy moved to intercept the doctor, who had parked on the double yellow lines and was getting her bag out of the boot, he was cut off in his turn by a young woman whose most obvious assists were a ponytail and a notebook. 'Are you a detective?'

'I'm sorry, ma'am. I can't speak to you just now.'

'I'm Fi Styles. I'm a journalist.'

'No comment. I have to ask you to keep away from the scene. We'll be issuing a press statement in due course.' Shaking her off, Doddsy succeeded in cornering the doctor, and when he looked back over his shoulder, he saw that Tyrone had Fi Styles in the queue with everyone else. The two hippies were standing to one side, he with his arms around her, and Tyrone was ticking the rest of them off his list and lining them up, either to the one side or the other.

More vehicles were converging on the scene now. Doddsy headed back up to hand the doctor over to one of the uniformed constables to take her down to the body. The CSI unit van had pulled up, and he relaxed. Tammy Garner, the best CSI officer he'd ever worked with, was on the case, pulling on her forensic suit and taking charge of the team who were with her.

'Have we closed off enough of the scene?' Charlie Fry was running an eye over the woods. 'Looks like there are a couple of ways out. I've secured the whole field but you might want to seal off the woods, too.

Doddsy checked the scene. There was a four-foot-high dry-stone wall abutting the woodpile, but anyone who tried to get away over that would have found themselves in an enclosed cottage garden, and there were no immediate signs of a great escape, though (he took a quick and cautious look over the wall) someone might have flung the weapon over it. The field opened on to the road and that was closed at both ends, no doubt to the huge inconvenience of anyone wanting to take a slow way round the lake. Cody Wilder would have to cross the cordon to get out of Coffin Lane, but that was a problem they'd come to later. A stile on the far side of the field led into the woods and that, along with the main road out of the village, looked the most likely escape route, but the murder weapon could be anywhere.

Another police car came to a halt. The place was getting busy, now. He strode over to where Tyrone, patient and meticulous, had taken control of the growing crowd. What else had he expected from Tammy's boy?

'Okay, boss.' Tyrone tapped the pen on his notebook, revealing the edge of a tattoo creeping below the cuff of his jacket. Efficient or not, he must be a man who pushed boundaries.

For an unguarded moment, Doddsy's eyes rested on him in appreciation. Tyrone, with his lithe lean figure, dark eyes and a narrow beard outlining his jaw, was a good-looking young man. Quickly, he recalled his duty. 'How are you getting on?'

'I've got the key witnesses settled in the cafe. It belongs to Mr and Mrs Gordon, who came to help Ms Twist after she discovered the body. They're the landlords, and they're happy to let us use the cafe as a temporary base. If I can have a couple of the guys who've just arrived, they can start getting the witness statements from them right now. You'll want to speak to Ms Twist and her partner yourself.'

Doddsy's phone buzzed. Jude. *I'll be there in five.* He allowed himself a quiet smile, knowing that Jude wouldn't be happy at being called up on a weekend when his new relationship was still firmly in the lust phase. Understandably. In Doddsy's view, Jude deserved a lot better than the treatment he'd had from Becca and in this barely concealed relationship with Ashleigh it looked as if he might have found it. 'Good man.' He gave Tyrone an approving smile and a flash of understanding passed between them. Tyrone would go far in the police. 'Carry on as you are.' In time one of the more seasoned hands would probably object to being given orders by a junior but you couldn't argue with the fact that Tyrone knew what he was doing.

'Okay, Doddsy.' Tammy tapped him on the shoulder. Her face bore a serious look but there was that familiar glow of determination in her eye. 'I'm taking the team on site, and I'll let you know what we find. In the meantime, you mind you look after my boy.'

Tyrone, overhearing his mother, shot her an exasperated look and then, with a resigned shrug, turned away.

Doddsy reminded himself that he had a duty of care, that Tyrone probably hadn't seen anything as savage as the butchered corpse in the field before and that these things could have delayed effects. 'Tyrone, your mum has a point. Are you okay about this? That wasn't a pleasant thing to see.'

Tyrone turned back, hands in pockets and put his head to one side, looking at the inspector with a long, liquid gaze. 'To tell you the truth, it was a bit shocking. I think I'll probably need a pint when I'm off duty. What do you think?' And he left his superior officer with a broad and totally inappropriate wink.

8

After a brief conversation with Doddsy to make sure everything was under control, the first thing Jude did when he arrived in Grasmere village was to check on Cody Wilder. As far as he was aware, there was no connection between Cody and the hippy community but crimes were too often built upon things of which the authorities were not immediately aware. Two deaths, though so very different, within a few hundred yards and a few days, was too much of a coincidence, even without the threats that formed so dark a background to Cody's colourful career.

It was a job he would normally have delegated but in the light of the non-specific nature of the threat, along with Cody's over-assertive unpredictable character, he preferred to take on the challenge himself. Rank might offer him some sort of protection from her sarcastic tongue. As he walked, he thought of Ashleigh and her assertion that Cody's brutal directness was protection against some secret fear. Less charitable himself, he preferred to ascribe it to downright misanthropy but Ashleigh had an instinct for these things. And others, too. He suppressed a smile.

There was movement behind the glazed panel in the front door of the cottage as he came up the path, and the door eased open as he reached it. The man who answered was tall, lean as a whippet, taut-muscled and active, with an outdoorsman's tan. He was clad in black jeans and black jumper and his expression was one of wary neutrality. 'Howdy.'

'I'm looking for Cody Wilder.'

Cody materialised at the man's side, as if she'd been waiting in the wings to decide whether she was ready to see him. That, and the scowl she always seemed to have for him, offended Jude's professional pride. 'Chief Inspector. Hello. Don't you have anything better to do than disturb law-abiding citizens on a Sunday afternoon?'

When Doddsy had called, Jude's mind had been firmly on other things – specifically, on Ashleigh. 'It's a courtesy call. I just thought I'd make sure you were safe and well.'

She opened her eyes wide, in mockery. 'Why wouldn't I be? You have your man in uniform floating around the village pretending to look after me, don't you?'

No one in the village could possibly be unaware of the furore that was taking place at the foot of Coffin Lane. From where they stood, the blue lights and police cars were obvious, and if those weren't enough, the visible white tent over Lynx's body told the world that someone had died. Her feigned lack of interest irritated him further. 'You obviously don't know there's been an incident in the village. I wanted to check that you're safe. Obviously you are, so I won't bother you any longer.' He turned away. He'd send someone up to interview Cody and her visitor later, in case they'd seen anything, but if they hadn't been on the scene, they weren't his priority.

'What kind of incident?' A sharp edge to her voice gave

her away. Yes, she was concerned, though whether for herself or for a stranger, he couldn't say.

He considered. Strictly speaking, he knew nothing other than the fact that the man known as Lynx was dead, but that information was all over the community. If she hadn't heard it, she'd find out the minute she set foot in the village, where the buzz was such that even those who were hostile to her would be willing enough to forget it to share their information and opinions. He turned back to face her. 'A man's body has been found down by the shore. A man known as Lynx.'

An expression of interest chased one of surprise across her face, like the shadow of a rainstorm over the fellside. 'That's hardly surprising. Those hippies don't have a grasp on the modern world. People who don't adapt to the benefits of science deserve to die young. It's called natural selection.'

There had been nothing natural about what had happened to Lynx. Cody, seeing the ambulance, the police cars, the buzz of activity and the flashing of blue lights, must know that now, if she hadn't guessed before, but she offered no sympathy, no thought for a fellow human. He shouldn't be surprised, because she'd reacted in exactly the same way to Owen Armitstead's death, and Owen, at least, had been someone she knew. Nevertheless, her hardness both repelled and intrigued him. 'Do you know the people down there?'

'You mean the hippies? God, no. Tree-hugging waste of space. This is supposed to be the age of progress, but they seem to want to go back and live in the sixteenth century.'

'You never spoke to them?'

'Maybe once, when I first arrived. There wasn't a lot of intellect there, to be honest. I couldn't even tell you who I spoke to. There were plenty of them there back then, and none of them could find a civil word.' She stepped back. 'I'll let you get on. I'm sure you have better things to do than stand on my doorstep.'

'You'll find there will be a restriction on where you can and can't go for a couple of days, especially while we have officers on duty.' Coffin Lane came out directly opposite the gate into the hippy camp, so she certainly couldn't be unaware of it. 'I thought I'd let you know.'

'Thank you.' She shouldered in front of the man and closed the door.

He was her brother, Jude judged from the matching accents and the broad foreheads, as he made his way back down to the scene to see what had come from it. So much the better. If she wasn't on her own, there was one thing less for him to worry about. 'Okay, Doddsy, where are we?'

'I've got the first witness statements in.' A man comfortable with a clipboard in his hand, Doddsy flicked through a couple of sheets. 'You might want to follow some of them up yourself. We'll need an officer to coordinate door-to-door inquiries. You want me to get Ashleigh on that?'

Jude nodded. Tammy was already at work on the scene but it would be a while before they got any results from forensic tests. The post-mortem wouldn't be done until the morning. In the meantime, his priority was to put someone on to finding out who the man was and why he'd died. Ashleigh could orchestrate the door-to-door inquiries and between them he and Doddsy, Ashleigh and Chris, would sit down and bring together the fruits of everyone else's work into a coherent plan and a solution to this man's murder. 'Where are our witnesses?'

'The owners of the coffee shop opened it up for us and let us sit in there.' Doddsy made an ironic face. 'They're our friends with the libellous banner, as it happens. They were the ones Raven called when she found him.'

'Is she okay?' Raven, so deliberately detached from a wicked world, might meet evil stoically or take it too much to heart. You never knew.

Doddsy shrugged. Who would be okay when they'd just seen the savagely butchered body down by the lake? 'You can try offering her help, if you want, but I doubt if she'll accept it. These people are too independent for their own good.'

This echo of Cody's rather harsher take on the matter was unkind, especially for Doddsy. Jude headed towards Tyrone, who was standing outside the cafe with his arms folded, ignoring questions from the interested public and turning aside the Sunday afternoon walkers who hoped for a quick turn around the lake before their evening meal. His expression lightened when he saw Jude. 'Sir.' That was for the benefit of the public, because Jude never encouraged formality, although there were those old stagers like Charlie Fry who refused to let go of it. 'Is there anything you need me to do now?'

'Keep doing what you're doing. I'm looking for a quick chat with our key witnesses.'

'They're in the cafe. Mr and Mrs Gordon are looking after them.'

Jude headed in. Young Tyrone, assuming he was responsible for this set-up, was a smart thinker. He'd rounded up someone to operate the coffee machine and that person – an older woman, looking gratified enough to be roped in to help – was shuffling cups of coffee and cake from table to table.

The cafe ran through the depth of the building and was deceptively large. At the back, plate glass doors gave out onto a deserted terrace with view of the misty lake. Currently, the views encompassed frantic activity as white-clad figures worked around a hastily erected tent, conducting fingertip searches of the encampment. Inside the cafe, Jude's attention focused on Storm and Raven, who were sitting in the corner of the cafe by themselves, staring at one another in shocked hopelessness. Two of the other tables were occupied by uniformed officers busy taking statements, and a couple of other local people were sitting waiting patiently around the counter for their turn to give their version of events. Fi Styles was there, chewing meditatively on her pen, and she gave Jude a speculative look as he passed, as if she were wondering whether she dared speak to him.

The uniformed sergeant tasked by Doddsy with supervising the witness statements approached him, with a couple of pages in his hand. 'These are the first statements we have. From the campers.' He nodded towards Storm and Raven.

'I'll have a quick word with them.' Taking the sheets, Jude scanned them, picking up the key information. He doubted very much that there would be anything more than the barest essentials, knew that Storm and Raven would answer only the questions they were asked, so immune were they to the sensitivities of the world around them. Anyone wanting to tease information from them would need to be as sympathetic to their world as they were skilled in interviewing. 'Okay, thanks. I'll just have a quick word with these guys.'

'Of course. If you want a coffee—'

'Yeah, why not?' Jude drank more coffee than he intended on these occasions but sociability sometimes did something to increase your credibility. He crossed the room to the table where the two middle-aged hippies sat holding hands across the table beneath a series of paintings of Grasmere and Rydal Water, all in primary colours and all for sale at an eye-watering price. 'Can I sit down?'

It was Storm – real name Kevin Foster, he'd learned from his quick scan of the sheets – who nodded. Raven just sat staring straight in front of her. He slid into the seat beside Storm, careful not to seem threatening, aware of his own prejudices. He liked the unpretentious, simple-hearted couple, out of place in this sophisticated cafe, but his feelings were irrelevant. They were witnesses, and until he knew for certain that they couldn't have done it he had to treat them as suspects.

That said, his job was to get information and sometimes you had to adjust your approach. Formality was something they might too easily perceive as hectoring or, worse, bullying, and now was the time to glean anything that would help. 'Are you all right?'

Raven nodded. When the woman left the counter and brought Jude a cup of coffee, she slid a plate of sugar-crusted shortbread in front of them too, and refreshed Storm's cup, but Raven's tea sat untouched in the table before her.

'I'm so sorry,' Jude said, his voice soft as he could make it. 'I know it must have been terrible for you.'

'It was a horrible thing to see.'

'Nothing ever prepares you for something like that. And he was a friend of yours, too.'

The pause answered that question. Lynx hadn't been a friend.

'I never met him,' Jude said, trying again to breach the wall of trust that encompassed the two of them, and the two of them only. 'He seemed to keep himself to himself.' In truth, he hadn't found himself in Grasmere more than a couple of times since the bulk of the campers had filtered away between the departure of the swallows and the fall of the autumn leaves. Both times he'd seen Lynx, as he now knew him, in the distance but the man had faded away before he could speak, just as he had done when Chris Marshall had pointed him out on the day of Cody's lecture a few days before. 'Was he with you long?'

'No.' Storm, at last, overcame his reluctance to talk, as if he understood that silence might harm them. 'He came in October, just when everyone else was leaving for the winter. He didn't seem to mind the weather. He said he was used to looking after himself. But he never talked about himself.' He lifted his coffee cup to his lips, but he kept hold of Raven's thin fingers with his other hand.

'You never asked?'

Raven let go of Storm's hand and turned to Jude, a weak smile on her face. Her long, grey plait lay over her shoulder and she flicked it back. 'You aren't very trusting, are you?'

'No.' Her remark was meant as a criticism and he couldn't help accepting it for what it was. 'I can't afford to be. As long as there are people who do things like that, I have to catch them.'

'I don't know why anyone would do that to him.'

Jude sipped his coffee, trying to read the body language and seeing fear and suspicion. 'Did you ever get any sense about who he was? Where he came from? Even if he didn't tell you, you must have had some idea.'

'He didn't talk. We never asked. Why is that so difficult to understand?'

'He was American,' Storm said, with a trace of doubt in his voice. 'Or perhaps Canadian. And he didn't have a lot to learn when he came to us. He knew what kind of a lifestyle we live and he wasn't afraid of it. Cold, wet. Some people would call it limited. He didn't always choose to abide by it.'

'We are very committed,' Raven explained. 'Lynx couldn't break himself free. He'd come into the village sometimes and buy a meal. We never did that. He was independent of us, just as we try to be independent of others as much as we can.'

Their independence was dependent on the goodwill of others. Jude knew that the owners of the cafe passed on leftovers rather than throw them away, and the open neck of Storm's hand-knitted jumper revealed a designer polo shirt that must have been a gift, but he wasn't going to take them to task for cherry-picking their philosophy. Everyone did that. 'Did he have any friends?'

They exchanged glances. 'We don't have friends,' Storm said. 'Friendship is an alien thing. We coexist. We treat others with respect and others do the same to us.'

'Our friendship has to be unconditional.' Raven looked at Storm and for the first time she smiled. 'Like love.'

With someone else, Jude would have been less patient, but he knew that there was no way past this mentality. There were as many ways of getting information out of people as there were reasons for withholding it and with Storm and Raven, only one way would work. They were right to distrust the police and the only thing that would help him was honesty. And hope. 'I know you think I'm prying.'

'It's your job. But it's something we've never done. Lynx came to us asking for nothing and he found friendship and companionship. He didn't ask us questions and we asked none of him.'

Only asking questions would solve the mystery of Lynx's death. 'What was he like?'

'Bright,' Raven said, with a sigh. 'Very bright. Hardworking and quick-witted. He was easily bored. I think he had an entrepreneur's mind. He was sharp, and quicker than we were to see an opportunity.'

'An opportunity?'

'For anything. For improving the way we were living, or getting something for nothing. He took over disposing of my weaving and he bartered it for what we needed, rather than money we didn't want.' Raven dabbed a tear from her eye and shivered. 'I think he was well-educated, but he never talked much. We don't talk about books or science or politics. We think about nature and the environment. We listen to the song of the Earth.' She lifted her tea cup and sipped.

'Did Dr Wilder ever come down to the camp?'

'Oh, she came.' Storm's normally gentle mouth twisted into an expression of contempt. 'Once. She came here for the first time when she walked round the lake, back in November. They had an argument, as I remember, about something she said. I don't remember what it was – something about the way we live – but it was arrogant and sarcastic and he didn't like it.'

'And how was that resolved?'

Truth shivered in the air, close but not close enough. They

weren't telling him everything. 'I don't recall.' Storm licked his lips. 'She never came back here. We saw her walking along the lane, but we never spoke to her.'

'Did he see her again?'

'I've no idea. We practise freedom, Chief Inspector. He did what he wanted.'

'Call me Jude.' Yes, it was bad practice, but there was no point in standing on your dignity if it would only end up costing you in terms of results. 'Sexual freedom, you mean?'

'We don't ask questions. But Cody Wilder strikes me as very… animal… in her approach to humans. Some people respond to the rhythms of their bodies rather than their hearts. Lynx was one of those, and I think she was, too. But that's speculation.'

That tied in with the Armitsteads' comments that Ashleigh had reported to him. 'And what did he think of her?'

'I don't know. The same, if I had to guess.' Storm's shrug dismissed the question. 'She's a good-looking woman, if you like that type.' He hesitated for a second, a man to whom asking questions was alien. 'When did he die?'

'I don't know yet.' The post-mortem would give them an idea, but possibly not a specific time. 'When did you last see him alive?'

'I never saw him all day.' Raven, apparently revived by the tea, reached out for the piece of shortbread, broke a piece off and nibbled at it with the timidity of a rescued child, keeping a wary eye on Jude as if she was worried he'd tell her off for it. 'Sometimes he'd get up very early and go for a walk. I was weaving and I had the tent open. I can see his tent from it, and if he was there, I'd have seen him.'

'I thought I saw him in the woods.' Storm reached out a hand for hers again. 'I went after him, but he was quite far ahead. But it wasn't him.'

Storm, Jude remembered from his quick glimpse at the witness statements the uniformed officers had scribbled down, hadn't been there when Raven had lifted the flap to the woodpile and revealed Lynx's body. 'Did you see who it was?' Because that was another person who needed to be traced, a probable witness and a possible suspect.

'No. I turned back as soon as I realised it wasn't Lynx.'

'Did you follow him far?' Jude suppressed a sigh of frustration. There was a lot to be said for dispensing with anthropogenic trivialities of the clock, but it did mean it would be virtually impossible to pin down a time at which this stranger might have been walking along the lakeside.

'A long way. He went up the lane and down into the woods and I followed him all the way up to…' Storm considered, a longer pause than should have been necessary. 'As far as the footbridge at the end of the lake.'

'That far?' It was a long way, a good mile and a half.

'I never thought.' Storm turned a bland look upon Jude. 'I don't think of time, or of distance. He was quite a long way ahead of me and I thought I'd catch him up. I just kept on walking until I realised it wasn't him, and then I turned around to come back.'

'I wonder where he was going.' Trying hard not to frame his questions too harshly, aware of how difficult it was to gain both Storm and Raven's trust, Jude resorted to thinking out loud and hoping they joined in.

'I don't know. I thought I might ask him. But as it turns

out, it was someone else and Lynx wasn't going anywhere, so it was an entirely academic question, wasn't it?'

With a sigh, Jude finished his coffee, thanked them, and moved on to see what other information had come his way.

9

'Are you happy with what you're doing?'

Ashleigh tucked the phone under her chin as she sat in the car just at the edge of the police cordon and watched a TV crew from the local news channel busy filming views of the campsite from a distance. They would be trying to establish a link, no matter how tenuous, between the death of Owen Armitstead and that of Lynx. Well, why not? It was something she knew Jude and Doddsy would be frowning over. 'Yes.'

'Good.' Jude's voice was brisk, but there was, she thought, warmth in it. 'I wanted to update you on what we're looking for. We're still waiting on the conclusions of the forensic investigation, but we do have the results of the PM and the initial crime scene report.'

'They won't make pleasant reading.' Ashleigh's conversation with Doddsy beforehand had indicated there was very little doubt as to the cause of death.

'They don't. We're still waiting on the toxicology results but Tammy tells me the evidence points to the fact that the victim died where he was found. He was attacked from behind by a right-handed attacker, or a left-hander using the right hand, and the extent of the injuries are so severe that whoever did it must have been covered in blood. There was a trail of blood leading down to the water so they may have tried to clean themselves up, but it's unlikely they'll have been completely successful.'

'Do we have a time of death?'

'He'd been dead for several hours when Raven found him. It gets light at around half eight and he was probably killed just before then. If that's the case, the killer probably escaped under cover of darkness, though that doesn't mean no one saw them.'

'I've got you. Then on those timings, whoever it was Storm followed into the woods isn't a suspect?'

'I don't think so, though I'd still like to talk to that person. They may have seen something unusual. So make sure that's one of the questions the guys are asking in the doors.'

'Right. I'm on it.' With interest, Ashleigh saw Fi Styles, floating around the film crew, watching them. She wasn't alone but she stood out among the knot of interested villagers, pushing to the front where they hung back, clicking photographs on her phone where they stood with casual hands in their pockets. 'What are your plans?'

'I have things to do in the office this morning.' Murder wasn't neat and tidy, and killers never waited for the loose ends of one case to be led up before they presented the team with another. 'Doddsy's your man in charge if you need anything before then. I've got Chris in charge of finding out as much as possible about Lynx, because I don't think we'll know why he died until we find out who he is.'

'Have we signed off Owen's death?'

'Not yet, but there's no reason why we shouldn't, other than time.'

Ashleigh watched as the TV crew packed their equipment away. Their film would appear on the lunchtime and teatime bulletins, with her in the background, interspersed with clips of whichever one of Jude or Doddsy had drawn the short straw of speaking to the press conference. 'Even if that's suicide, do you think the cases are linked?'

'I don't know. That's something we can discuss at the team meeting this afternoon. I'd like to know a little more about the disagreement between him and Cody. There does seem to be some link, even if it's tenuous. Storm and Raven implied that.'

They should probably refer to the hippies by their real names rather than the ones they chose to go by, but Jude must see there was a benefit in a softly-softly approach. 'Should I go and talk to Cody about that? Apart from anything else, she may have seen something.'

'We certainly can't pick her up with the casual door-to-door inquiries.' A lone bird – a robin or a blackbird, she thought – filled the stillness left by the film crew's departed car. 'I'm not sure it's fair to ask you to do that one on your own. I'll come down after my morning meeting and we can have a chat to her then. I've spoken to her about it, and she's as happy with that arrangement as she's ever going to be.'

'Is it her brother staying up there?' There had been a few raised eyebrows at the mention of the new man at the Wilders' cottage. Grasmere was used to all sorts but this cowboy, with his mid-western drawl and his cantankerous stare, had made a few ripples.

'It is. Apparently he was due to arrive for the lecture but had a transport nightmare and didn't make it. I'm a little bit happier about her welfare with him there than I would be if she was on her own.'

'You still think there's some risk to her?'

'There has to be a possibility, though I suspect it's small.' At the other end of the phone, rustling was followed by silence. He must have turned away, as if someone else was after his attention. 'Right. I have to go. I'll give you a call when I get down and we'll talk to the Wilders together. And in the meantime, you might want to chat to the Gordons. They'll be about.'

When he'd rung off, Ashleigh got out of the car and headed towards the lakeside cafe which had become, by default, a *de facto* operational headquarters. Graham and Eliza Gordon, landlords of the hippy camp and proud owners of the banner which had caught so much attention with its accusation of murder on the day of Cody's big reveal, turned out to be a middle-aged, middle-class couple who had allowed their burning fury to get the better of them and now showed every sign of being slightly embarrassed by what had seemed like a good idea at the time. They had turned their cafe over to the police, allowing Ashleigh and her interviewers a secluded corner at the back of the building and moving tables from the middle of the cafe to create a buffer between them and the store of onlookers who came in to buy coffee and Lakeland plum bread or, if the tables were full, some handmade chocolates to take away. The arrangement seemed to be working to everyone's advantage, not least increasing footfall in an establishment which, even in a tourist honeypot like Grasmere, surely wouldn't normally have been doing a roaring trade on a Monday morning in January.

The Gordons were hovering in a corner. Ashleigh had read their witness statements, detailing how they'd been sitting down to lunch when Raven had come screaming and crying to fetch them, how, unable to make sense of what she was saying, they'd gone down to see what the problem was and come across the mangled body. They'd called the police and then, some time later – neither of them was quite sure exactly when – Storm had reappeared, red in the face and out of breath, to be followed very quickly by the police.

Charlie and Tyrone, first on the scene the day before, were on shift again, sitting in earnest conversation in the corner with a couple of other uniformed officers. She crossed over to them. 'Okay guys. How's it going?'

'We're ready to get out on the doors.' Tyrone, who had that particular kind of charm that would get him a long way, turned a dazzling smile upon her, and shifted his seat along to allow her to sit down. With one eye on the clock, she ran through what they needed to know from Jude's update, and sent them out to talk to the good folk of Grasmere and see what, if anything, they could glean from the villagers' humdrum observations. Most of them would have nothing to add, but one or two insights could prove valuable. And the man in the woods might yet emerge from their morning's work.

That done, she looked around for Graham and Eliza Gordon. He was standing behind the counter tinkering with the coffee machine, she arranging cupcakes on a plate. When they saw her looking across, they exchanged a quick word and then Graham Gordon left his post and threaded his way across the room towards her, barging chairs out of the way with his hip as he did so. 'Sergeant O'Halloran. Is there any news?'

She shook her head. People always seemed to think that the police would tell them everything, and in a sense that was fair enough because weren't the police always the ones asking questions? But in this case, there was nothing to tell. 'It's still at a very early stage in the investigation.'

'It's shocking. I can't believe such a terrible thing happened so close to home.' He ran nervous fingers through his thin beard but not, she thought, in a way that suggested he had something to hide. 'To think that anyone could do something so terrible to those gentle people.'

'Did you know Lynx well?' Ashleigh motioned to him to sit down, and he did so, ready to talk.

'No, not well at all. The relationship we have with these people is a strange one, I suppose. Technically, Eliza and I are their landlords, although no money changes hands. It's a historical thing. When we bought the property, the previous owners had always allowed travelling folk to camp there for free, and it became a permanent deal over the years. We help them out, where we can. We understand their thinking. Raven and Storm have been here for a long time. People know them. Our daughter was a bit of a hippy herself.'

Ashleigh sensed a tensing of his jawline beneath the beard, a quivering of emotion that he struggled to hide. 'I'm sorry to hear that you lost her.'

'Yes. She was a peace-loving young woman, who would never have harmed anyone. She was vegetarian, couldn't bear any kind of cruelty, or to use any living thing for her own convenience. Unfortunately she fell in love with a cruel man, and there was nothing she could do to change him.

Turning the other cheek was all she could do, but standing up to him would have been as bad. She was true to herself.' He paused for breath and rushed off the subject. 'I've never charged Storm or any of his friends for using the field, and they've never given me a moment's trouble. It's so-called civilised people who don't know how to treat human beings. They're the problem.'

He threw a fierce glance up Coffin Lane. Ashleigh remembered Jude's concerns about Owen, about how much more sense there would be in a theory of murder if Cody had been the one found hanged. The same applied here. They'd be having a very different interview if she'd been the victim, rather than Lynx, and if the Gordons' whereabouts weren't firmly established for the deaths of both Owen and Lynx.

'You know Storm and Raven well?' They nodded. 'Did you know anything about Lynx?'

'Nothing. He'd come in from time to time for a chat. Not often, and the chat was never about him. it was about the weather and the trees and the phases of the moon. You'd say he kept himself to himself for most of the time. But when he did come in, he was friendly enough.'

'You don't know where he came from? Or his name?'

He shook his head. 'None of those things. I don't think I even knew the name he went under until today. He was just someone who dropped by from time to time, and I never had any need to ask his name. There's no formal arrangement over the field, so nothing ever needed to be signed. If it had been, it wouldn't have been him who signed it. He always said he was just blowing through.' He glanced back to the counter, where a queue had formed. 'I'd better go back and help Eliza out. Excuse me.' He slid away.

Ashleigh looked from the scribbled witness statements to the bleak lakeside and back. No one knew who Lynx was. No one, it seemed, really cared. And by all accounts he'd had nothing, so perhaps his death, with its apparent robbery, wasn't what he had but what someone might have thought he had. Or it was a bluff, something to conceal the real cause of death.

Yet no one, it seemed, had any reason to dislike the man.

At the back of the cafe, where the patio doors gave onto the garden with its terrace for smokers, Raven sat with a shawl around her shoulders and a pack of tarot cards spread out in front of her on a rickety table. Unable to resist the lure of a shared interest and aware that such a connection could easily prove beneficial, Ashleigh slipped out of her seat and through the door onto the terrace. 'Excuse me.'

Raven waited a moment before she turned a thin, sad face away from the cards. She didn't say anything, merely nodding towards Ashleigh.

'I'm DS Ashleigh O'Halloran. In charge of the door-to-door inquiries. I just wanted to say—' Ashleigh floundered to a halt. Just wanted to say what? Just wanted to intrude on someone's misery? Jude had interviewed Raven, after a fashion, after Tyrone had taken the initial witness statement, and he seemed already to have won their trust. There was surely nothing more that Ashleigh herself could learn, and yet something at the back of her mind suggested that there was. 'I'm sorry to interrupt.' She looked down at the cards, fanned out on the table in front of Raven. The Sun, the Star, the Eight of Swords, all reversed so that they represented misery and pain. It was so complete a selection that Ashleigh almost wondered if Raven was doing the same as she herself had done, tweaking the reading to make it reflect the world as she saw it rather than listening to what the cards were trying to tell her.

When she saw Raven sneak a look down at the upturned pack, pick out another card and turn it over and over in her fingers before setting it down, her suspicions were confirmed. The card was Death, and Raven's gaze, distracted from Ashleigh herself, flicked from it to the camp where the police were still working around the tent that had covered the woodpile. Apart from the tent and the police activity, everything was as it must have been at the moment when Lynx's body was found. Through a lifted flap of another tent she saw a loom, a piece of fabric half-completed. A man's clothing hung on the line, though it had been so wet over the past couple of days that it would never have dried. 'I hope someone's looking after you.'

'Yes. Gordon and Eliza have been very kind. They've taken us in and found us a bed.' Raven laid the card down on the table and used the end of her shawl to mop up the puddle from the seat next to her.

Taking that as an invitation, Ashleigh sat down. 'I'm glad to hear that. I don't know the exact progress of the operation, but I expect you'll be able to go home soon. Maybe even later on today.' She was an instinctive judge of character, and all that she could feel from Raven was goodness. Even the thoughtful, sad eyes, passing gently over the scene of Lynx's murder, spoke of forgiveness without sorrow. Hating herself, Ashleigh suppressed the surge of sympathy she felt, not to its extinction but to a point where it didn't affect her judgement. It was a mistake to feel too much for someone, witness or even victim. All it did was distract you from what needed to be done.

'I don't believe in ghosts,' Raven said, shuffling the cards, 'but it's the memories that are a problem. I'll never look on this place again without thinking of him.' She cut Death back into the pack, and looked down at it, held tight in her arthritic hands as if an idea had suddenly come to her. 'He was a fellow traveller. We all are. I hate no one and I try to love everyone.' She gave Ashleigh a shy, sidelong smile. 'Would you like me to read your fortune?'

The turn of phrase tripped Ashleigh's interest. No one with any credibility used the cards to tell fortunes. Maybe Raven was tempering her language to make the idea more easily accessible, or maybe it was something else. She'd find out. 'Yes, why not?' Because it wasn't about interrogating the Fates, which was something that she could do very well for herself, for what it was worth. It was about seeing how Raven interrogated them on her behalf.

'Of course,' Raven began, flicking the well-worn deck of cards between her fingers with surprising dexterity, not looking at them, not dropping any, 'there are no certainties.'

There never were. 'I understand.'

'There are many ways to read the cards.' Raven had adopted a sing-song voice as she shuffled. 'I lay five of them out in a horseshoe. They'll tell you the answers to your questions. Pick a card.' She passed a hand over them like a magician waving a wand over a top hat, then withdrew the hand to a protective position in front of her left breast and held the pack out.

Pretending to be hesitant, Ashleigh picked a card between finger and thumb and laid it on the table, face up, where Raven indicated.

'And another.'

She repeated the action, a third, fourth and fifth time until the cards sat in a semicircle like a Greek chorus. Only then did Raven look down at them, staring with a slight frown, switching them deftly around on the table into a certain order. 'How fascinating. The Five of Wands indicates anger. It's an unhappy card. Here's the Queen of Swords.' Her gaze flicked up the hill towards Cody's cottage. 'She represents an unreliable female with uncontrolled desires and secrets to hide. The Four of Cups… ah, that's a card. That's a warning to all of us to look over our shoulders. Poor Lynx. As he should have done.' She bowed her head, sighed and went back to the cards. 'The Eight of Cups shows us someone on a journey. I'm seeing a dark man, travelling alone. And lastly, the Hermit. He's a stranger to us. A single stranger.' Her hand hovered over the five cards. 'A single stranger, travelling through the woods.'

Ashleigh stared down at the cards then back to Raven. The woman's eyes were bright but her face was pale beneath the stains of outdoor life. 'And did you ever see a tall dark stranger in the woods?'

There was a pause. Raven passed a hand over the cards as if she were wafting her lies away from them, shuffled them up and returned them to a tattered box. 'Yes, but at a distance. A tall man in a black jacket. Someone who doesn't belong here.'

'When was that? Today? Yesterday?'

Raven's eyes flipped up to meet Ashleigh's then down again. 'It was the day of the big fuss in the village. The day that poor boy died.'

*

'Of course,' Ashleigh said to Jude as the two of them walked up from the village centre towards Cody's cottage, 'the reading she did for me was complete hokum.'

'Well, of course,' he said, amused. Ashleigh's fondness for the tarot, at odds with her professional position, had troubled him from the moment he became aware of it. Later, as he got to know her, he'd become reassured that she wouldn't let it impinge upon her judgement but he was still uncomfortable when it came into the realm of her police work. 'And I take it you put her right? Did the two of you sit and discuss different interpretations of a random selection of cards?'

'No, we didn't. You're completely missing the point.'

'Then what is the point?'

'There's a code in reading tarot. Of course, no two people interpret the cards the same way and I'm not saying that Raven is any kind of a fraud. I suspect she knows perfectly well how to read the cards but she chose not to.'

He sensed her exasperation with him, but he stuck to his guns. There was nothing as important as the facts and the evidence. 'Why would she do that?'

'She doesn't know I'm interested in that sort of thing. I never told her. She was busy telling me that it answered my questions, but she never asked me what the questions were. She'd have said the same thing regardless of what came up.'

'So she was trying to mislead us?'

'I think so. She told me the cards pointed to a cruel woman, with secrets to hide, and a tall dark man who'd travelled a long way alone. We were to look at the woods.'

'Oh, I see. Cody Wilder, and her brother. Is that right?'

'That was the clear implication. I imagine she'll have

heard about Brandon in the village if she hasn't seen him, since Cody's all they ever seem to talk about in the cafe and the two of them are pretty exotic by local standards. But she tripped herself up. She claims that she saw this man – who she wants us to think is Brandon Wilder – in the woods on the day Owen died.'

'When he wasn't here.'

'Yes, though we need to check the passenger lists to be sure he wasn't. But in actual fact there was no coherent reading from the cards. She never intended there to be one. She barely looked at them before she launched into the interpretation, and she arranged them into a particular order, which you never do. The order they come out in is significant.'

'Past, present, future and the like?' Pausing as Cody's cottage came into sight, Jude took a look back down the hill. The CSI team had finished in the field, although there was a boat moored just off the shore as divers scoured the water in search of the murder weapon, and a couple of police cars remained parked outside the Gordons' cafe, base for the door-to-door inquiries. Those would be finished soon, because so many of the properties covered were holiday lets and had been empty. There had been very few people out and about on that dark January morning. 'She was telling you what she wanted us to think.'

'Yes. I believe that's exactly what she was doing. Though whether she genuinely believes it was Cody and Brandon who are guilty, is open to question.'

'Interesting point. I get on well with her and Storm, though I wouldn't say we were bosom buddies. But I don't understand why, if they wanted to tell us that they think it was Cody or Brandon or both who killed Lynx, they couldn't tell us directly. They've had plenty of opportunity.'

He looked back down to the camp again, frowning. He was the first to pull Chris Marshall up on the casual assumption that anyone who was different was the first to be questioned on suspicion of a crime, but this was something he had to look at more closely. 'Which begs another question. Are they trying to distract us from something they don't want us to look at?'

'I wondered that. I wondered if the man Storm allegedly followed through the woods really existed.'

'He said he followed him for a mile and a half before he realised it wasn't Lynx. I don't know if you know that path. You can see the beginning of it from here.' Jude pointed to where the line of the path followed the shore. 'Some if it goes through the woods, but at this time of the year, with no leaves, it isn't hard to identify someone, even at a distance. And there are long parts of it where you get a clear view along the lake shore, even in summer.' And it wasn't as if Lynx, with his long hair and dark woollen clothing, would be easily confused with the typical Lakeland walker.

'It looks as if they're trying to pull the wool over our eyes, doesn't it?'

This thought depressed him more than it ought to because he already suspected them of lying. He tried to make light of it, turning to carry on striding up the hill. 'So what did the cards really say? No answers to any of your questions?'

'I didn't ask them any. And actually there was no coherence to them. They were a completely random selection.'

Even though it was early afternoon, there was a light on in the cottage. Through the small-paned window, Cody was visible, sitting at a table in the living room frowning over her laptop, with Brandon by the fire holding a broadsheet newspaper up in front of his face. Although for the life of him he couldn't find a connection between the deaths of Owen Armitstead and Lynx, Jude couldn't bring himself to rule it out. 'Let's see how we get on. Though as the good doctor is formidably short with people like us, I don't imagine we'll be here for very long.' He lifted his hand to the door.

It was Brandon who answered, flinging the door open as if they were welcome guests. 'Come on in. You must be the detectives. Come to tell us who killed the poor dude down by the water?'

'I wish I could.' Jude held out his hand in greeting and Brandon clasped it in a tight, redneck handshake. 'I'm DCI Satterthwaite from Cumbria Police. This is DS Ashleigh O'Halloran. I wondered if we could ask you a few quick questions?'

'There's no need for you to come in.' Cody bounced in from the living room, her ponytail swinging in indignation. 'I'm really busy right now. This whole business has been very trying. More to the point it's been very disruptive. And I have work to do.'

'Honey,' Brandon said, turning to his sister with an engaging smile, 'these guys are doing their best.'

'Doing their best is bumbling around like the keystone cops, or so it seems.' She turned her glare on the visitors. 'It shouldn't be taking you this long to decide that Owen killed himself when everybody knows it. You should be focusing all your attention on what happened down in the field.'

'That's why I'm here.'

'I already told you I didn't see anything. I was quietly minding my own business.'

'I was here,' Brandon offered, semi-apologetically, 'but I didn't see anything. Can't say I'd have been much help if I was. I was so jetlagged I barely knew which side of the world I was on.'

'Brandon had a difficult journey.' At last Cody showed some fellow feeling to someone. 'Another reason we don't need to be disturbed. And don't feel you need to patronise me by coming to keep me informed. I'd far rather be left alone.'

Jude stiffened a little. Beside him, he could sense Ashleigh was at least as irritated. 'I haven't forgotten that there have been threats made against you. It's my job to make sure you're safe.'

'That's great, but I have Brandon and that's all I need. I've been around the world in far more dangerous places than this. I can look after myself. Thank you.'

She moved to shut the door but it was Brandon who put his foot in it. A power struggle played out between the two of them, and he won, turning back to Jude and Ashleigh with a charming smile. 'Guess it's not a good time for you to ask questions right now. Maybe you can come back. I'm sure you've got other things you can do.'

'I've answered all the questions I could possibly answer,' Cody snapped. 'I'm tired of questions. Owen's death has been traumatic but I don't even know the man who's dead. Maybe they had some trivial fallout. Those people are like that. It's nothing to do with me.'

'Did you ever speak to him?'

'Once, maybe, when I first came. I vaguely remember trying to be polite. Not that they were polite in return.'

'What we were looking for was some background information about yourself, Dr Wilder.' Ashleigh, attempting to lower the temperature by changing the direction of questioning, would fail just as Jude himself had failed with Cody in this belligerent a mood, but he had to credit her for the attempt.

'Why do you need it? Everything about me is in the public domain. Isn't that what you pay your hundreds of detectives to do?'

'Cody, honey.' Brandon's voice held the shade of a warning and his sister, after a moment, heeded it and managed a too obviously false smile. 'It won't do any harm. A few questions don't hurt. It's no more than you'll have to tell your journalist friend when she comes.'

Brother and sister fought a second round in their silent battle of wills and again, he won. 'I'd forgotten about her. I've agreed to give an interview to that journalist woman, Chief Inspector. Persistence pays, I'll say that for her. You should try it.' She paused as if to invite an answer, then carried on when she didn't get one. 'Perhaps you just want to send one of your detectives to sit in on the interview. It'll save a lot of effort for both of us and spare me a lot of stress.' The smile was even more fake, her lips pinned back to reveal the slightest hint of perfect teeth. 'That's what we'll do.'

Jude took a moment to think about it. A journalist wouldn't ask the questions he wanted to ask, but he couldn't force Cody to answer so there was nothing to lose. 'Yes, all right. I'll meet you halfway on that one.'

Brandon seemed to think that was uproariously funny, but he took the chance to end the interview. 'Sure. Send someone along. Cody'll let you know when to turn up. Have a good day.' And he closed the door.

'This is starting to get to me.' Cody wound her scarf around her neck and tucked the ends of it into her coat. It wasn't an admission she'd have made to anyone but Brandon, and she wasn't even prepared to tell him everything. Somehow Wordsworth, whether William or Dorothy, found the right words for her mood which, today, was melancholy. *How fast has brother followed brother, From sunshine to the sunless land*. 'Let's get outside and get some fresh air.'

'Sure.'

Brandon was never much of a talker. The wilderness did that to you, or to some people, turning them into silent types who'd learned there was rarely any point in wasting words when they too often got ripped from your lips by the wind or, worse, floated away over miles of plains, clear as a bell as they echoed off the rocks and were heard by no one. It had the opposite effect on her. She'd learned how wonderful words were, how they made good companions in a desolate silence and enriched lives through generations. Once that secret had dawned on her it had almost been inevitable that she'd go on to study language in its richness.

She stepped out into the lane, blanking out the grim truth of what had happened to Lynx and looking instead to the circling hills. 'The Wordsworths loved this area. It's hardly surprising.'

'It sure is pretty.'

She shot a sideways glance at him. She'd have expected

him to have got over his jetlag by now, but he was still uncharacteristically distant from her, tired and unlike his enthusiastic self. His sleeping patterns hadn't settled down, either, and he'd been rumbling round when any other sane person would have been asleep. It had its advantages – the dishwasher and the washing done, the kitchen cleaned before she got up, but really. Anyone would think he was the one who was the focus of all the suspicion, that death had come calling in his home not hers.

She averted her gaze from the field as they reached the bottom of Coffin Lane. She wasn't quite sure why she'd denied knowing Lynx to the police. Her liaisons with him belonged to a shared past, but it surely wasn't anything to do with her and his threats were meaningless. He was a man who liked to play rough in bed, but out of it he'd cared for nothing. Whoever was hating her now, whatever had produced the endless stream of invective that had played its part in driving Owen to his death, was a more modern intolerance. Some people couldn't handle freedom of expression. William Wordsworth would have had a few things to say about that, too.

'Afternoon, Dr Wilder.' The policewoman on duty in Coffin Lane stepped aside to let her past. Cody turned towards her with a forced smile, trying not to look at the scene beyond. She'd miss Lynx, who had been kind to her, but life had taught her the hardest lesson and now she knew you couldn't trust the people who ought to care for you. Only Brandon, to whom she was tied by the double lock of blood and secrecy, had never hurt her.

'Howdy, ma'am,' Brandon said to the policewoman, falling into step beside Cody as she moved on. His deliberate adoption of the stereotypical cowboy's speech and manner irritated her further. *Dear God*, she said to herself, *surely I'm not letting this get to me?*

'Cody.'

She skidded to a halt, alerted by his tone. Brandon never called her by her name, always *honey* or *baby* or, occasionally, *sis*. 'What?' Her mind jumped back a quarter of a century. 'What have you done now?'

He stopped, too, and turned towards her as if he'd made a decision, though he wouldn't look her in the eye. 'What do you mean?'

'Last time you spoke to me like that was when—'

He raised a hand in warning and wisdom prevailed. The words died on her lips. *Look where your last good idea got us*, she wanted to shout at him, but she knew what he'd answer. He'd say: *it got us out of hell*. 'Ssh!'

They didn't talk about it. They didn't dare. 'So what is it this time?'

'It's all good. You'll be pleased for me, baby. I'd have told you before, if there hadn't been so much going on. The whole reason I came over here is to tell you. I've met the best girl in the world and I'm going to marry her.'

Brandon, marrying? Hitching his star to another woman's wagon? 'I'm sorry, honey. I thought you came to hear my presentation.'

He was by no means stupid but with him everything boiled down to brutal necessity and sarcasm always washed over his head. The wilderness did that to you. 'Sure. That, too. But while I was here, I wanted to tell you my news.'

'Married?' The thought appalled her, on too many levels. 'You've found some girl who's prepared to go and live twenty miles down a dirt track and see no one but you for weeks on end?' To her disgust, his sheepishness gave way to a bashful, boy-in-love smile. In response, she forced a smile but dread and guilt and anger welled up in her heart. At the end of that track, Brandon and his unsuspecting wife would have kids who'd be stranded out in the back woods just as she and Brandon had been, isolated in a way that would make them both dependent and interdependent. History threatened to repeat itself. Her stomach lurched at the thought. 'It'll never last. She won't cope.'

'Guess she will. She's prepared to take me on.'

He was looking at her furtively, as if he was unsure of her response, and it gave her the opportunity to be generous. She saw Brandon little enough and was confident enough to believe he'd always come when she called, that if she ever needed him, no wife, no kids, nothing would come between them.

'Well, sweet.' She leaned towards him and hugged him, offering him an untypical peck on the cheek to show him how open-hearted she was. 'I can't wait to meet her. What's her name? What does she do?'

'She's called Laura,' he said, setting off more jauntily as if he'd passed some difficult hurdle with ease. 'She works for a tech company in LA.'

'LA, huh? Wyoming's going to be a change for her.' Catching up with him, she smiled as they passed the Gordons' cafe. 'That's where those nutters live who think I killed their kid.'

'Jeez. Did you tell the police that?'

'They already knew. They weren't exactly subtle about their banner.'

'I wish I'd made it here in time. I'd have ripped it down myself and made them eat it, shred by shred.'

In reality, Cody cared nothing for the Gordons. 'Let's go and find somewhere for a coffee. There's a proper American diner around the corner that does waffles and pancakes. Scones and weak tea are real authentic but right now I need a kickass coffee.'

They negotiated their way past the cafe and into the village centre, and even there she was attracting stares. Normally that wouldn't have bothered her but that sudden thought, that memory of life on the ranch alone with Brandon and her parents and its inevitable brutal outcome, had unsettled her. Violence extended through the years and she was powerless to stop it. 'These guys are as bad as snakes,' she said loudly to Brandon, as they crossed the road to the churchyard.

'Worse than snakes, honey. Snakes don't pretend to be anything they're not.'

That was true enough. The majority of those who stared with such intense curiosity weren't hostile, and the chances were that whoever had killed Lynx wasn't among them. But she couldn't be sure.

Outside the church, a mother with a pushchair, a child and a dog occupied the pavement as she unpacked her bag in search of something or other. The child, bored, sat on the pavement sorting scarlet yew berries into a pattern and as Cody and Brandon stepped out into the road to pass by, the woman lifted her head to stare.

'Stare all you like, honey,' Cody heard herself saying. And then the woman's dog jumped up at her and she squealed and kicked it out of the way. 'Get that beast on a lead!' She jumped and ran a few steps, mortified at her weakness, at how fast her heart was beating.

'So sorry, ma'am.' Brandon intervened. 'My sister's terrified of dogs.'

Did she really need him to smooth things over when she was perfectly right to be annoyed? 'I am not scared of dogs. But they should be kept under control. If you can't do that you shouldn't be allowed to have them. Or children. Look at your kid. Sitting on the sidewalk playing with poison berries? Do you realise how dangerous that is?'

Ears back, tail still, the dog flattened itself against the tarmac and growled. The woman stared, speechless. The child, sensing aggression, broke into a doleful wail.

'Honey.' Brandon took charge once more, linking his arm through Cody's and steering her away before more people could gather. 'Let's get somewhere quiet, huh? Let's get you that coffee.'

Tension pained her like a rope around her head, so that she even wanted to scream at Brandon, cursing him for his folly in dragging some poor woman out of the modern world and back into the brutal wilderness, but she fought it back. 'Sure. Or maybe something stronger, huh? To celebrate your good news.'

10

'Let's get on.' It was already later than Jude had intended and a team meeting scheduled for three o'clock had slipped until its completion would take them way over the time when everyone hoped to leave; he'd end up negotiating the murky water of who was entitled to overtime and who was being asked to do just too many hours. With that in mind, as well as the need to keep information as tightly controlled as possible, he'd called together Doddsy, Chris and Ashleigh to summarise the day's activity. Outside the incident room in Penrith's police headquarters, the damp January night rubbed up against the windows, condensation blooming where heat met cold. 'Okay, Doddsy. How's it going?'

Doddsy pushed back his chair. They were sitting in their usual place, in the incident room beneath the whiteboard that supported maps and pictures of victims and the scenes. When Jude looked up at it, he saw photographs of Owen, sophisticated and modern, and of the luxury cottage where he'd died, alongside images of the damp, dreary campsite in the rain. There were no pictures of Lynx alive. 'I feel like it's Christmas and I'm doing a jigsaw puzzle with Auntie Gladys. Two puzzles, in fact, mixed up in the same box. One of them's cute little Grasmere and the other's the Wild West.'

This was an unusual bout of levity from the usually dry inspector. Something had got into Doddsy, Jude mused. Maybe he'd started counting down to early retirement and realised he only had another decade in the job before he could think about getting out of it. He lifted an eyebrow, but it was a cheerful one. After all, he himself was noticeably more relaxed than he used to be, he had Ashleigh to thank for that. 'It does feel like that, doesn't it? My gut tells me that two deaths very close together like that have to be connected, but there's no evidence for it. We'll treat them separately just now.'

'Shall we start with Owen? That looks like the straightforward one.'

'Go ahead.' Jude had decided to bring the two cases into the same incident room and put them up on the same board, but they were still officially separate.

Owen's death was Doddsy's project, so he took the lead. 'There's no evidence of any other involvement in his death. He seems to have been a nice enough guy, although I've had people talking with his friends and former colleague and he was known for being mentally frail. He didn't perform well under pressure.'

There couldn't be much that was more stressful than dealing with Cody Wilder in the immediate run-up to a major presentation, even without the added piquancy of death threats from person or persons unknown. 'So what do we conclude?' Jude asked. 'That he just cracked?'

'It looks like it. Chris found out a little bit about what might have driven him over the edge, and I expect the coroner will be very interested in it, as will the boy's parents. But it's not enough for a criminal prosecution.'

Jude looked across the table at Chris, who was looking down at his laptop. 'I think you've probably guessed. When his parents said she was a sexual predator they weren't far off the mark. According to one of her previous researchers, sexual favours are a de facto part of the job. I didn't get the impression that that necessarily bothered that particular young man, and he certainly didn't seem to think anyone else was bothered about it either. Sex with a dominant older woman? Turns some people on, I suppose.'

'But maybe not Owen?'

'Maybe not. Or maybe it did, and maybe he got tired of it and she wouldn't let go, or vice versa. I'm not sure I'd be in a hurry to get on the wrong side of her if she was my boss. Either way, it seems to me that she has some questions to answer, if only of her own conscience.'

Silence. Everyone was looking at Jude, expectantly.

'You're not happy, are you?' Doddsy picked up an empty coffee mug and sighed into its depths. 'There aren't even any biscuits. I had a packet. God knows who ate them. We should make an incident board for that, too. I can think of a few suspects.'

On the matter of Doddsy's missing biscuits, Jude's conscience wasn't entirely clear. It would certainly be a case more easily solved. 'No. You're right. I keep telling myself it's straightforward, but I can't convince myself.'

'What have we missed?'

'I don't think you've missed anything, but you know me. I can't abide a coincidence.' Two deaths, so close in time and space. And the medication. What did you say the toxicology report said?'

Flicking through a pile of notes, Doddsy read out the

relevant section of the report. 'Double dose. Technically an overdose.'

'But he could have taken more. Is that right?'

'Yes. He had two weeks' supply of tablets in his room.'

'Okay. So why didn't he just take the whole lot? Isn't that very much easier than finding a rope and then jumping off a table?' And if you wanted to kill yourself, why wouldn't you do it the easy way?

Doddsy laid his notes down. 'You don't want me to pass that on to the coroner, then.'

'I don't think we can. Not without the answer to that question.'

There was an awkward silence. Doddsy broke it. 'We'll leave it live, then. See if anyone can come up with some answers.'

'What about Lynx?' Ashleigh, who'd been hitherto silent, moved the conversation on. 'I know we have the PM results, and I know Tammy's finished on the crime scene.'

Jude would have liked to get Tammy down to talk them through it, clear, concise and always ready to answer questions, but she'd been busy elsewhere. 'Did you speak to her, Doddsy?'

'Yes. We had a long and interesting chat. But I'll do the PM first. That was interesting too.' He consulted his notes. 'Multiple blows from a large knife. Blade around six inches. Struck by a right-handed person, from above and behind, to the right.'

'Someone taller than him?' Chris nodded. 'How tall was he, anyway?'

Jude checked his notes. In his mind, the figure of Lynx, at a safe distance on the day of Cody's lecture, ducked back out of his sight. Was he shy, or a man with something to hide? 'He was just under six feet, which would imply someone much taller. That said, and bearing in mind where he was found, it seems more likely that he was bending over the woodpile when he was attacked. In which case, that doesn't tell us anything about the height of his attacker.'

'He died where he was found,' Doddsy confirmed. 'The time of death is put at about eight o'clock, give or take half an hour. That's the crucial thing, I think. It would have been dark, or more or less. There might have been a little light in the eastern sky, and some light from the fire or the brazier, both of which had gone out by the time he was found but were still hot, so would have been alight when he died.'

That meant there would have been enough light for someone to see a figure but not necessarily identify it. 'What did Tammy have to say? Anything specific?'

'We won't know about the forensics until we get the results back from the lab. Similarly, with the toxicology tests. I think we know what they'll show, because there was a stash of weed under the floorboards of his tent. Not that that's really a surprise.'

When Jude first visited the camp, there had been the faintest scent of marijuana about it, and rather to his shame he'd chosen to conclude that it wasn't strong enough for him to be certain, that he didn't need to get involved. He'd thought of Mikey, and his brother's youthful misdemeanours. It had taken him a long time to learn the consequences of being heavy-handed.

Lynx had learned, too. When the place had been flooded with police the previous week, the only fragrance drifting out from the camp had been the unmistakably innocent smell of woodsmoke. Maybe if they'd gone into the hippy camp on a drugs bust, he'd still be alive. They'd never know. 'Did the findings confirm the PM?'

'Pretty much. The way the body was found seems to indicate that Lynx had gone there of his own accord and that he was surprised by someone as he bent over the woodpile. There were marks going down to the water but the ground was too soft to get any decent footmarks.'

Jude looked across at the photos pinned onto the board. Even with decent equipment, the greyness of the weather in Grasmere meant that the pictures appeared in monotone, like arty prints on sale in the village's many galleries, and the images of Lynx's lifeless body reminded him of the covers of paperback thrillers. There were no pictures of Lynx alive.

'What else did she come up with from Lynx's tent?'

'There were no finger-marks, but someone had been looking for something. Not the drugs, obviously, unless there were more. If that was what they were after, they'd have taken them.'

Jude took the conversation back a stage. 'Think about the half-light when he died. Could it have been mistaken identity?'

'You meant someone thought they were killing Storm? Or Raven?'

'Possibly so.' Jude doodled a picture of a campfire on his pad, deep in thought. There were so many options, so many possibilities. Which of them would lead to the truth? 'On balance, I think not. If so, why search the tent?'

'A red herring.' Chris looked cheerful, as though the discovery of the marijuana had confirmed his view of the doubtful nature of the Grasmere camp. 'Or one of them could have done it.'

Sitting back, Jude chewed the end of his pen, thoughtfully. His gut told him that neither Storm nor Raven was capable of such violence even if they'd shown any particular dislike for Lynx, and their tolerance and forbearance of him, as of anybody else, was both admirable and difficult to fake. 'They could. Let's think that one through. Ashleigh.' She'd been mainly quiet until that point, but silence didn't mean a lack of engagement, just that she was someone who processed information internally whereas the rest of them tended to think aloud. 'Any ideas?'

'Too many.' She folded both hands in front of her, like a schoolteacher in a bad mood. 'I can't sort out what's going on. Too many people are lying.'

'You have to be sure before you can accuse anyone of that.' Chris, who was sometimes inclined to patronise his superiors, shook his head.

'I am sure. Raven offered to read the tarot cards for me, and I said yes.' She avoided Jude's eye, as if she wanted to keep her own relationship with the tarot a secret. 'My grandmother used to read the cards, so I know a bit about them. Anyway, what Raven turned up was a completely random selection.'

'Surely it's that anyway?' Chris flipped the cards aside, his youthful impatience showing through.

Ashleigh ignored him. 'The story she proceeded to spin me wasn't explicit. I think she's too clever for that. But it pointed us to a strong woman up a hill.'

'Cody Wilder.'

'Yes. And there was a mention of a tall man who'd made a long journey.'

'Brandon?'

'I think that's what she wants us to think. She claimed she saw a man fitting Brandon's description in the woods on the day Owen died. I went back and showed her a picture of him, and she gave us a positive ID.'

'You checked Brandon's stated flight time against the passenger lists, didn't you?'

'Yes. He flew out from Chicago on the Thursday morning, as he said.'

'So Raven can't have seen him.' Ashleigh sighed. 'Maybe she was mistaken, but I think she was deliberately pointing us towards him. And then, there was that reference to a man in the woods.'

'The man that Storm saw.'

Ashleigh folded her lips together. She liked Raven, Jude knew, just as he did, and he could tell how hard she was fighting to retain her objectivity. 'The man he says he saw. Because this man was specifically covered in the door-to-door questionnaire and nobody we've spoken to saw anyone fitting anything like the vague description Storm gave us of him. He's the only one who says he saw him. Even Raven says she never saw anyone. And there's something else.'

'Go on.'

'It's been cold. It's been wet. What do we know about Storm and Raven? We know they reject most of the things we think of as necessary. We know they keep the place tidy—'

'They aren't what you'd call clean, though, are they?' Chris shook his head over this shortcoming.

There was, indeed, a faint human smell that hung around the camp, and about its occupants. 'They don't really have the options, to be fair.' Jude sighed. 'If they want to have a bath or wash their clothes, they have to make a huge effort. Sometimes the Gordons help them out.'

'That's exactly my point.' Ashleigh nodded. 'After I'd been to see Raven and she'd read the cards, I went along and looked to see what I could see. And do you know what I saw?' She looked around the table at their expectant faces. 'Look at the pictures of the site.'

They turned to look at the board. 'Clothes.' Doddsy wrinkled his face, as if a missing piece of Auntie Gladys's puzzle had revealed something surprising and unpleasant.

'Yes. On the line. Drying. They're a man's clothes and they weren't there the day before.'

'It's always bloody wet up here.' Chris was a southerner at heart. 'No chance of getting them dry. So why wash them unless you've got something to hide?'

'Exactly.'

A theory formulated in Jude's brain. 'Let's see. Both Storm and Raven claimed they were in their tent asleep at what we know is the time of his death. They wake up with the light, they said. But that might not be true.'

'It surely can't have been Raven who killed him.' Ashleigh gave them all an apologetic glance, as if she were aware of her own vulnerability, her tendency to care too much. 'Whoever killed him must have been strong, and she's incredibly slight. She couldn't have inflicted injuries like that. But if Storm killed Lynx, he might have persuaded her to lie to cover his tracks. And they'd have pointed us to Brandon because it was easy. He stands out like a sore thumb so she could be reasonably certain her description would point us towards him.' Raven so obviously adored Storm, and the two of them lived in their own world, wrote and abided by their own rules. 'If he did do it and she knew, I don't think she knew straight away. She'd have backed up his story about a man in the woods.'

There were more questions than answers. Jude looked at the clock. 'I don't know if there's much more to gain from this tonight. Time to head off. We'll reconvene at some point in the morning.' They could stay there all night chewing over the possibilities. 'The main thing to come from this is that we need to find out everything about Lynx, and why someone might have wanted to kill him.'

'Leave that with me.' This was exactly the kind of challenge Chris relished.

'One last thing.' Jude motioned Ashleigh back, as the other two got their coats. Chris's last glance over his shoulder and a half-wink to no one in particular indicated that the relationship, though not public knowledge, was now an open secret in the office. 'I meant to ask you. Cody Wilder. She's emailed me to say that she's giving her interview to this journalist tomorrow and has invited me to send any one of my detectives along to sit in. What do you think that's about?'

Deep in thought, Ashleigh twined the end of her ponytail around her finger in a way he could never stop looking at. 'One of two things. Either she genuinely does want to save the effort of having to go through the story of her life twice, or else she doesn't want to be on her own with the woman.'

'I think it goes without saying that I'd like you to do it.' Chris and Doddsy had left the room, and so he felt emboldened to smile at her in a way he might not have done in their presence.

'One thing's for certain.' She pulled on her coat and picked up her bag. 'I'm not likely to allow my sympathy for Cody Wilder to affect my judgement.'

'Excellent. I don't know whether she'll take questions from you, but you might learn something.' Ashleigh was a good listener and an instinctive judge of character, of right and wrong, someone who knew when she was in the presence of a liar. They could do with more people like that.

'I'm worried about Cody,' she said out of the blue.

'Oh?' He turned to watch her as she slid her arms into her coat and buttoned it up, tempted to wait and walk down to the car park with her, but equally sure that someone, somewhere would think it didn't look good.

'Yes. Tyrone said she laid into a complete stranger in Grasmere today. Over her dog, and the fact that the woman's kid was playing with yew berries. He thought he was going to have to go over and intervene, but her brother sorted it out and took her off. Perhaps it isn't surprising the pressure's getting to her.'

'All the more reason to catch whoever killed Lynx.' And to find out if anyone had killed Owen. 'Good luck with it. I'll see you back in the office tomorrow.'

She whisked out of the room. He locked the drawer of his desk, picked up his laptop bag and followed her.

'Isn't DCI Satterthwaite taking you home for a personal debrief tonight?' Superintendent Groves was saying to Ashleigh, with his meaningful chuckle. He must have been walking along the corridor as she walked out and she couldn't have seen him, or she'd surely have dodged back into the office.

Annoyed, Jude took a few long strides along the corridor. 'No, Ashleigh and I are going our separate ways this evening. Another day we might not. Is there a problem with that?' He strode on, leaving Groves in his wake.

It took Ashleigh a few sprinted steps to catch up with him. 'Thanks for that, but really. I could—'

'Yes. But why should you?' Did he really care whether people thought his behaviour towards her was unprofessional? It was a whole lot better than what he'd just witnessed. 'That wasn't okay.'

'He's harmless, Jude. He's like that with everyone.'

'He isn't like that with me.'

'You know what I mean. With every woman. People just learn to ignore it. And anyway, he won't do anything. The whole place has worked out we're sleeping with each other by now. Did you really think they hadn't?'

They'd reached reception by then, and headed out into the car park. Ashleigh's car was parked closer to the building than his, so they paused for a moment next to it. 'It's better that I said something than you.'

'If the secret's out, perhaps you can kiss me goodbye in the car park without caring?'

He laughed at her, but he accepted the invitation, though it only partly eased his irritation at Groves's attitude. The dislike between him and his boss was mutual, and Groves wasn't a man to forget an insult, but he was ready enough to take that on.

It had always been like that. When he stopped to think about it, he'd seen those attitudes, whether conscious or subconscious, casual or crassness disguised as clumsy wit, but he'd never done anything about it before.

Times were changing. Groves would retire in a year and then they could all start anew with someone who wasn't a dinosaur.

11

The detective sergeant, thank God, arrived before Fi Styles. True, there was something of the devil and the deep blue sea about the interview and when she reflected on it, Cody, more than a match for either woman, could only imagine that the police presence had somehow made her more nervous than she felt.

'I must have been mad,' she said to Brandon as she watched Ashleigh stepping smartly up the path. 'Why did I agree to speak to the journalist anyway?'

'Honey, you agreed to speak to her so she'll shut up and go away. And she will.'

She might, but Cody couldn't quite rid herself of the fear that Fi Styles's terrier-like determination to get an interview owed less to her plan for a scoop for the arts section of the national papers and more to a desire to dig out something that might have wider and, for Cody herself, more damaging implications. An ambitious journalist was one thing. Cody's own conscience, only just waking from a lifetime of slumber, was quite another. And there was that telling little line that had caught her unawares – Fi Styles's claim to be a friend of Owen's.

Maybe that was all it was — a claim, and a false one.

One thing was sure. She didn't know which and she didn't dare be wrong. 'And the detective?'

'It saves you having to talk to the police separately and having her here will stop your journalist getting too stroppy with you.'

Nothing ever fazed Brandon, who had an answer for everything. She smiled at him. 'You're right. It's an hour of my time. The police are taking a while to decide Owen killed himself, but they'll get there, and then we can go.'

'He did kill himself. Didn't he?'

Ashleigh O'Halloran rang the doorbell. 'Of course he did. He was weak as water and he couldn't handle me. I could have been a bit gentler with him, I guess, but he knew my reputation before he signed up.' Owen must have been so full of dread at what she might do to him, the damage she might inflict on his career and his studies. He should have known better than to threaten her. 'Nobody made him do it.'

'You were sleeping with him, huh?'

'Are you jealous?' She hoped so. Jealousy was such a creative emotion. Even her jealousy of Brandon's fiancée had a sweet tinge. It had been hard for him to break the news to her and his relief at her acceptance had been palpable. It was proof, if she'd needed it, that even with a wife in tow he couldn't afford to cast her off.

'No. What do I have to be jealous about?' He moved towards the kitchen. 'I'll get out from under your feet.'

The doorbell rang again and the time for talking was over. Cody swooped on it before Brandon could get there. 'Detective Sergeant. Let's hope you don't find this a complete waste of your time. Obviously your boss is determined to finger me for something I didn't do but I can assure you, he's fighting the wrong dog.'

'DCI Satterthwaite is only trying to get to the truth.' The woman said it with her lips tight, as if she were trying not to laugh. Too late, Cody remembered that the police had no reason to connect her with Lynx and that she'd made the rookie error of protesting too much. This wasn't going to be quite as easy as she thought.

'Am I late?' Fi Styles ran the last few steps up the path, as though terrified she was missing something.

'Not at all.' Cody stepped back to invite them into the cottage and ushered both women through to the living room. 'The police were keen to talk to me and so I thought I'd kill two birds with one stone. You can do their work for them and DS O'Halloran can have an hour off.'

'Isn't that irregular?' Fi Styles flashed an irritated look at both the detective and at Cody herself.

If she wanted to play hardball, let her try. 'I don't think so. You both seem to want the same thing and my time is precious. Tea? Coffee?' It was ready on the table, so she poured them both the coffees they asked for and helped herself to some peppermint tea. This wasn't a meeting she planned on lasting a long time. 'I have another appointment at eleven.' Which was a lie, and she was pretty certain both of them knew it, but that didn't bother her. They could challenge it if they wanted and she gave them a fraction of a second to do so, like a minister limiting the opportunity for the public to object to a marriage, but neither of them responded. 'All right. Let's go.'

She sat down facing Fi Styles and cutting the detective out of the conversation. Ashleigh O'Halloran was there to listen, not to talk, and Cody would keep her firmly sidelined. She concentrated on her interrogator, staring straight at her. Brandon had warned her about the wisdom of being conciliatory and the risks of getting on the wrong side of a journalist, but she was confident she was big enough to beat aside any collateral damage from a would-be headline maker who didn't even have a buyer lined up for her story. Fi needn't think she'd get anything spectacular from the interview.

'Thank you so much for agreeing to speak to me, Dr Wilder. Of course you don't mind if I record the interview.'

Cody nodded. That just meant she'd have to be doubly careful what she said. Despite her bullishness, there was a flutter of nerves in her gut. What did Fi know, and how much of it was true?

'You're a controversial figure, Dr Wilder,' the interviewer purred, looking sideways at her as if she might take it as an insult. 'Perhaps there are reasons for this? You've spoken before about your tough upbringing and how it's forged you—' she checked her notes '—into *a woman of steel.* Could you talk me through your childhood?'

Out in the garden, Brandon was pottering about, poking without any real interest into the innards of some unspecified dead plant. Cody drew in a deep breath. 'Sure. My parents were ranchers, out in the ranges of western Wyoming. We lived in a cabin twenty miles down a dirt track off Interstate 80. There were the four of us, and it was more than a little lonesome. When I was a child, there were cattlemen who lived on the ranch with us, but as soon as Brandon was old enough to help, they left and he and Pop managed the ranch together.'

'Is that unusual?'

It was very unusual. Brandon Wilder Junior had been a man

so introverted and antisocial he preferred to work himself and his family into the ground rather than put in the effort it took to retain employees. He'd been mean, too, though he'd died without spending any of the money he'd saved. Not that there had been a lot of it, but there had been enough to make everybody's lives easier, if he'd chosen to do so. That was something else she'd never forgive him for. 'He was proud and an independent man. He wanted everything he owned to be something he'd earned, something he'd worked for. That's what he taught me. Among other things.' Yes, there were a lot of things she'd learned from her father that had shaped her, and she wasn't going to tell Fi Styles what they were. 'He made me the person I am. Every time I achieve something, every time I succeed, I think of him.' In its way, it was the truth. She composed her expression into one that she hoped showed admiration, rather than hatred. 'Every time I publish a paper. Every time I speak at a conference. Every time I see my name on the cover of a book.'

Fi was scribbling enthusiastically. It was a good quote. Cody's heart sang like the whirring of the recording device on the table.

'Every time I come across someone who abuses me, every time I meet someone who tells me I can't do something because I'm a woman, every time I hear someone tell me I should stay silent and sit in the corner, I think of him, and I rise up.'

'Life in Wyoming was hard?' Fi underlined whatever she'd written in her spidery shorthand and put a star next to it.

This was the easy bit, the embroidery over the frame of a brutal upbringing, with an abusive father, a weak and increasingly frail mother and only Brandon on whom she could rely. 'It was hard, but it shaped me.' She could talk for hours on this, and rattled into her standard speech on the rare good side of her childhood. The black velvet of the night sky, the huge moon hanging low, the howl of the wolves in the distance and sometimes not the distance, the drifts of snow in the winter. The isolation. The cold. Working in the daytime, studying in the long winter nights, driven by an unwavering determination to be out of that place and into the real world.

Wyoming had been her personal hell, but its cold isolation had forged her steel soul. Did she regret what she was, she wondered, briefly, as she prattled on, but she caught herself up. She couldn't afford to ponder on the philosophy of life with Fi Styles sitting in front of her, ready to slip in a sly question when her concentration had lapsed.

'So the big question.' Fi put her head to one side, almost coquettishly. 'How did you come to be interested in the classics?'

Those cold, hard winters had been dark and lonely. 'The snow was feet thick. We couldn't go out. There was little to do but we had a lot of books, so I read. One of the books was a collection of poetry and that's where I learned about Wordsworth.' It could have been any other book she'd picked up at that moment when her soul was ready to fly. It could have been Shakespeare of Longfellow or Austen but chance had chosen a damp copy of the *Prelude*, its pages spotted with mould, to spark her lifelong obsession and she'd fitted too easily into a world where a brother and sister were so dangerously interdependent. 'His poetry spoke to me. *I was taught to feel, perhaps too much, the self-sufficing power of*

Solitude.' She paused. William, Mary and Dorothy, at once domestic and unconventional, had become an alternative family into whose lives she'd escaped. 'But there was no way, or seemed no way, to fulfil my dream to become an academic. And one day my life changed.'

'Your father died?'

'Yes. I couldn't stay on the ranch. There were too many memories.' She was about to quote William again but she could tell Fi wasn't interested, so she stopped.

'So you left Wyoming and went to the big city. What then?'

'I didn't leave it.' Cody hated inaccuracy. 'I went to the University of Wyoming, in Laramie. It's hardly a big city.'

'But it must have felt like it to you.'

Cody was off again, another tour through the comfortable parts of her life. She couldn't believe how easy a ride Fi Styles was giving her. 'Coming to Laramie was a step up for me. I adapted very quickly to a socialised environment.' Maybe she should show a little humility. 'My past made me what I am. Sometimes maybe I should be more sympathetic to those who didn't have to endure the hardships that I endured when I was growing up.' That was as far as she was prepared to compromise. 'That said, I have to be true to myself. Young people these days have no idea what hardships other people have to endure. They care only about their tender sensibilities, about their own safety, about being able to do what they want when they want. They believe that democracy means getting what they want. They believe that their right not to be offended overrides anyone else's right to speak. Well, I can tell you that I shall continue to speak out, within the law, in the defence of freedom of speech, and I will speak out on behalf of those who daren't speak out, even if I disagree with them. *We must be free or die*, as William wrote.'

This, she could see, was the sort of thing Fi Styles was after. The woman was nodding and making notes, not asking any questions but allowing Cody to rattle on. She dared a glance at Ashleigh O'Halloran, and found the detective watching her in silence. Let her make what she wanted of that.

'And so,' Fi said, when the story of Cody's career had followed seamlessly on from that of her upbringing, 'tell us about your breakthrough in the story of the Wordsworths. Your findings are controversial at best.'

There was nothing new to say. 'You attended my lecture. You have the press pack. You have my book. Everything is in there, the process of my research, how I came here to Grasmere in October last year to show the Trust the papers, how excited they were about them. Of course, I can outline for you the moment when I realised I had something special.'

She paused and lifted the cup of peppermint tea, which she'd been holding throughout the interview, to her lips. It wasn't unpleasant when cold. 'I knew, of course, that the last reference to the complete Alfoxden Journal placed it in the possession of Wordsworth's biographer, Professor William Knight, in St Andrews. I had put out feelers there for some time and eventually it paid off. Sebastian Mulholland got in touch. He's an antiquarian bookseller and he has a phenomenal memory for detail. He told me he remembered seeing something, many years before, in a bookshelf in a private house. The owner of that house had died and the house was to be sold.'

She sipped her tea again, savouring the memory. 'I instructed him to ask if he could buy the books on my behalf and he did. I told him I would take them all, unseen, for five hundred pounds. And it turned out Seb had been right. The books included Dorothy's handwritten journal.'

Even thinking about it set her heart hammering, and it got better. 'As you know, the contents of the journal were disappointing. I shouldn't say that, of course. It was – it is – a very precious document and I can tell you that I intend to gift it to the Wordsworth Trust.' Fi Styles could have that nugget of information for nothing. 'They were very helpful to me during my research.' And they'd been discreet when she'd shown them the papers. That was one reason for giving them the journals. She no longer had any academic interest in it, and it could be used by others who wanted to analyse William's relationship with his sister.

'How incredibly generous of you. And the letters?'

The letters were different. There was something about them that Cody, as a historian, couldn't let go. 'It was what was in them that really changed everything. Folded at the back of the journal were letters written by Mary Wordsworth, William's wife, that clearly indicated that the relationship between William and Dorothy was closer than society considered decent. Mary asks Dorothy to take *the best care* of her husband when she's not there and *tend to his every bodily need*. At one point she asks about Dorothy's condition. She recommends herbs her sister-in-law can take. The implication is clear – that Dorothy, so devoted to her brother, was carrying his child.'

A tiny vein fluttered in her own belly as she thought about it. How had Dorothy responded? Had she wanted to keep her baby, or was she content to sacrifice it for her brother's reputation? What sins had these two siblings committed for each other's sake? 'I'd suspected it for a long time. At last, I had proof.'

'What a wonderful moment for you.' Fi nodded, encouragingly, as if Cody were a child who'd correctly answered a difficult question. That put Cody's back up even more, if it was possible. How had she come to let this aggressive young woman sit in her living room and question her in the first place? What had come over her?

Ah. She remembered. It was because the girl had been talking to Owen and he, in an unbalanced state of mind and with revenge at the forefront of his heart, might have told her anything. Lies or truth, it didn't matter. Owen would have sought to do as much damage to Cody's career as he could, by any means. That was why she was here. It was why the detective, unwittingly, was there. She forced a smile. 'It was.'

'And these letters. They're genuine. You had them verified?'

Oh, so that was it. After all, it was a pity Ashleigh O'Halloran was there, or she'd have ripped into Fi in a way that would have made her a prime suspect for something, for sure. 'Naturally.'

'Independently?'

'Yes. By an expert in New York.'

'George Gould, I believe.' Fi shook her head, an exact mimicry of Cody's own mannerism.

'That's correct.'

'Is that George Gould the independent expert you are rumoured to have had an affair with?'

Jesus. No wonder Owen had killed himself, if he'd told

Fi that. He'd have been terrified of the consequences, and rightly so. Cody's fury towards him gathered strength, even though he was beyond her reach, but her battle, for the moment, was with Fi and it wouldn't be won by fury, but by disarming honesty. 'Honey, you need to understand. They were verified by the foremost independent expert in the field. It isn't a large field of expertise. It so happens that this man is someone I knew well and had been close to. Yes. Socially and academically it's all pretty incestuous. But there was no affair.' It was a safe lie. George would deny it as hotly as she had, and there was only the word of a dead troublemaker to say otherwise. 'Not that it's your business, and not that I care what people think. You know about me. If I'd wanted to sleep with George, I'd have done that. I won't let other people's morals hold me back.' But in reality, George hadn't been that interested, and there had been other people around at the time so she hadn't needed him. Not in that way, at least.

'That's not what Owen said.'

'With respect. There's no way Owen could have known. It wasn't something I felt the need to discuss with him.'

Fi's smile betrayed her. She must already be writing up the article in her head, probing for the sensational angle. 'What kind of relationship did you have with Owen, Dr Wilder?'

'No doubt Owen told you that. I prefer not to discuss my personal relationships with strangers.'

'I'm sure that's the case. I'm sure you have every reason.'

Cody sat for a moment and stared at Fi's pretty, little-girl face, the simpering green eyes. Did she think that by playing it simple she'd make any kind of breakthrough? 'We know that poor Owen was unstable. I don't think it's appropriate or respectful to cover this topic.' Bowing her head to try and shame Fi off the subject, she chanced a look at the detective, who sat curling the end of her plait round her finger in silent fascination.

'The letters.' Fi resumed the attack, though subtly. She, too, spared a quick look at Ashleigh. 'May I see them?'

'I don't have them here. They're precious documents.'

'Is there any doubt at all about their authenticity?'

'No.' Cody sighed.

'Then you won't mind me approaching Dr Gould on the subject.'

'I can't stop you, but even if I could I'm very happy for you to do so.'

'Thanks. This has been a most helpful interview.' Fi had achieved whatever she came to achieve. She got to her feet, and Ashleigh did likewise, and Cody saw them off the premises.

So that was it. Before he'd killed himself, Owen had sown the seeds of his revenge and now they were blooming. Fi Styles, Cody was sure, was no investigative journalist looking for a big story, but an aspiring one seeking a breakthrough. Owen's story might give her that, but at what cost to Cody? It wouldn't take much of an allegation for her enemies to rally round and her reputation as a researcher to be besmirched.

And that wasn't going to happen. She paused for a while to be sure they'd gone. George had assured her the letters were genuine, and she believed it. That wouldn't stop someone trying to cause trouble.

Swiftly, she moved to the drawer in the bureau, turned the key and pulled it open. The letters were in there, in a cardboard folder and three layers of acid-free tissue paper. They should be in controlled conditions in a fireproof safe somewhere but without them she felt deprived. Instead she'd brought them with her and then taken the ridiculous notion that Owen might try to destroy them if he couldn't destroy her and in the end he, in his weakness, had chosen to destroy himself.

And yet she felt jumpy about them even after he was dead, unable to bring herself to leave them with Lynx. Fi's questioning of their authenticity only sharpened her concern. She got them out, partly to be sure they were there and partly for a quick adrenaline fix. It was unbelievable how much they mattered to her – more than any human ever had, except Brandon. Any psychologist would have a field day with so strong a reliance not just on something material but something rooted so far in the past.

She frowned down at them. She always put them in the folder the same way, the heading to the right so that whenever she opened it Mary Wordsworth's handwriting seemed to greet her. *My dearest darling...* Today they were the other way round.

A stranger to self-doubt, Cody knew immediately what had happened. Someone had been in the drawer. And that meant someone had been in the house.

But the letters were all there, and all undamaged. She snapped the drawer shut, locked it, and put the key in her pocket.

12

'I can't wait to hear how you got on with the mad professor.'

Chris and Doddsy were at the table in the incident room when Ashleigh came in, and Jude was a couple of steps away from them on the other side of it, trying to sign off a phone call without sounding rude. 'I'll get back to you. Yes, as soon as I can. Certainly by the morning. What's the latest I can call you?' He wrote something on a pad, made an extravagant face, and ended the call. 'Okay. Sorry about that. Yes, Ashleigh. Let's find out what you learned from Cody Wilder.'

She watched him as he slid into his usual seat beneath the whiteboard and glanced down at his pad. Jude was an inveterate doodler and almost certainly gave his thought process away more often than he realised. Today, it was revealed to anyone who cared to see it in a series of question marks. It was going to be that sort of day.

'Did she talk to you?' Chris's bad mood of the previous couple of days had improved. That meant he had something up his sleeve he was dying to reveal.

It would wait. They were looking to her first. 'I never said a word.'

Jude threw back his head and laughed. 'There's a first time for everything.'

She smiled back at him. 'Sometimes it's better to watch and listen, though there wasn't much new.' She checked down at the notes she'd made that morning. It would have been good to have a tape recording of exactly what Cody had said, because the clues were in the inflections, in the tension between interviewer and interviewee. 'There was one thing Cody said that struck me, but which may be coincidental.'

'Go on.' Doddsy suppressed a sigh, as if his mind were elsewhere.

'Fi Styles had been talking to Owen Armitstead. Apparently, he'd suggested to her that there's some doubt about the provenance of the letters on which Dr Wilder's research is based. Fi challenged Cody on it. Cody denied it.'

Jude rubbed a hand on his chin. 'I read up about her and none of the reports of her launch questioned the authenticity of the letters.'

'That was what I thought.'

He scribbled over one of the question marks, almost in frustration. 'That's not a reason for Owen to kill himself, though I can see why he might have wanted to use that to get back at his boss if she was making his life miserable. How did Cody react?'

Ashleigh thought about it. Sitting silently, watching the interplay, had been revealing. Cody's response to the accusation had been realistically appalled. 'She insisted that the letters had been independently authenticated, but Fi challenged her further on it. She suggested Cody had had an affair with the expert who undertook the verification and Cody denied it, although not particularly strenuously.'

'That's damaging for her, is it?'

'Potentially. I don't imagine there's anything criminal about a soft verification and if there was, it isn't our jurisdiction. But it's interesting.'

'What was the body language like?'

'Tense, but you'd expect that. I don't think Cody wanted to give the interview in the first place, and I still haven't worked out why she agreed to have me sit in on it. I think she may have regretted it, but decided she couldn't pull out of it. And I also thought that she was very uncomfortable with some of the questions Fi Styles was asking her.'

'In what way?'

'I'm not sure. I don't think she was lying, but I certainly think she may have been withholding some of the truth.' Recalling Cody's stiffness as she'd faced down Fi Styles, switching from good cop to bad cop, from aggressor to victim with the switch of a subject or a turn in a sentence, Ashleigh struggled to make sense of it. 'Is it bad to say I felt sorry for her?'

Chris, who'd been patronised to hell and back by Cody Wilder, shook his head with amusement and Doddsy, who gave all humans the benefit of a certain degree of doubt did the same with a touch of understanding, but Jude's scowl bore no regard for any relationship between them. 'I can't afford to have you feeling sorry for her. At best she's a witness in a murder case and probably played a significant part in driving a young man to his death. I don't think she needs our sympathy.'

'She had a very tough upbringing.'

'That may be what she wants you to think.' Doddsy seemed to have taken Jude's reprimand to apply to himself as well, and was fighting a valiant rearguard action against his better nature. 'In reality, she's highly privileged. What she calls a tough upbringing isn't an excuse to walk all over other people the way she seems to have done.'

'Is that all you have to say on Cody?' Jude clearly wasn't in the mood to go over the morality or otherwise of Cody's behaviour.

'No. There's one other thing that did catch my eye. When she talked about Mary Wordsworth's letters.'

'If that's what they are.' Chris, it appeared, was ready to believe in Cody's villainy. He yawned and stretched out in his seat.

'I don't know if they are. I think she genuinely believes they are. There's a lot about Cody I'm not sure about. There's a lot about her manner and her approach I think is put on, though whether that's because she wants to con the wider public or whether she's trying to deceive herself I don't know. But I'm one hundred per cent sure that she's dedicated to her subject, to an almost frightening degree.'

Jude thought about it for a moment. 'Okay. Anything else?'

'There's one thing. Fi Styles asked if she could see the letters and Cody said no. Why do that if you were sure of them?'

'Maybe she didn't have them.' Chris was the one who was closest to Ashleigh's line of thought.

Jude made another note. 'We can come back to that. Meantime, I meant to try and catch Tammy before she left but I never got the chance. Did any of you manage to speak to her?'

'I did.' Chris couldn't suppress his grin. He loved to be the man who produced the show-stopping piece of information, and if he couldn't do it himself, Ashleigh knew he was just as happy delivering information from someone else. 'You don't know?'

'I have three cases running at once.' Jude was struggling not to get irritable. 'I'm sure there'll be an email in my inbox. I'll read it when I get a moment.'

'It'll be worth it. The results are back from the samples the CSI team took from the murder scene.' He allowed himself a dramatic pause.

'And?' Jude's patience, it was clear, was running out.

'Cody Wilder's DNA was all over Lynx's tent. Hair, fingerprints, the lot. She'd spent time there in the previous couple of days and they'd had sex.'

Silence, in which Jude's face froze into a mask of concentration as he reviewed the implications of this remark. Cody had lied. Ashleigh, thinking of her confrontational approach, her challenging attitude, could understand why. The controversial American, so obviously, was someone who trusted nobody but herself.

'Okay.' Jude rapped his pen on the table. 'So there's a relationship we didn't know about. Let's call a spade a spade. No, let's call a suspect a suspect. That's what she is. There's a relationship she lied about. I'll talk to her about it tomorrow.'

Something flicked into Ashleigh's mind. What was it Cody had said? 'She first announced the date of the lecture back in October. Isn't that the time Lynx arrived at the camp?'

'There's no point in asking those Flat Earthers,' said Chris, with a note of contempt. 'They don't even bother to tell the time, let alone keep track of the date. And they probably wouldn't tell us the truth if they knew.'

'Clearly they didn't.' Jude tapped his pencil impatiently on the pad again. 'She isn't the only one who lied about it, is she? Both Storm and Raven said she hadn't been down there. They must have known she was there, and you can hardly avoid the conclusion that they knew what the two of them were up to. What else do we think they've been lying about?' He reached for a file and flicked through it. 'There's nothing in this that suggests they're anything other than sweet-natured hippies, I grant you. But what if that's not right?'

With a sigh, because people lying to the police was inevitable but always made things complicated, Ashleigh looked down at the bullet points she had in front of her, the latest results from the door-to-door inquiries. 'We've been contacted by a local resident who stopped his car on Red Bank Road to answer a phone call at three minutes past noon on Sunday. We know the time from his call log. He saw someone matching Storm's description walking along the shore. At speed, he said. He was carrying a bundle and there was no one else in sight.'

Jude sat for another few seconds in that fierce stillness, then bounced up and crossed to the map pinned up on the wall. 'On Red Bank Road?' His finger traced the line of the path. 'That's a hell of a place to stop. The only place he could pull in on this side of the village is where the path takes off down to the shore. There's a gateway and a clear view from there. He's sure there was no one?'

'The call lasted thirteen minutes. He says when he started the path was clear, that he only saw one person, and his description of that person fits Storm.'

'Okay. So we have three liars. Storm, Raven and Cody Wilder. Now I want to know what Storm was carrying and why he was in such a hurry to get it away.'

'The murder weapon?' Chris shifted in his seat a little.

'Possibly.' Jude took a long look towards the darkness. 'There's not a lot of point in trying to look for it tonight, but I think in the morning we'll get a search going up in Deer Bolt Woods. Anything else?'

They shook their heads.

'Then we'll get off. There's plenty for us to do tomorrow. Doddsy, I'm going to leave you to take charge of the search for the weapon. Chris, I want you to keep on looking for anything you can about Lynx. I take it we don't yet know who he is?'

'No. There's no match for his DNA on record so he's obviously never been in trouble with the law, either here or in the States or Canada. I'm waiting for a result on dental records. And he had no papers that we've been able to find.'

'They'll be locked in some left luggage place, somewhere, I expect. Or else he was serious about cutting himself off from the world and he really did destroy them.' Doddsy was getting his coat on already, with an unusual eagerness. 'I'll be away, Jude. I'll be down in Grasmere first thing tomorrow.'

'What's the hurry? Got a date?' Chris bounded up and followed him out through the door and down the corridor.

Jude took one long last look at the incident board, hands deep in his pockets. Pushing her chair back, Ashleigh went to stand behind him, more closely than she would if anyone else was there. In front of them, the complex and widely differing pieces of two different puzzles took on no recognisable shape, made no obvious sense. 'There is an answer to this, isn't there?'

'There must be. But it would help if people didn't try and hide things.' He sighed and turned back. 'Anyway, I'm done for today. I need an evening off. Doing anything tonight?'

'I don't believe I am.' Ashleigh looked at him, thoughtfully. 'But you are. Aren't you? I thought you were going out for a pint with Doddsy.'

'I usually do on a Wednesday. Not tonight. He's stood me up.'

'I'm sure I'm a poor substitute, but yes, I'll fill the gap.'

He grinned at her. 'You'll do. I'll see you in the Dockray Hall at eight and we can stop thinking about Cody bloody Wilder for an hour or so.'

But they wouldn't. Both of them would keep chewing the matter over and over until the mystery was solved and Lynx's killer apprehended.

13

Becca was just getting comfortable with her first glass of wine at Adam Fleetwood's birthday drinks when Jude walked into the bar and ruined the evening, for her at least. She was fortunate enough to be the one facing the door so she saw him before anyone else, even before he saw her, but she wasn't quick enough to turn away. He was usually good at concealing what he thought but they'd been together for too long, so that he couldn't hide it from her. His eyes narrowed, shoulders stiffened under the sharp cut of his overcoat and he turned his head, quickly and scanned the room.

He would be early, because he always was. For a moment Becca felt almost sorry for him as his gaze came back to her and settled on her companions. It wasn't just her. There was Adam, his former best friend, sitting to her left and a few places along was Mikey, the younger brother who barely spoke to him.

Beside her, Adam turned, saw, and placed a deliberate hand on her arm.

Jude's expression deepened from disinterest to an inimitable scowl, but he banished it, almost immediately. You had to hand it to him. He tried. It was a couple of months since Adam had come out of prison and even in a town as small as Penrith it was easy enough to avoid someone when you wanted to. Jude's problem was that Adam didn't want to avoid him, flaunting his rehabilitation and his acceptance back into society in the face of the man he believed had put him behind bars in the first place.

It wasn't quite like that. As Jude had never tired of saying when they were together, things were never that simple, but there was no question in Becca's mind that his attitude and actions had been high-handed beyond endurance, and things had fallen apart between them as a result. Hard drugs were one thing; a little dabbling, as Mikey had done with Adam's encouragement, quite another. Who, apart from the overly puritan Jude, hadn't done that? On this matter her sympathies were entirely with Adam.

It's because I value friendship, she told herself, still watching Jude as he hovered just inside the doorway, a man in two minds about whether to stay or whether to go. It would have been good to keep him as a friend, and the offer was always open to him, but he was too proud to meet her on the middle ground after she'd rejected him. Surely that proved she'd been right to let him go.

'There's Jude,' someone else said, a few chairs away.

'Judas,' someone else corrected, to general laughter.

On the other side of the bar, Jude flipped a quick text, rammed his phone into his pocket and turned to leave, but thought better of it. His gaze flicked across the room, rested for a moment on Adam, and then he walked towards them.

The ten or so people around the table, all of them friends of hers and many of them once friends of Jude's, the people who might have joked about whether they were on the bride's side or the groom's side at the wedding everyone assumed they'd eventually have, stilled in anticipation. Adam stood up. The wall lights behind his head gave him the unlikeliest halo.

'Happy birthday, mate.' Jude stopped and held out a hand.

Becca found that she was holding her breath.

The silence persisted just long enough to remind her that Adam was both a clever man and a wronged one, to bring his friends inching closer around him in the expectation of a confrontation, and to leave Jude's gesture of friendship hanging in the balance and his attempt at reconciliation looking like foolishness. Only when the tension had built so high that someone couldn't suppress a nervous snigger did Adam move. 'Thanks, pal.' He took Jude's hand, shook it briefly, let it go. 'Care to join us for a drink? I'm buying.'

Jude's serene expression never wavered. 'I'd love to, but I'm supposed to be meeting someone else.'

'Your friend can join us, too.' Adam sat down again and replaced his hand on Becca's arm. Trying not to be too obvious, she shook him off. Her sister thought Adam had a manipulative streak though Becca herself liked him – maybe more than liked him – but she was quite capable of rubbing Jude's nose in his misdemeanours for herself.

'Not tonight. We've just had to rearrange.' Jude managed to deliver the line as if it wasn't blindingly obvious he'd just texted whoever it was and headed them off. He was good at excuses, but he was good at twisting everything to make it fit his own agenda, so that he looked noble and everybody else looked small-minded.

'Shame. Well, no doubt we'll bump into one another around the place.'

'I expect so.' With every sign of relief at a situation defused, Jude turned once more for the door.

He had reckoned without his brother. With a sinking heart, Becca saw that Mikey had risen from his seat as Adam had spoken and was threading his way round the back of the group to cut him off. His spiky silhouette bristled with attitude. 'Jude. What the hell?'

'Nothing. I'm leaving.'

'You came here to check up on me, didn't you?'

'No. I wouldn't have come near the place if I'd known you were going to be here. Any of you.' His look darkened in Becca's direction.

Fortunately, Adam had turned away to laugh with his friends, a clear signal of dismissal. That wouldn't stop Mikey. Nothing ever did. He was as pig-headed as Jude himself, though he'd yet to learn how to look as if he was being reasonable. Ready to intervene if required, Becca shuffled in her seat.

'You knew we were meeting here.'

'I had no idea.'

'Mum knew.'

'She doesn't tell me everything you do. And Mikey…'

'What?'

'You can meet your mates anywhere you like. It's nothing to do with me. But if I want to meet my girlfriend in a particular pub, I don't need your permission.'

'Girlfriend!' Mikey said, his mouth slack with surprise. 'You kept that one quiet.' But if Jude heard he couldn't be bothered with the discussion, and slid out of the door, as unobtrusively as possible.

'Did you hear that?' Mikey asked Becca, oblivious. 'A girlfriend? Why didn't anyone tell me?'

'Yes. I heard.'

'Why didn't I know about it?'

'I didn't know, either.' She picked up her glass and sipped and Mikey, the bone of contention removed, slipped back down to his seat and his pint.

A girlfriend was no real surprise. Jude wasn't a bad-looking man, a bit of a catch if you liked them mean-looking and weren't too desperate for a casual smile. (That was harsh. Jude smiled a lot, in private, when he was happy.) And she'd hazard a sportsman's guess at who the woman was, too – the blonde, overtly sexy detective sergeant with whom he'd been so obviously smitten when she'd seen the two of them together a couple of months earlier. The woman wasn't the most beautiful in town, but she had a figure that any red-blooded male might take a few risks for and she compensated by accessorising for impact. Her blonde hair was unjustly natural. The whole effect, and the confidence that came with it, gave her the knack of making people – man or woman – look at her with interest and more. Perhaps it was as well Jude had bailed out of that particular date, or Becca would have spent the evening sneaking little looks across the pub at them, wondering whether she and Jude would still be together if she'd done things differently, and that would have put Adam out just when things were beginning to move forward between them.

Jude was a detective. He always got his man – or woman.

'Good luck to you,' she muttered, after his departed figure. 'And I don't need to know who she is. Because I really don't care.'

Because, she assured herself, she really didn't.

'What was all that about?' Ashleigh must have been almost at the pub when she got his text, because she was doing her best impression of an undercover cop, loitering in Angel Lane, on the other side of Great Dockray.

'I'll tell you later.' Reaching her, he gave her a longer and more obvious kiss than was strictly necessary, a gesture of defiance aimed at Becca even though she wouldn't see it, then turned along the street with her hand clasped firmly in his. 'We'll try Xavier's. They have about fifty types of gin and you're bound to find one that suits you.'

'Don't be cheeky. I'm easy to please.'

His mood, which had been soured by the unexpected encounter in the Dockray Hall, mellowed as they progressed through the town centre, hand in hand, and arrived at a wine bar that wasn't to Adam's taste and where, if the birthday party moved on, they could be reasonably certain of being undisturbed. 'My turn to buy, I think.'

'I'm not sure it is, but I can't be bothered to argue.' She slid out of her coat and settled herself down in a corner of the wine bar with a sigh, and when Jude returned with the drinks she was already measuring him up with that quizzical look that warned him he might as well tell her what was bothering him, if only to save her the effort of working it out. Ashleigh was smart and had an instinctive understanding of people she'd never met before. Those she knew had no chance of hiding their weaknesses or disguising them as strengths.

Fortunately for him, she was generally forgiving of his many faults, and there was no denying that it was very much less complicated dating someone who understood how much he loved the job and why he sometimes had to let it take priority over everyone else, than it had been dating Becca, whose patience had eventually run out.

'Here you go. Cheers.' He lifted his pint. 'Thank you for sparing me from a lonely evening at work.' He smiled at her and drank. After all, Becca had been right and all work and no play did no good at all.

'So who's Doddsy stood you up for? I thought your little man-to-man chats were sacred.' She curled her hands around her glass and the ice cracked inside it.

In all the time Jude had known Doddsy his friend had remained single, a cautious celibate unwilling to take a risky step. 'I don't know for certain, but I've a sneaking suspicion the better offer came from Tyrone Garner.'

'Oh, really?' Ashleigh obviously couldn't have seen the two of them together, or she wouldn't have been so surprised. 'I thought Doddsy had been a bit more cheerful recently.'

'Yes. I might be wrong but I overheard the two of them discovering a shared interest in folk music and there's a band on at the Gate Inn in Yanwath tonight. Who knows where that'll end up?' He grinned. Being in the police didn't leave you time for friendships, but the ones he forged were solid and long-lasting and Doddsy, so unlike him in almost every way, was the person on whom he could always rely.

'That's very sweet.' Ashleigh, who was as fond of Doddsy

in her own way as Jude was, smiled at him over the rim of her glass. 'There's quite an age gap there.' Tyrone was twenty, Mikey's age, and the two of them had been at school together, though their paths had diverged early.

'Yep. Twenty-five years.'

'That'll get people talking.'

'I expect it will. But they're both over the age of consent and we're all grown up and tolerant, these days.' Remembering how DS Groves had leered over Ashleigh in the corridor, he revised his best estimate of human nature downwards. 'Well, most of us are. And those of us who are still dinosaurs will be retired before we know it.'

She lifted her head as if she were about to say something, then stopped.

'Well?' he said to her. 'Out with it. What's on your mind?'

'Nothing. I was just going to ask you what caused the last-minute change of venue.'

'Oh. That.' It was in his mind to play it down, but she'd know. 'I bumped into someone I know.'

'Oh, I see. You're ashamed of me.'

She said it with a laugh but he couldn't risk her taking him seriously and seized the opportunity to close his warm hand over her cold one. 'No, of course not. Even my mum knows about you now. Amazing no one found out before, but there you go.'

She didn't look at him but disentangled her fingers from his and stroked the back of his hand with her forefinger. A tingle ran up his spine. 'Was it your old mate Adam Fleetwood in the pub?'

'Yes and no.'

'As in, he was there but it wasn't him you were avoiding.'

'Yes.' Letting go of her hand, Jude drank deeply from his pint, once more reviewing and reconsidering his behaviour of a few years before, checking every aspect of it and finding himself guiltless even though everyone else still judged him for it. 'It's his birthday. When we were younger, we always met up. His birthday's two days before mine and we always used to celebrate together. It was fine. I met his eye, I shook his hand and left.' There had been a challenge in the look that Adam had given him, one that promised his sins weren't forgotten and would never be forgiven, but Jude hadn't risen to it. He could be proud of himself.

'So if it wasn't him, who was it? Becca?'

Jude met her gaze. He'd been in love with Becca for long after she'd ended the relationship, but he thought he could be honest with himself and say it was over now. It had annoyed him to see Adam flaunting their friendship and hinting that it could be so much more, annoyed him even more that Becca didn't seem to see just how cynical his attentions to her were, but that was all it was. She could do whatever she wanted with whoever she wanted and it wouldn't bother him now that he had Ashleigh, who understood him to a fault, who was as good in bed as he could have hoped she would be, and who was also once bitten and not looking for a complicated romance. 'She was there, as it happens. She hangs out with that crowd. But she wasn't the reason I left. It was Mikey.'

'Ah.'

He wasn't a man who worried about things beyond his control, but Mikey haunted his dreams and his nightmares. In the two months he'd been building that tentative relationship with Ashleigh he'd told her a lot and there was a lot more she'd guessed, but he hadn't told her quite how deeply he worried about his brother. 'I know he's twenty but he's still a kid. He's still got a lot of growing up to do.'

'Twenty's an adult.'

Once again, Jude made the comparison between Mikey and Tyrone Garner. 'But a very young adult. He's hanging round with friends my age, not his age. They tolerate him, but they aren't what he needs. And it's all about me. It's Adam and Mikey, the two of them, for their own different reasons, punishing me for having let them down.'

'You didn't let either of them down. You did what you could for Mikey, and Adam let himself down.'

He shrugged, a gesture that represented his helplessness. 'Mikey needs a father and he won't let me help him.'

'He never sees your dad at all?'

'No. He hasn't spoken to him since Dad walked out on us. Not on me, strictly speaking. I'd left home by then. But he walked out on my mum and he walked out on Mikey. She'd been diagnosed with cancer the week before.'

'I didn't know that.' He could tell from her expression that it was only a half truth. She might not have known the detail but she'd have guessed there was something there. 'Do you still see your dad?'

'Yes. It's something else Mikey holds against me.'

'And do you get on with him?'

'Not as well as I'd like to. Better than Mikey thinks he deserves.' He shook his head, a wry grin on his lips. 'Mikey doesn't hold his drink that well. That's why I left. Because if I'd stayed and he'd had a few, there would have been a scene. I don't want that, and you shouldn't have to sit through it. So it's best avoided.'

'You're both right, of course,' she said, after a moment, and the blue eyes darkened a little, as if her heart had hardened at a difficult memory. 'Some people don't deserve to be forgiven, or don't deserve a second chance. But just because they don't deserve it does that mean we shouldn't give it to them?'

He took it as a rhetorical question, knowing that she was thinking of Scott and the number of times she'd forgiven his infidelities. He suspected that she might have given in once more if her husband hadn't turned up drunk and tried to win her back by aggression, but Ashleigh was a woman who couldn't be bullied and that had been Scott's final, futile roll of the dice. She had Jude, now, instead of a philandering wastrel, and he had her instead of an emotional butterfly with no understanding of his motives.

With that, the conversation ground to a halt. He'd told her as much as he wanted to about Mikey, and was on the edge of revealing his deepest fear – that what he'd done for Mikey wasn't enough to protect him from the effects of what he'd done to Adam Fleetwood. And he could tell from the rueful expression on her face that she was regretting that last glimpse she'd let him have into her heart and the part of it that would always belong to someone else.

'I'll get us another drink,' she said, with a sigh, 'and after that we'd better get back. Because it's not as if tomorrow's going to be a quiet day, is it?'

Walking her back home, Jude passed the Dockray Hall with a certain degree of trepidation, almost expecting Adam and Becca and Mikey and their friends to come rolling out and

Mikey, with a drink or two inside him, to get bold and try to cause a scene, but the walk up to Castletown passed without incident.

'Coffee?' she asked him, before she turned to unlock the front door.

He was tempted, as he always was, but with Ashleigh he could refuse without offence. 'Better not.'

'No, you're right. We spend far too much time having coffee together. Maybe next time we're both off together we'll find time for something a bit more exciting.'

The roguish wink tempted him into a more intense goodbye than he'd intended, and it was a moment before she extricated herself, with a giggle. 'Behave yourself.'

'I behave myself in the office but I can't keep it up all the time. I'm only human.'

'I love your humanity,' she said, stepping away from him into the shadows and rearranging her hair. 'By the way, I had one thought. It could wait until tomorrow, but it's something that just occurred to me. About Cody Wilder.'

'Go on.'

'If you're going up to talk to her tomorrow, you might like to ask her about her letters. Ask her to show them to you.'

'Do you think she won't?'

'I don't know. But she wouldn't show them to Fi Styles. And then it occurred to me. She obviously knows Lynx. Pretty well. And she obviously really values the letters. So maybe she gave them to him to look after. And maybe that's what someone thought it was worth killing him for.'

14

Ashleigh O'Halloran's unexpected silence hadn't marked the end of the police's interest, nor even their retreat in the face of Cody's brusque manner. Cody hadn't really expected it would and throughout the interview she'd given to Fi Styles – which had passed with less hassle than she'd expected – she'd been aware of the sergeant, sharp as a ferret, sitting in the corner and making the occasional notes, but mainly watching in silence.

Perhaps it was the silent approach that had unnerved her. She was used to people who couldn't keep their own counsel in the face of her outrageous assertions, who abused her publicly to her face and anonymously through social media. With those people she could give as good as she got, but in her considerable armoury she had no defence against silent evaluation and the sense that the woman understood her too well. For that reason, she was relieved when it was Jude Satterthwaite who appeared on her doorstep the next morning, even though irritation clouded his brow like a swarm of summer midges on the surface of a lake. She could reasonably expect a fight with him, and she'd a chance of coming out of it as the victor.

'Chief Inspector.' She folded her arms firmly across her

chest, blocking the entry she knew she'd have to concede and aware of Brandon's shadow behind her. She knew, without looking, that he'd be smiling. 'What is it now?'

'May I come in?'

'Is it important?'

'Misleading the police is very important.'

She stepped aside to let him in as Brandon headed towards the kitchen. They'd found out about Lynx, then. It had been a matter of time. 'Who's alleged to have done that?'

'This isn't an allegation. You claimed you never went down to the New Agers' camp at the bottom of the lane. You said you had nothing to do with them. The forensic evidence proves that wasn't the case.'

'*Proves* is a very strong word.' She turned and stalked through the narrow hallway into the kitchen, leaving Jude to close the front door behind him and follow her through. Brandon, a man who was happier tinkering with the engine of a pickup truck, was standing by the kitchen unit fiddling with the finer features of the coffee maker, frowning at it like a master watchmaker dissatisfied with the work of an apprentice.

'Honey,' she said to him, with a wink that Jude Satterthwaite couldn't see, 'you'll see we have an uninvited guest. But I like to be hospitable. Would you make us some coffee?'

Brandon pressed a couple of buttons and the machine fizzed and hissed like a miniature steam train. 'Coffee, Chief Inspector? Black? Sugar? Have a seat.'

The visitor sat down, the expression on his face relentless in its annoyance. For the first time, Cody felt the very slightest shadow, a chilling sense of doom, as she too sat down at the table from which Owen had stepped to his death. Eventually, things came back to haunt you. Owen's suicide had removed any threat he might have posed to her and for that reason she'd welcomed it, but Lynx's murder implied a threat from another direction. Perhaps it wasn't wise, after all, to be so fiercely independent and to turn her back on those who might help her, but what help could any of them bring her when she had the unconditional support of Brandon, always watching her back. 'Biscuits? Or we have some chocolates.' She tried to stare him down and failed. On reflection she shouldn't have lied to him about knowing Lynx, or about the time she'd spent at the New Age camp, but she hadn't thought it mattered and everyone needed some happy secrets. 'The chocolates are handmade. Lynx gave them to me.'

'Your coffee.' Brandon turned on his most charming smile, and she could see Jude Satterthwaite looking at him as if he were trying to make sense of him, why he was there.

The detective waved the chocolates aside with a word of thanks, and turned back to Cody, who was beginning to get the impression that he wasn't, as she'd previously thought, no match for her but had chosen to go soft on her for reasons of his own. Maybe she should have told him everything she knew about Lynx earlier, but that was the devil in her. He hadn't needed to know and she couldn't abide the entitlement that always came with men in senior positions when their female colleagues had to fight for it. 'Okay, Dr Wilder. Can we talk?'

'You want to talk about Lynx.'

'I do. But before that I want to make a few things clear

to you. The evidence points to Owen Armitstead's death as being suicide, but with Lynx we're dealing with a violent murderer. I don't need to remind you that threats of personal violence have been directed at you.'

'If it's my safety you're concerned about, it would be easiest for everyone if you let me return to the States.'

It was obvious that there was nothing he'd like more than to see the back of her, and she took that as a small victory. 'You're a potential witness in a murder case at best, and it's in everybody's interests for you to cooperate fully with the inquiry. The sooner we can finish it, the sooner you can leave.'

At best. For the second time in a few minutes, she felt a qualm. The man was looking at her with eyes that threatened judgement. She swatted the fanciful thought away. Conscience was weakness and she was strong in her own defence. 'So you want me to tell you everything about Cain, Chief Inspector.'

'Cain?' He glanced out of the window in the direction of the lake, though from where she sat a bank of bushes that settled in the crooked elbow of Coffin Lane obscured the view. 'You knew his real name?'

'Yes. His name was Cain Harper.'

'He told you that?'

'I've known Cain for a long time.' Using Lynx's given name did more than establish herself as the owner of particular information. It kept a contact with a memory of an older, even a kinder, time. She shivered at her own weakness. When had she become a prey to sentiment?

Uninvited, Brandon took a seat at the table beside them and helped himself to a chocolate, but what she had to say was so painful and so personal that she couldn't bear him to hear it. He knew the story, but he'd never had to hear her tell it. 'Brandon.'

Her look to him was the nearest she ever got to seeming apologetic, but he read it well. 'Everything okay, honey?'

'I just realised. We don't have any milk.'

'I'll run down and pick some up.' They drank their coffee black but he was quick to go, hooking his jacket from the back of the chair and over his shoulder in one fluid movement. When the front door had clicked behind him, the chief inspector pulled out a notebook and pen and began to write. 'Fire away. I'm interested in everything you have to tell me about him.'

He wrote fast and neatly, in a bold hand that sprawled across the page. Cody had never studied graphology, but his self-confidence spilled out from the tip of his pen. 'Is this a witness statement?'

'Yes. I'll get it typed up and sent to you for signature. And in view of our earlier conversation, I'll add the warning. You already know that lying to the police is an offence. We also take a hell of a dim view of people who withhold information from us, if that information might help us to find a killer.'

Ruthlessly, Cody smothered the whisper of her conscience. Life was a long game and her role in it was to tell the police enough to preserve her innocence. 'Your forensic evidence has likely shown that I slept with Cain.' The phrase had an apocalyptic ring to it, so much so that she regretted using it.

'Yes. Care to tell me about it?'

'He was a former lover.' Irritated by the way he tapped his pen on the word *former* after he'd written it in his notes, she rushed onwards, past the barrier of his judgement. 'I've known him for a long time.'

'Can we go back to the beginning? When and where did you meet him?'

'Way back when I first went to university. As you'll no doubt know from my interview with Fi Styles, I left the ranch and came to Laramie. Cain was at college there, a couple of years ahead of me. He was already a bit of an outlier. He was different and so was I. It was natural that we were attracted to one another.'

Time played tricks on some, but not on others. Twenty-five years before, Cain had seemed old, sophisticated and world-weary to a girl who came from the wilderness. 'His parents were traditional hippies – San Francisco in the Sixties, flowers in your hair, free love and so on. He was brought up on a commune and a part of him yearned to be conventional, which was how he came to Laramie. But when he came to a conventional place, he wanted to be different.' Some people could never be satisfied. That had been Lynx's curse, doomed to wander the world like a modern-day Flying Dutchman, caught between two worlds and able to settle in neither. She stopped talking as she thought about him and once more Wordsworth offered comfort, almost as if he'd known Lynx, *the sleepless soul that perished in its pride.*

The detective let her think for a while, longer than he needed to and she found herself strangely grateful for that, but his patience wasn't endless. 'And after he left Laramie?'

'I don't know. We lost touch. But now you know who he is, you'll likely be able to find all that out. Maybe let me know, too.' Because there were things he hadn't told her, so keen was he to leave parts of his life behind him. None of them would be traumatic, but she'd like to know them, if only because there would be no one else to tell her.

'You were close to him?' he asked.

After all, this chief inspector was smarter than she'd thought. He understood that having sex with someone needn't mean anything but that there were people who kept a piece of your soul even when you were no longer together. Cain's earthy scent, the rough touch of his skin, his animal hunger, had gone, but they'd always be a part of her. 'I suspect you think I may have killed him, or at least had something to do with his death. I didn't. So perhaps you'll let me explain.'

'Go ahead.' He reached out his hand for his coffee cup, and tried to meet her eye, but she looked away. There were things you should only think of when you were concentrating on something harmless, to take the pain away. Instead she stared out of the window and saw a robin, feathers fluffed up against the cold, shouting indignantly at the world from its place on a branch. At least she could smile at that.

'You'll have heard worse stories than mine. I'm not self-indulgent and I don't want your pity. I was brought up on a ranch in the wilds. You'll know that. But you won't know – or you might think you know but not understand – how isolating that was. If you need help, there's no one. If you meet a bear, or a coyote, or you run across the tracks of a wolf pack, there's no one. If a tree falls across the track, you move it yourself. If you tread on a rattlesnake, you die. But I learned young that the biggest danger out in the wilderness is the same as it is everywhere else in the goddamned world. It's other people.'

He wrote that down on his pad and threatened her with

another empathetic pause but she ploughed on before she could dwell too long on it, before her heartrate rose and the memories overwhelmed her. 'My father was a loner and a violent man. He raped and abused my mother. He did the same to me.' Lynx, of course, had known. 'I fell pregnant and my mother took me to a clinic in Laramie for an illegal abortion. I was fourteen.' There. It was out and she could roll the stone back over the dungeon door of history. 'No living person knows that but you and Brandon, and I want to keep it that way.'

'I'll be discreet.' He didn't write that down, and though he made no promises she almost believed in his sincerity.

The story wasn't over. 'Mom died not long after that. You can imagine the turn my life took then.' A shiver, one she hoped Jude Satterthwaite didn't see, crept across her skin. 'Fortunately, karma paid Pop back with an equal measure of brutality. Three years later he went out to look at the cattle and never came back. Brandon went out to look for him and found his truck empty. There was no sign of him, and he never came home. As soon as we realised he must be dead, I applied to go to university, and the first person I met there was Cain.'

'You must have been seventeen? That's very young.'

The robin strutted its way along the branch, skipped down and fluttered across the damp and moss-ridden lawn. A couple of sparrows, nervous, took off in front of it. She smiled, a thin smile at how life had dealt with her after her father died. 'In many ways Cain was a rough man. He knew neither subtlety nor security. I was drawn to him because he was the first man apart from my brother to treat me kindly.' The clock ticked. The coffee machine emitted a strange sigh as it cooled down. 'That was why he was special to me. He was the first man I willingly had sex with and I learned a lot from him, but we grew out of one another. When he left Laramie it was easy to let him go, but I always wondered what had happened to him.'

'Were you surprised to see him here?'

'Not especially.' Nothing Lynx did had ever surprised her. 'He told me he'd been bumming around Europe in different places, but he must have kept up with the world somehow, because he'd seen something about my work. He came to Grasmere on the off chance of finding me and I wasn't there. But he found the New Agers and he joined them.'

'Was he keen to see you again?'

'I don't know if he was.' She turned her back on the robin, now busy probing the mossy lawn, listening for worms in exactly the same thoughtful way Jude Satterthwaite was listening to her account for mistakes or treasures or things she'd wish she hadn't said. 'Cain – Lynx – was always very ... casual. He never planned anything. I think he turned up here, found a connection, stayed to see if anything came of it. It did, but if it hadn't, he'd have drifted on somewhere else.' Poor Lynx; he'd been the most profoundly unsatisfiable man. 'He was an old friend and a good lover. That's how I came to be in his tent before he died. For old times' sake.'

He sat back, nodding. 'Thanks, Dr Wilder. That's helpful.' He even managed to mask what must be his annoyance at not having had the story sooner. 'It's no consolation, but I understand why you didn't want to share the full story.'

'Remember what I said. I want to keep it secret.'

'And as I promised. I'll do my best.' He held back a

moment in uncertainty, then must have decide to risk the compliment. 'That must have taken courage.'

A swell of gratitude rose within her, and she forced it down. Was she so desperate that she needed sympathy from a policeman? 'No courage at all, Chief Inspector. I hated my father. He died and we all lived on. I put the trauma behind me.' She sat back, as if the interview was over. That night, she knew, she would have nightmares.

He put the pen down. 'One more thing. The tent had been ransacked, as if someone had been looking for something. Do you have any idea what that might have been?'

'No. I don't.'

'I wondered if you'd given him something to look after.'

He, or someone in his team, was very smart indeed. 'If it's relevant, I did think about asking him to look after something for me. But in the end, I decided not to do it.'

'That wouldn't have been Mary Wordsworth's letters, would it?'

'I take it it was your detective sergeant who worked that out?'

He smiled. 'Yes. She could tell that you seemed attached to them. So much so that you seemed reluctant to show them to Fi Styles. We wondered if part of that reluctance might have stemmed from the fact that you don't have them. And whether you might be concerned about them.'

There was a reason people withheld things from the police. If you gave them even a little information, they would extrapolate from it and sometimes they were correct. 'I didn't show them to the journalist because I don't know she understands. They're precious documents – not necessarily valuable, but irreplaceable. They should be kept in controlled conditions and I shouldn't have brought them with me, but they mean a lot to me and I couldn't bear to leave them behind.' That had been a mistake, too. The letters had been copied and scanned and she had all the information she needed for her work on her laptop but she'd brought them with her in a moment of weakness, like a child dependent upon a security blanket. 'That's the reason I decided not to ask Cain to take them.'

'Do you have them there?'

'At the moment, yes. It isn't ideal. When I return to New York, I'll make arrangements for their permanent care. But I do have them.'

'And they're genuine?'

She scowled at him, as if he'd questioned the paternity of her child. 'I'll be astonished if they're not.'

'And he knew how much they mattered to you?'

'No.'

For a second he stared at her as if he were about to ask to see them, but the key in the front door heralded Brandon's return. 'That's fine, then. I'll get this typed up and someone will bring it through for you to sign.' He got up and picked up his coat.

'Do you know who killed Cain?' She asked him in an undertone, as if it mattered that Brandon might overhear.

'No.'

'Or why?'

'If we find the answer to that question, I might be able to answer your first one,' he said, shrugged on his coat and left.

*

Still mulling over what Cody Wilder had told him, Jude had barely got as far as Grasmere village when his phone rang. He pulled up on a double yellow line to answer it, justifying it to himself as important when he saw that the number was Doddsy's. 'Have you found it? The murder weapon?'

'Yes.'

'What is it? Where? And where are you?'

'About ten yards from you. In the cafe.'

Looking up, Jude saw Doddsy standing laughing at him in the window of the cafe which had somehow become a base for their inquiries within the village, with Ashleigh at his shoulder. So much the better. 'I'll join you.' He drove on and squeezed the Mercedes into the car park at the back of the garden centre, then jogged back to the cafe.

The investigating team had taken up their position at the back of the room and Graham and Eliza had set out the tables in such a way as to give them an element of privacy and had placed reserved notices on the closest tables for good measure – something they probably couldn't have afforded to do in the summer. But crime was an ill wind and the Gordons' takings would be well up on normal as a result of Cody Wilder and the little local difficulty she'd brought down upon the village.

'Okay.' He slid into the seat beside Ashleigh, not looking at her but nevertheless with a comforting sense of her presence, and addressed himself to Doddsy. 'What is it? And where?'

'It's pretty much as the PM and the forensic evidence suggested. I've packed it off to the lab.' He flicked up pictures on his phone and handed it over.

Image after close-up image of a six-inch hunting knife

wedged into a cleft in the rock, its blade dull in the sunless conditions, flicked across the screen. Enlarging the image, he frowned over it. It didn't look as if whoever had hidden it had tried too hard. 'Blood?'

'Yes.'

'But not much.'

'I'd say it's been badly cleaned. Of course,' Doddsy reprimanded himself, 'I say *the murder weapon*. It may not be.'

'Let's hope it is, or we'll have something else to worry about.' With one last look, Jude handed the phone back.

'I think we can assume it is. I've leaned on the guys in the lab and they're going to get me the results as soon as they can.'

'Where was it?'

'One of the search teams found it up in Rydal Caves. The biggest one. Right at the back. Tucked under an overhanging rock, as you can see, but not well hidden.'

Turning to field Ashleigh's questioning look, Jude reached for a paper napkin, fished out a pen and sketched out a quick map of the area for her benefit. 'Rydal Caves are some disused slate quarries. You find them all over the place here. These ones are a known beauty spot.'

She looked out of the window as if trying to match the map to the landscape. 'That's quite a distance. What is it? Two miles to the far end of Rydal Water?'

'Nearer three. Probably two and a half to the caves.' With the blunt end of the pen, Jude traced a possible route from the spot where Lynx's body had been found, along the shore and up the hill.

'That's too far for Storm to have covered in the time he

had, then.' She frowned at the puzzle. 'Chris could do it, I suppose, but he's a runner.'

'I could, too.'

'Of course.' She spared his male pride an indulgent smile. 'But Storm couldn't. And the time doesn't fit with our witness who saw him.'

'We spoke to Storm again,' Doddsy said. 'No good. He just closed up on us.'

'I'm not surprised. They don't trust the police, and I can hardly blame them.' Having just dealt with Cody's refusal to cooperate, Jude felt rather more sympathy with Storm and Raven, but understanding their attitude didn't make it right. There was a balance to be struck between procedures and people, but the New Agers, rejecting everything that smacked of modernity, pushed it too far, freezing with terror at the sight of a uniform or any kind of questioning, any challenge to their simplicity. 'Did he just refuse to answer?'

'Not exactly.' Ashleigh, tapping her finger on the desk, looked as if she knew where they'd gone wrong and wished she could try again but trust, when it was lost, couldn't easily be regained. 'He insists he followed someone he thought was Lynx through the woods, as far as the footbridge at the end of the lake, then lost sight of him and came straight back. And in fairness to him, he had time to do that, though not much more, and it's just about plausible that the person he was following had either cut off the path before our witness saw Storm, or else was much further ahead of him than we thought.'

'And the parcel Storm had?'

'He flatly denied having had anything. Maybe you want to talk to him about it.'

Would that achieve anything? Probably not. 'I think I'll leave that until tomorrow. They aren't going anywhere, and we have a couple of leads to follow up.'

'That's progress, at least.' Doddsy's to-do list, Jude noticed with amusement, had the words *find murder weapon* scored out. 'Did you get anything from your academic?'

'Yes.' Jude turned to smile at Ashleigh again. 'You were right. There's a connection between Cody and Lynx – old friends, lovers way back. Current lovers, as the forensics show. And she'd thought of asking him to look after her letters from Mary Wordsworth to Dorothy.'

'Is that what someone was looking for?'

'I don't know. She says she changed her mind and never gave them to him, and no one else knew she'd thought about it. She said it was a passing thought and she never followed it up, but I suppose it's possible that someone else might have thought that was what she'd done. Heaven only knows what else they might have thought he had. But at least we know who he is. I can get Chris onto that.' Chris would come up with a profile of Cain Harper by the morning and there would surely be answers to a few questions in there – not least corroboration or otherwise of Cody's story, though quite why it needed corroboration wasn't so clear. He remembered his promise. Something would have to be said, but he'd spare her the exposure of every detail. 'I'll head back and brief him.' He looked across at Doddsy. 'Will I see you up there?'

'I'll go back and check what's happening at the caves,

if they've turned up anything else. I'll see you back in the office later on.'

'Great.' Jude pushed back his chair and stood up. 'I'll see you later then. See you tomorrow, Ashleigh.'

So were they any closer to finding Lynx's killer, he wondered as he negotiated the A591 on the way back to Penrith? Was it someone pretending to be Lynx who led Storm along the path to Rydal Caves, or was Storm, improbably as it seemed, either a killer or an accomplice in a murder?

Doddsy wound his weary way up towards the incident room via the canteen. He never pretended to be inspired and he valued the chance to think things through, and even though he seemed to spend half of his working life in canteens and coffee shops and meetings with biscuits, it somehow never seemed to translate into large quantities of food.

He checked his watch. There were a dozen things he had to deal with in addition to the killing of the man they now knew to be Cain Harper. Despite Jude's reservations, he was ready to hand Owen Armitstead's death over to the coroner.

There was no real doubt in his mind that it was suicide and the only thing that concerned him was why. In the final reckoning, Cody Wilder would have to account for how she'd treated her young researcher, for her lack of care and her callous pursuit of him. No doubt she'd use her tough upbringing to excuse her behaviour.

'Doddsy, do you have a minute?'

He looked up at the woman who'd accosted him. Strictly speaking every minute of his day was accounted for, but there was something about Aditi Desai's face, as if she'd taken a while to approach him, which rather surprised him. Aditi, who was one of the younger detective constables working with Chris on the background to the Grasmere murder case, was normally one of the most relaxed people around. He didn't think he'd become impossibly forbidding overnight, so it must be something else. 'Sure.'

Still she hesitated, so he indicated the chair opposite. 'Sit down. No hurry.'

'It won't take a minute. Just I wanted to ask you something.'

'Fire away.'

'I may be making a fuss about nothing. I don't know.'

He smiled at her. He liked Aditi, though he found her a bit too kind for the wicked world she'd chosen to inhabit. 'I won't know either, if you don't tell me.'

'I was in Sainsbury's yesterday and I bumped into Superintendent Groves. He asked me out for a drink. Of course I said no. But he said if I changed my mind…' She turned her engagement ring over on her finger. 'It wasn't the first time. I didn't think that was appropriate.'

'It's anything but.' Groves had an eye for the ladies, and it had already cost him two wives. Now, it appeared, he might be bored with his own company.

'No. Because he said something about talking about how we could advance my career. I think it was a joke, but it made me feel uncomfortable. I mean, that's really not right, is it?'

'Definitely not. You need to mention that to Professional Standards.' But he could see the way the conversation was going to go.

'That's what I thought. But I just... you know it isn't just me, Doddsy. It's happened to a few people.'

He knew, without really thinking about it, that it had always gone on. The attitude of some of his colleagues was mired in darker parts of the last century. Didn't he know that, and hadn't he, as a gay man learned to keep his head down? What had changed was that most people no longer found it acceptable. 'They need to report it, too.'

'Yes. I wondered if you'd mention it to Professional Standards for me.'

People always approached him for this kind of thing, and there was as reason for it. He was the softest of touches. 'Yes, okay. Why not? Leave it with me.'

He was, he realised, when she'd gone, going to have to sacrifice his break. Picking up his coffee, he turned a couple of corners and opened the door to the Professional Standards department.

They clearly had less to do than he had, because he'd walked in on some kind of relaxed chat, and he had to clear his throat loudly before someone – Lorraine, an older woman, who'd done her hard work somewhere else and was marking time in an office – spun round on her chair to take up her position at her desk. 'Doddsy. What can I do for you? Come with a complaint?' She picked up a pen and sat with it poised above her pad, almost as if she was expecting it.

He nodded.

'Okay. Let's have it. Who's been behaving inappropriately to you?'

'Not me.' He outlined Aditi's comments and the woman scribbled industriously. 'I don't think Aditi will mind giving you the details. She just didn't want to make the first approach.'

'Okay. Thanks for telling me.' She frowned down at the paper. 'Sure you don't have anything to add?'

'Nothing. Should I?'

'I probably shouldn't tell you, but this isn't the first complaint I've had about him.'

That wasn't surprising. Groves had acquired a reputation. 'I think we can be reasonably sure he hasn't made a pass at me,' he said, and grinned at her.

'Oh, God,' she laughed. 'No, I didn't mean that. The opposite, really. Just that these days we need to make quite sure no one's being discriminated against over anything.'

'I'll tell Aditi you'll be in touch.' And Doddsy backed away towards the door, deep in thought.

15

Cody had expected the nightmare. She'd fought the memories when Fi Styles had pressed her on her history, but Cain's death had shown her that she'd have to acknowledge them. Jude Satterthwaite had been sympathetic but she knew how his people's minds worked. They'd be checking up on everything she'd said, attempting to verify the years of abuse she'd received, and maybe they'd decide it was relevant to the trial of whoever killed Cain and bring her own personal Armageddon down upon her. And so came the nightmare, in which she had to stand up in court and testify to every detail of something that should have stayed buried for ever, in front of a shadowy figure in the dock.

The killer had her father's face, of course. She knew enough psychology not to be surprised, but not enough to help her cope.

She woke about four, in a hot sweat on a cold night and lay there, tossing and turning as she thought about everything, anything but the past. Sometimes she dozed off, woken by the echoes of a man's footsteps in the corridor, and just as she had done then, she pulled the pillow over her head and hoped the nightmare would end. The modern footsteps were a figment of her imagination but the fear they engendered was not. In the end, as it always did, time won, ticking on beyond the nightmare zone. The clock in the living room chimed a tinny seven and it was time to start the day.

Not soon enough. In the kitchen, she made herself a coffee and sipped it, but she was still restive. Brandon, who was an early riser, would normally have been up by now but he'd probably be lying in his bed crooning sweet nothings to a sweetheart on the other side of the world. The scent of his ultimate abandonment hung around her and even if it hadn't, her nightmares were so raw she couldn't bring herself to face him. He knew everything that she knew, and their relationship had at least meant some good had come out of the bad, but the two were linked. Most of the time she prided herself on her positivity, but just then she couldn't face anything that reminded her of hell.

She drained her coffee and set her mug in the sink. The first glow of dawn was fading into the eastern sky, though there was still a while to go before the sun climbed the far side of Heron Pike and made itself known. The living room clock ticked and wakefulness proved no escape. The silence and the fear that seemed to inhabit the chilly, slate-floored kitchen in Coffin Lane echoed the early mornings in Wyoming when she'd waited to find out what kind of mood her father was in, whether it was to be her or her mother who'd take the brunt of it.

Coffee helped her to shrug her shoulders at her own weakness. Her father was dead and the dead couldn't hurt you. Only the living could do that, and she genuinely thought there was no one alive she was scared of. Hadn't

Owen folded under her challenge, when all he'd needed to do was take her on, so much stronger than she? And Lynx, who had threatened her for fun in an unintended echo of her father, was dead and those joking shadows would never haunt her from his direction again. Men were like dogs – pack animals, who needed only to know who was boss.

She snatched at her coat and let herself out of the front door, still pulling her arms into the sleeves against the cold air as she headed down the path with no idea of where she might be going. There would be nowhere open for breakfast, unless one of the hotels would rustle up something for a non-resident. What mattered was that she was outside, escaping her memories, in the chilly damp dawn of Cumbria.

A beauteous morning, calm and free, she misquoted wryly to herself, though still finding comfort in the words. It had been raining heavily, and the standing water splashed up under her feet. Down on Red Bank Road a dog barked. Knowing her luck, it would be that couple who ran the cafe, so detached from reality that they held her responsible for who-knew-what. It was too bad. She wasn't in the good mood she'd been in the last time, and if they wanted to take her on today, they were welcome to try it.

It hadn't been a windy night, but something lay across the ground in front of her like a branch fallen from a tree. In the cold, grey morning light, Cody dropped to her knees beside it. Her fingers reached out to touch it in the deep shadow of the wall and felt the slippery fabric of a Gore-Tex rain jacket. The soft silky texture of a woman's ponytail. The sticky touch of fresh blood.

In the lane, the dog barked. Someone called its name.

Behind her in the cottage a light went on in Brandon's room. *The earthquake is not satisfied at once.*

With Fi Styles's blood fresh on her fingers, Cody remembered to scream.

This time there was no need to look for the murder weapon. It was lying next to the body, a sharp piece of Lake District slate, its leading edge still bright with blood under the drizzle and matching the deep gash in the side of Fi's skull. Jude stood looking at it from a respectful and non-interventionist distance, with Doddsy to one side of him and Ashleigh to the other. At the bottom of Coffin Lane, outside the blue and white tape that Tyrone was unwinding to seal the place off, another car pulled up to join the haphazard collection of vehicles already there.

'Here's Tammy and the CSI guys. Let's get off and leave this place to the experts.' He stepped back. 'Where's Dr Wilder?'

Charlie Fry was on duty, once again displaying his uncanny knack of being first on the scene whenever there was a crime to be investigated, and taking even this in his world-weary stride. 'Her brother took her down to the cafe. It was the people who owned it who came up to help her. They were walking their dog in the lane. They called the police and got her off the scene.'

'The Gordons?'

'That's right, sir. Graham and Eliza Gordon. They walk their dog every morning before setting up the cafe for the day. They say they didn't see anybody coming down the lane.'

'Shall we get down there?' The hint of anxiety in Ashleigh's voice suggested that she, like him, was wary of the irony of the Gordons, with their vitriolic hatred of Cody Wilder, being the ones to come to her rescue. 'Has she got anyone else with her?'

'Mr Wilder's down there.' Charlie stepped past Jude and held a hand up to stop Tammy and the two white-clad forensic investigators with her. 'The doctor hasn't finished yet.'

'Sure, I'll wait.' Tammy pulled the fine mesh mask up over her mouth and ran an expert finger round her hood to check it was sealed. 'It's hardly going to take him long to certify the poor woman's dead, though.'

Fi's body sprawled ten yards from them, and even as they spoke, Matt Cork, the pathologist stood up, picked up his bag and stepped back. 'Confirmed dead.' He shook his head. 'It all stands to be verified but it looks as if that piece of slate nearly took the back of the poor woman's head off. Death would have been instantaneous.'

'Can we get on?' Tammy sidled past him to stand and survey the scene, deciding where to start.

Jude liked Matt, a man who understood the need for haste and how to balance it with accuracy. It meant he always gave the police something to work with while the information was of some use to them, even though his first impressions sometimes required amendment. It would be a couple of days before they got the detailed post-mortem results and though there might be surprises, the cause of death was surely clear. 'When did it happen?'

'Recently. Not much more than a couple of hours ago. I'll firm up the time later.'

It was half past nine. The 999 call had come in to the control centre at about half past seven. Cody had been on the scene at or about the time the murder had been committed. 'Thanks, Matt. That's helpful.'

'I'll be in touch when I can tell you more.' Matt moved off down the lane, past Tyrone, and the crime scene operation swung into operation around him.

'Okay.' Jude reviewed his priorities. 'Doddsy, I'm going to leave you in charge here. I want to get down and speak to Dr Wilder. Ashleigh, it's the same drill as last time. I want you to do the witness interviews and the door-to-door inquiries. Someone might have seen something.'

'Of course.' She fell into step beside him and they headed down the lane together, ducking under the tape and past the crowd of onlookers who were visibly concerned over a second murder when they'd been curious at the first. 'What do you reckon? The same killer?'

'Possibly. It's the same modus operandi, more or less – attack from behind with what passes for a sharp instrument. And the same time of day.'

Ashleigh cast a rueful look back up the hill. 'But why Fi Styles?'

'I don't know.' But an answer to that question was beginning to form in his head, an answer framed by the sight of Fi's blood-soaked ponytail spread out on the gravel lane where the sharp edge of the slate had sliced it from her scalp. 'The first question we need to ask is what she was doing there at that time of the morning.'

'Do you think she disturbed someone?'

'Possibly.' As they paused outside the cafe, he got the chance to see Ashleigh's expression. She'd seen far worse than this, but her face had lost some of its colour. If they hadn't been standing in the full glare of the public, he'd have loosened up enough to give her a hug, but he couldn't afford the smallest, most innocent gesture of affection. 'Or she was mistaken for someone. Or she was meeting someone.'

He pushed open the door to the cafe. The sign on it had been turned to *Closed* and there was a uniformed policewoman outside. Eliza Gordon, her face as white as the milk she was frothing to put in the lattes, was going through the motions at the coffee machine. Her husband sat by himself at a table with his head on his hands, the dog lying at his feet. In a seat by the window, Cody stared out across the lake with the frozen self-possession of a statue, while Brandon, his dark shadow stretching across the table, stood beside her, an expression of concern on his face.

Jude and Ashleigh separated, he to speak to the Wilders, she to the Gordons. 'Mrs Gordon,' he heard her say, with all the sympathy available for them that he hadn't felt he could offer her. 'Let me get the coffee. Sit down. That was an awful thing for you to have to see.'

With some difficulty, he turned his attention away from Ashleigh and focused it instead on Cody. 'Dr Wilder.'

Brandon shuffled sideways, resting his hands on her shoulders when Jude spoke, as if it were the two of them against the world.

'Chief Inspector.' She looked at him, all defiance, chin out. The band holding her characteristic ponytail had slipped down to the nape of her neck, giving her a defeated look. Dried blood picked out the edges of her fingernails, seeped into the cuticles of her right hand, insinuating itself under the nails. 'It's getting closer to me, isn't it? You aren't doing a great job keeping me safe.'

He pulled up chair and sat down opposite her. For the first time, he didn't trust her. 'You must have had a terrible shock.'

It was easy to be brave when death was at a distance, less so when it came calling at your door, but Cody Wilder was made of sterner stuff than Jude had expected. 'Only very briefly. I told you, Inspector. I had a traumatic upbringing and I experienced a flashback when I found her.'

Brandon's fingers, he noticed, tightened slightly on her shoulders.

'Of course,' Cody went on, 'I recovered. People die and I wouldn't be true to myself if I pretended to be sentimental about it. But that's not what you're interested in. You're interested in what I saw. Or rather, what I didn't see.'

'Honey. You don't have to talk to anyone.'

Her brother was as bad as she was. 'The more you can tell us, the sooner we'll catch the person who killed Ms Styles.'

'And Lynx, too?' Perhaps now she regretted not having told him what she knew earlier. 'Let's get through this quickly, shall we?'

'The first thing you need to do is to make sure my sister is safe.'

Cody looked up at Brandon over her shoulder and smiled at him. 'I have you as my bodyguard.'

'Yes, honey, and I'll watch over you like I always did. But these guys need to kick some ass. I can't stay here for ever.'

'I'll make quite sure you're safe, Dr Wilder. Assuming there's a threat to you.' Cutting Brandon out of the conversation, Jude nevertheless noticed the scowl that passed over Cody's face at that last remark. 'Talk me through what happened.'

She composed herself, shaking Brandon's hands from her shoulders and delivering a concise explanation of where she was and what she'd seen. It was a slender tale, one that offered no opportunity for anyone to vouch for her movements. By her own admission Cody had been alone and unseen within yards of Fi Styles when death had struck. 'Thanks, Dr Wilder. I'll get you to give a full witness statement to DS O'Halloran in a moment.'

'Thank you.' She nodded, as if to dismiss him from her presence, then thought of something. 'You've taped off the lane. Can we go back to the cottage?'

'Perhaps you'd be better relocating to a hotel for tonight. Let me know where you are. I hope we'll be clear of the place tomorrow. I'll send someone up to the cottage with you to pick up some stuff.'

That visibly irritated her, but if she was innocent of Fi's death she must be sensible enough to understand the situation was serious. Leaving Ashleigh to deal with the witness interviews, Jude took himself once more along Red Bank Road and down into the field where Storm and Raven clung resolutely to the last of their innocent way of life. A kettle sang like a bird on the brazier near the main tent and the sides of the canvas shack where Raven did her weaving were looped up to let in the air and light, but the tent was empty. Stepping through the hissing smother from the brazier, Jude took in the single branch of an early-flowering shrub that someone – presumably Raven – had laid against the woodpile. Goodness knew where she'd found it – culled from someone's garden, perhaps, or given as a gesture of goodwill.

In the main tent, he found the elderly couple sitting on the floor staring out at the lake in a companionable silence. Raven, he noted, had laid tarot cards out beside her but she wasn't looking at them. He cleared his throat. 'I'm sorry to bother you both again.'

Storm scrambled to his feet. 'I'll make us tea,' he said to his wife, and to Jude, he said: 'Come over with me. You'll want to ask us questions and I'll answer them.'

Jude stood aside to let him pass, then followed him over to the brazier. Three chipped mugs sat on top of a box next to it, and a knitted square sat over a jug that must contain milk.

'You'll have some tea. Sir,' added Storm, in his first, uncomfortable concession to the realities of life.

'Just call me Jude, okay?' Jude curled his hands around the mug that Storm handed him, shaking his head at the offer of milk that would make the tea unpalatable. 'Strictly speaking, you probably shouldn't. But let's keep this a bit less formal than usual, shall we?' Storm and Raven, unlike Cody, resisted questions on a matter of genuine belief rather than political principle, and what was the point in hammering home your authority when people were already broken by it?

'You want to know about the girl who died.' Storm tossed his head in a gesture towards the tent. 'We've talked about it. You can leave Raven out of it, and I'll tell you everything I know. Come away over here, where she can't hear us.'

Another carload of police arrived at the scene and headed into the cafe for instructions. Doddsy, his hands plunged into his pockets and a look of philosophical acceptance on his face, strode away from the police tape and into the cafe after them. 'Go on. Tell me what you know about Fi Styles.'

'Was that her name?'

'You didn't know it?'

Storm chewed a charcoal-blackened thumb. 'I think she introduced herself, but we don't need names like you do. It didn't stick.'

'She came down to the camp, then?'

'Yes, a couple of times in the past week. Wanting to talk about the woman up Coffin Lane. I told her Raven and I knew nothing, but Lynx found time to talk to her.'

Jude couldn't allow himself to sigh. People always found their tongues when it was too late, but who knew whether Storm's information might have saved Fi's life, at least, if he'd revealed it earlier? 'What did he say?'

'I don't know. She took him into the village and bought him lunch. He wasn't quite a part of our world, you know. Not as much as he thought he was. Not as much as we are.'

'I see that.'

'And there was something Raven overheard one night. When Cody was down in the camp.'

'That'll be one of the visits you seem to have forgotten about when I asked you the first time.'

Storm tugged at his beard. 'You know about it now.'

Undeniable. 'Why did you lie to me about it?'

'If I'd told you you'd have turned it against me. I know what you people are like.' Storm's words were at odds with his submissive body language. 'You're like everyone else. You see someone who's different and you blame them for everything wrong. All you modern, sophisticated folk are the same. See how the villagers talk about Cody Wilder and her brother. I never liked her but I live and let live. I never gaped at them like they're exhibits in a zoo.'

It was useless to argue. In any case, there was some truth in it. People did look at Cody with intrigued eyes, stared in fascination at Brandon's tooled leather cowboy boots. 'Okay. So tell me about the last time Dr Wilder was down with Lynx.'

A sidelong, guilty look acknowledged the earlier lie. 'It was the day of that palaver in the village, when she did her talk or whatever it was she was doing. She came down late at night, after we'd gone to bed. I was asleep, but Raven doesn't sleep well.'

Cody had been with Lynx, in a coupling that the two New Agers must have heard. Why had they claimed it had never taken place? 'What did she hear?'

'Lynx told her that he could tell people things about her, but she didn't seem to mind. She just laughed. A couple of times he talked about her father.'

They didn't like her. Jude sensed it by the way Storm fidgeted, by the way his mouth twisted a little when he talked about her. Sometimes he had to remind himself that Storm wasn't just an ageing hippy but had lived another life in which, the background reports had assured him, he'd been highly thought of in recruitment, a sound judge of character and temperament. It was easy to see how Cody's aggression might have grated upon their gentle withdrawal from any kind of conflict.

'That follows.' Lynx couldn't reveal Cody's nightmare now. Would he seriously have done so?

Storm stayed still, looking at him with wide eyes. 'Is it all over?'

'Who knows?' Jude allowed himself a shrug, then moved the conversation on. It wasn't as if he didn't have anything else to do. When he'd had a chance to review the information that would soon come flying at him from every direction, there would be a moment to send someone back down to take both Storm and Raven through their relationship with Cody, tenuous though it was, in more detail, but he was aware that the fund of goodwill he was building up could too easily be dissipated by an overly harsh approach. 'I hope so.'

'Can we just get on with our lives?'

'Of course.'

They walked back towards the tent where Raven had begun turning the tarot cards over, looking at them with exactly the same expression of deep thoughtfulness that characterised Ashleigh's readings of them. He paused for a while and watched as they were flipped over, trying to see what they were from a distance and failing, not sufficiently familiar with them. A King and a Queen, he could see that. He watched as she shuffled and dealt again, and again they came up – a different king, a different queen.

'Goodbye.' Acknowledged only by her nod, he turned and walked back up towards the village. The cards were nonsense, but sometimes they caused people to think in a particular way. He only wished he knew what was going through Storm's mind.

16

Jude had kept his phone switched off when he was down in the camp, aware that his best chance of getting any information lay in meeting the New Agers halfway. When he flicked it back on, there were half a dozen messages flinging themselves at him like angry wasps around a jam jar, but it was the one from Chris that caught his attention. *Murder weapon forensics*, it read, a message fraught with capital letters and spotted with exclamation marks.

Chris liked a bit of theatre, sometimes to a fault, but he wasn't prone to exaggeration. Ignoring all the other calls on his attention for the minute, Jude called him straight back, holding the phone clamped to his ear as he headed up towards the cafe. 'Okay. What's the bombshell you've got for me on the knife?'

'Mixing your metaphors there.' A breakthrough always put Chris in high good humour. 'The lab phoned. They've found blood and they've found fingerprints. Someone has tried to clean it up – washed it in the lake, probably – but they haven't made a great job of it.'

A ray of sunlight drifted from behind a shred of broken cloud, a finger of light pointing down towards the cottage on Coffin Lane, and Jude's mood lightened with it. 'It was definitely the murder weapon?'

'Yes. There are traces of Lynx's blood on the joint between the blade and the handle.'

'And could you get a match for the fingerprints?'

Chris could never help himself. He held the news back for a few seconds, for effect. 'We ran them through the system. They're Storm's.'

Stopping dead, Jude turned to direct a hard stare towards the New Age camp. A bare fifty yards away, Storm crossed from the tent to the fire and busied himself with something or other he must deem important but the rest of the world would see as trivial. The dislocation between the life of the Flat Earthers and everyone else was, Jude now saw, so significant that it would take more to learn their story than simply winning their trust. Storm had sworn that he'd told the truth and the whole truth, but he hadn't. Jude cursed his own weakness. He should never have been quite so ready to give them ground. 'Really?'

'Yep. And if you have any doubts about whether there could be a mistake they'll disappear when I tell you the rest. Because there was someone else's blood on the blade, and that was Raven's.'

In the field, Raven had left the tent, her tarot reading presumably complete, and had strayed over to where Storm was standing by the fire. Apparently oblivious to Jude's gaze, she slid her arms around him and the two of them stood locked together against the world in a moment of shared affection.

Was that for show or for real? 'Okay. That's very helpful. I'll get right onto that.' And he'd do it before Storm, who must think in his naivety that they'd got away with it, had time to work out an answer to the questions he was about to face. 'I'll speak to you later.'

He was outside the cafe by then and Ashleigh, fortunately, was standing in the middle of it having just ended a discussion with one of the uniformed teams. In turning, she spotted him, responding immediately to the gesture that summoned her out into the street. 'Is everything all right?'

'As far as I know. I've been speaking to Chris about the forensics.'

'Doddsy just told me.' The wind ripped a strand of hair from her ponytail and flicked it across her face, and she twisted it back behind her ear. 'Could there be a mistake?'

There could always be a mistake, but he couldn't see how that particular one could have been made at the lab. 'Yes. It was my mistake. I should have hauled the two of them in under caution and put the fear of God into them to start with, instead of treating them with kid gloves to spare their delicate sensibilities.' Maybe Cody was right about the snowflake generation after all, and a short, sharp shock would be an effective remedy and good for everyone's soul. 'I think it's time we put that right.'

'Steady on.' She placed a restraining hand on his sleeve. 'Going in there all guns blazing won't work.'

'The softly-softly approach didn't work either. I'm willing to give the alternative a try.'

She lifted an eyebrow at him. 'I wondered at the time if Doddsy and I went in too heavily with them to start with. That might be the problem.'

'They lied to us. It's their fault, not yours and Doddsy's. There are no excuses.'

'No. But what are you trying to do? Make a point about the primacy and inviolability of the law? If that's it, fine. Cart them off in handcuffs and interview them under caution. You won't get any information from them. If they haven't told us anything it's because they were scared of what we'd do with the information.'

'They've every reason to be worried. The forensic results on that murder weapon make Storm a prime suspect in a murder investigation.'

'They also suggest he injured his wife, and that clearly isn't true.' Her gaze followed his to the field beyond which the grey surface of the lake was frilly with wind-driven wavelets. 'So there's got to be an explanation, and the quickest way to get it is if they give it to us voluntarily. That's your objective, isn't it? To find out the truth.'

'It's a part of it.' Ultimately, his objective was to protect the innocent and bring the guilty to court, but the truth was an unmissable step on the way.

'Right. Then first we find out the truth of it, and then we see what we have to do from there.'

She was right, but from that point on he wouldn't be able to take anything Storm told him on trust. 'Fair enough. But I don't like being manipulated.'

'I don't think you are being. Even if Storm did kill Lynx, you'll get the story out of him, bit by bit. He doesn't understand our thinking, and he isn't equipped to resist it.'

'He's a former recruitment consultant.' With his usual thoroughness, Chris had prepared a profile which established Storm's previous life as astonishing only in its banality. There had been nothing extraordinary in his ten years in the peloton of the rat race.

'That was years ago. People can change their mindsets.'

'Then we'll ask him now. Can you spare me a moment?'

She checked her watch. 'I think so. If anyone needs me, they'll be able to find me easily enough.' She fell into step beside him and they headed once more towards the camp.

When they reached the gate Storm, who had been watching them, leaned over to Raven, said something to her, then detached himself from her orbit and headed up towards them. He'd begun walking with purpose but by the time they met his steps had slowed and his expression was the sheepish one of the child about to be caught out in very obvious mischief. 'Jude. Did you forget something?'

Ashleigh was right, and anger would get them nowhere. Jude knew it, but he had to keep reminding himself. Scenes like those at the woodpile and in Coffin Lane made the blood run hot as well as cold and Storm's refusal to cooperate, even if it had no criminal foundation, might end up costing another life. 'No, it isn't that, but there's something else I'd like to ask you about. Something that's just come up.'

'Of course.' Storm licked his lips, avoiding Jude's gaze.

'Shall we go somewhere else?' Looking at Raven, Ashleigh must have picked up Storm's desire not to involve her, as Jude himself had done. 'Did I see a seat over by the water? We can go there.'

'We'll go up the lane.' Storm walked past them, along Red Bank Road, past the bottom of Coffin Lane and the policeman whose attempt to stop him was deflected by Jude and Ashleigh's presence, up the hill. His concentrated, purposeful stride was at odds with his shabby appearance – body swathed in misshapen knitwear, hair long, the hems of his trousers dragging on the damp ground. After a quarter of a mile he stopped and swung his way over a stile and there, on a low viewpoint overlooking the lake and the scene of police activity, he stopped. 'What is it?'

Jude opened his mouth to level a challenge but Ashleigh pre-empted him, stepping forward and cutting him out of the conversation as if she didn't trust him to handle it. 'Tell us about the knife.'

Storm leaned back against the fence and glanced at the two of them with a look that was an echo of his days in business, calculating and rational. It lasted barely two seconds before he was back to a haunted face, as if he was wondering where it all went wrong. 'You know it all already.'

'No. We know a lot already. But what I want to hear right now is your side of it.'

A dog walker passed through the stile, a young and bouncing collie at his heels. Moving out of the way, Jude put a hand down to pat the dog, took a few steps downhill and took up his station on Storm's other side. He didn't think the man would make a break for it and if he did, he'd be easily caught, but pre-emptive action was always the best.

Storm turned his head away from Ashleigh, towards the mist-shrouded crag of the Lion and the Lamb. His eyes were bright with unshed tears.

'What happened? You should have told us where it was. You must have known we'd find out. You were the last person to handle it.'

'You are so smart,' he said, under his breath. 'Work it out for yourself.'

How could Storm be so naive? Reviewing the profile of

him once more, Jude shook his head over it. A university degree in economics was almost fifty years behind him and for forty of those fifty years he'd rejected everything but instinct and the feel of the environment. Once upon a time Storm must have known the power of science, but he'd let that knowledge slip away from him and any developments in forensics would have passed him by. He could never have stopped to contemplate the inevitability of being caught and now here he was, wriggling under Ashleigh's gentle questioning, trapped like a butterfly in a lepidopterist's net. Liars were rarely so easily and so completely caught.

'I think I have worked it out.' Ashleigh turned once more to look at him, her wide blue eyes playing on his innocence, inviting him to trust her. 'Is Raven ill?'

A wood pigeon grumbled at being disturbed in the woods behind them and the wind fretted the surface of the lake below. Storm had been standing with his back to the dry-stone wall, elbows resting on it in the negligent pose of an executive switching off by the water cooler, but at that comment he clenched his fingers tightly into the palm of one hand. 'How did you know?'

'I can tell.' Ashleigh's hand fluttered around her body in a sexless way, one that mimicked and exaggerated Raven's slow and deliberate gesture. 'She's so pale. And the way she unfolds herself from the ground when you get up so easily. She must be ten years younger than you.'

He nodded.

'And the way she holds her hands. All the time. Protecting herself as if she's in pain.' Her hand recreated a gesture that Jude had noticed but never really understood, hovering in front of her left breast. 'Is she in pain?'

He nodded.

'Then you have to take her to see a doctor. Because that looks to me—' She shifted around, turning her back on Jude, shutting him out. 'Storm. You have to trust me, for Raven's sake. I know you hate the modern world. I know you think medicine does more harm than good. But this won't work.'

'Would someone like to let me in on the secret?' Jude shifted round so they couldn't ignore him and found that once again Ashleigh had found a way to make a witness talk. With Storm's reluctance to talk overcome, she stepped back and left the interview to Jude. 'Well?' he asked the older man, with a sigh.

'It's a spell.' Storm let go of the wall and took a step forward as if to take himself closer to Raven in the distant field. 'Nothing else worked. We tried herbs and we tried diet… we tried everything.'

Except medicine. 'And how does the spell work?'

'You need a weapon. A weapon that's been used to kill someone. And you use it to prick the place where there's pain, and the pain goes away.'

Tolerance got you so far. Jude forgot himself so far as to open his mouth to protest but Ashleigh raised a warning hand to stop him. 'Storm. You aren't telling me you killed Lynx just to get hold of a murder weapon?'

'I didn't kill him at all.' Storm's face had turned the same colour as the winter sky, an even paler shade of grey than his ragged beard. 'I found him by the woodpile in the morning, when I got up. It was just light. The knife was in the water. And that's when I remembered someone telling me, in the summer, that that was what we should do to get rid of the pain.' His breath rippled uncomfortably from between parted lips.

'And what did you do then?'

'I took the knife out of the water and I hid it behind the wall.'

'Why didn't you call someone?'

'I couldn't help him. He was dead.' Storm turned dull eyes on Jude, then towards Ashleigh in a mute appeal for support. 'When Raven said she was going to look for him, I knew I had to get rid of it. You'd find it and I couldn't use it. So I took it and hid it.'

Still fighting a losing battle against the insistent wind, Ashleigh twisted hair from her eyes again. 'Was there ever a man in the woods?'

'No. I lied about it. To you. To Raven, too. I wish to God she hadn't found him, but I couldn't stop that. If I had I wouldn't have been able to hide the knife.'

'Where did you hide it?' By the most generous calculation, Storm hadn't been away from the camp long enough to get to Rydal Caves and back. Jude's methodical mind set to working out how he might have done it. Step by step, that would be it.

'Up in Deer Bolt Woods, in some tree roots. Under some leaves. The next day I went back. I took Raven with me and we walked along to the woods. She loves that walk.' He shook his head. 'That was when we tried the spell. Then I took the knife to the caves and hid it up there. In case we needed it again.'

'You must have known we'd find it.' Jude sighed. 'Didn't it occur to you that it would be easier just to tell us about it?'

'You'd have taken it away.'

Irritation fought with sympathy and sympathy won, but it was close. 'And do you think it worked?'

'Time will tell us.' Storm turned away, but the droop of his shoulders betrayed his lack of faith. 'What happens now? Do you arrest me?'

'No,' Ashleigh said, before Jude could get a word in. 'We need to check everything you've told us and we'll be in touch with you. And we'll want to talk to you again.'

You could fight modern life all you wanted, but in the end it kept you in its trap. Storm's understanding of that painful truth showed in his face. 'I don't have any choice, do I?'

'I'm afraid not.' Ashleigh stepped towards the stile. 'Shall we go back? I expect you'll want to get back to Raven.'

'Will you want to talk to her?'

'I promise we'll be kind.'

It would take Jude a lot of creativity to account for how they'd dealt with Storm and Raven in writing up the case, whatever its outcome, and he should metaphorically rap Ashleigh on the wrist for perpetuating a lack of professionalism, but he couldn't bring himself to do it. Sometimes the alternative way was the only way, though he doubted the alternative approach would give a happy outcome for Storm and Raven. 'Let's get back. We need to get on.' Because this episode hadn't, in the end, got them any further forwards.

'So what the hell was all that about spells and witchcraft?'

Coming round the corner to where Jude and Ashleigh

stood opposed in what looked for all the world like a full-on row next to Jude's car, Doddsy allowed himself a wry smile. Jude couldn't help himself. He got too involved, too easily frustrated and had to sound off. There were many people who could have been intimidated by it if he wasn't careful, but Ashleigh wasn't one of them.

'Jude. You have to understand how other people think.'

'Don't tell me. Your granny was a witch as well as a fortune teller.'

'She was interested in white magic, yes. And she did have a book of spells.'

'A book of spells? For Christ's sake, is this for real? It's a police investigation and people have died.'

'Yes, and tuning into other people's wavelength got an answer that shouting at them didn't. I'd heard the idea of a murder weapon as a cure-all. I believe the theory is that the inherent goodness in the object cancels out the evil use by humans. Obviously I don't believe it, but it fitted with what we know of Storm and Raven. Not just their thinking but their actions. So we have to consider it. Fair?'

'Chris is right to call them Flat Earthers. I've never seen anyone quite so benighted.' Jude turned away from her, running his hand through his hair in frustration, but his mood wasn't serious and he broke into a grin when he saw Doddsy. 'Not even our detective inspector.'

Doddsy returned the grin, saw Ashleigh shaking her head with a smile of her own and concluded that all was well. It amused him to see how hard the two of them tried to put up the front of a purely professional relationship but there were enough clues if you knew and it warmed his heart. He was an old sentimentalist who liked a happy ending, though

God knew he saw few enough of them. 'I'm guessing you've got something useful from our friends by the lake.'

'You could call it that. Storm claims to have discovered the murder weapon in the lake, purloined it in order to use it to cure Raven of some undiagnosed illness and then hidden it up in Rydal Caves in case he needs it again.' Jude rolled his eyes.

'Good luck writing that up in the case report.' Doddsy nodded at Ashleigh as she took herself back down to the cafe to carry on supervising the door-to-door enquiries. 'I think I'm done here for the moment. I wondered if you were heading back up to the office, so I can cadge a lift. I came down here with the uniformed guys and they'll be here for a while yet.'

Jude nodded at the car and opened the door. 'Your timing's perfect, as always. I was just heading back.' He turned around and waved at Ashleigh, a signal to everyone who saw it that they needn't read anything into a professional difference of opinion.

Doddsy went round to the side of the car and got in. As Jude headed away from Red Bank Road towards the village centre, they passed Tyrone, standing in conversation with a colleague. He looked up as they passed and smiled.

Warmed by the sight of the young constable, Doddsy accompanied a faux-regal wave with a reciprocal smile. Jude would spot it, just as everyone else spotted the smiles he himself shared with Ashleigh but allowing a personal relationship to impinge, ever so slightly, on the working day needn't damage your ability to do the job. 'What do you reckon?'

'To what?' Jude must have seen the smile and the wave.

'About who killed Fi Styles. About who killed Cain Harper. About the story about the murder weapon.'

'It feels like we have three jigsaws in our box right now, not two, but I think we'll get the picture in the end.' Pausing at the exit onto the A591 to let a stream of traffic pass by, Jude tapped his finger on the steering wheel. 'We have to consider the Gordons, because they were nearby, even though we know they're in the clear for Lynx's killing. But our wild academic was right on the spot for both murders and doesn't have an alibi for either.'

'Why would she kill the journalist? Because she was asking too many questions?' Cody had never struck Doddsy as the violent type. That was what he couldn't work out. Everything he knew about her suggested that her approach was forceful but that her violence was purely intellectual.

'Maybe. Or she was asking the wrong sort of question. But I'd like to know what she was doing up there at that time of the morning. I'd like to know if anyone knew she was going. And if not, could we be looking for someone who thought they were killing Cody Wilder?'

The bobbing high ponytail had been a strange feature of Fi Styles's appearance, as if it was intended as some subliminal compliment, intended to flatter Cody into answering questions. One way or another, the young journalist had paid a high price for her enthusiasm. 'That might be the Gordons then.' But he couldn't quite believe it of them.

'It might. There might be some clue on Fi's phone, or among her belongings. Where was she staying? In the village?'

'Yes. In a B&B. She told the owners she'd be out early this morning but she didn't say where she was going or why.'

Jude flipped the radio on and subjected them to a blast of cheesy Eighties hits as they drove up Dunmail Raise and dipped down to Thirlmere, in a contemplative silence. 'Jude. Can I ask you something?'

'Sure.' Jude turned the radio down and swung the car confidently round a couple of corners, slowing to sit behind a minibus, driving sedately along the lakeside.

Doddsy was a diffident man, a quiet soul who minded his own business except on the rare occasions when he chose to share it with his few close friends. Jude, the closest of them was the main beneficiary of what passed for his secrets. 'Did anybody ever mention the boss's behaviour to you?'

It was a moment before Jude replied, as if the question made him uncomfortable. 'Not until recently. Why?'

'Aditi complained to me about it.'

'Right.' The slightest frown crinkled Jude's brow, as if he was bothered by that. Doddsy understood why. His friend prided himself on his management, on how tightly he ran his team and the fact that they could approach him for any reason. The fact that one of them had chosen not to was something he'd interpret as a failing. 'She never said anything to me.'

'It was just because she bumped into me, I expect.'

'Hmm.'

'So I took it up to Professional Standards, and they gave me the impression that it wasn't the first complaint.'

'Generally speaking, people don't complain. That's always been the culture. Not that that's a good thing. The opposite. We need to complain more.'

'I'm glad you said that. Because I've made a complaint on my own behalf.' It had been at Tyrone's suggestion following an appalled silence during the conversation they'd had in the pub earlier in the week. 'About something he said to me about not wasting my time and his applying for a promotion because it wasn't the kind of thing for people like me.'

Silence, while Jude turned the car to the right, off the main road and up towards St John's in the Vale. 'You didn't tell me.'

'I never thought to mention it.'

'You were quite right to complain. Let's hope someone smacks the guy's wrist before he gets to retirement.'

No matter how disapproving Jude might be of his boss's behaviour there was no alternative to dealing with the devil. Groves was increasingly tetchy but there was a job to be done. As the afternoon ticked on, Jude made his way up to his superior's office and found the door standing, as usual, ajar.

Groves looked up when he came in and the expression of relief was swiftly succeeded by one of irritation, as though Jude weren't the person whose arrival he'd been dreading but nor was he particularly welcome. 'Satterthwaite. How are things going with the furore down in Grasmere? I seem to spend half of my time fending off the press. I have better things to do.'

Jude bit back a smart remark. He himself hated dealing with the press but Groves, who enjoyed it, was always high risk. One day someone would notice, if they hadn't already done so, that the best way to get your question answered was to find a good-looking woman to ask it. 'I think we're making some progress.' Perhaps that was an exaggeration, but Groves wouldn't accept *I've got a suspicion* as a justification for any action. What Jude really wanted was to search Cody's cottage, but he didn't have enough evidence to persuade a magistrate to grant him a warrant. 'There's something I'd like to do and I need you to submit the application to the Chief Constable for it.'

Groves sat back. 'Right. And that is?'

'I'd like to get audio surveillance placed in the cottage where Cody Wilder and her brother are staying.'

'I see.' Groves allowed himself a moment of silence. 'This is Dr Wilder who's been the subject of numerous threats of physical violence and whose stay in Grasmere had caused us to spend a significant proportion of a limited budget looking out for her. Is that right?'

'Yes. But that was before three people died.'

'Her researcher's death was suicide. I do read the reports you people send me.' Half a smile, half a sneer.

'Right. Then you'll know that she knew Cain Harper. The man who was murdered in the camp. She has no alibi for that time. You'll know that she was the one who found Fi Styles and that she has no alibi for that time either.'

Groves, at last, stirred himself to action, though not with any great enthusiasm. He flicked something up on his laptop and scowled at it. 'No alibi doesn't automatically mean—'

'Dr Wilder told us that she didn't know Cain Harper and she later admitted that was a lie. Maybe she lied about other things, too.' Cody and Lynx, with so long a shared history, had two decades of potential secrets to share. 'I have a witness who claims that he heard Harper threatening Dr Wilder. The threats were non-specific, other than that he said he had things he could tell the world about her. Now he's dead.'

For all his faults, Groves was a rapid processor of information and a man who came to a decision quickly. 'And the journalist?'

'Fi Styles was very keen to speak to Dr Wilder, who made certain that when an interview took place, she wasn't alone. One of my officers sat in on it. I have a suspicion that the reason she was outside the cottage in Coffin Lane that early in the morning was that she was trying a second time to speak to her alone.'

'But you've no evidence?'

'Nothing that isn't circumstantial, no. But as Dr Wilder has her brother staying with her and they're very close, it's possible that they'll talk about it, and I'd very much like to know what she says.'

Groves turned a heavy gold signet ring around on his little finger. 'What could a New Age traveller and a young journalist possibly have in common? Have you established any link?'

'Not yet. Except that we know the journalist had been down at the camp. I may be wrong, of course.' Groves was always susceptible to a touch of humility. 'But if nothing else, we may get enough to rule Dr Wilder out of the inquiry.'

'It's an unusual step, of course.' Groves turned his big office chair around and looked out of the window, as if he could see twenty miles and through the mountains to assess Cody Wilder and the scene of two murders for himself. 'But I grant you. It's an unusual case.' He spun back again. 'Put together an outline application for me and I'll see what I can do.'

17

'It looks like we have another visitor, honey. But this sure doesn't look like one of your usual fancy men.' Standing staring out into the grey morning, Brandon chuckled.

In some irritation Cody joined him at the living room window, where the two of them stood twitching the net curtain like a pair of elderly spinsters. At the gate a grey-haired man in a grey overcoat over grey trousers, a grey canvas bag over his shoulder and only a pair of shiny black shoes to relieve the monotony, hesitated at the gate and strode up the path. 'Oh, please. This is all I need.'

'You know him?'

'It's Sebastian Mulholland. Someone else who knows too much.' Brandon wouldn't understand what she was talking about, but who cared? 'What the hell is he doing here? He went back to St Andrews after the lecture.' Cody's nerves, over which she'd thought she had complete control, were betraying her just as everything else did. All her life she'd expected betrayal from every quarter at some stage, and only Brandon had ever shown her anything passing for fidelity, but it had come to something when she couldn't trust herself. 'You'd better let him in.' Hope flared in her heart. Maybe he'd discovered something else in some dusty attic in Fife.

Maybe there were more of Mary's letters, exhumed from a long-lost archive. 'No, I'll do it.' She swooped on the front door. 'I know this will be good news. And about time too.'

Brandon was looking suddenly and unusually anxious. 'Just so long as this dude doesn't try and take a pop at you too.'

A month before – even a week before – she'd have laughed that remark off as the joke she knew it to be, but nerves still troubled her after another bad night. 'No, he won't. That's one thing I can be sure of.' Like Owen, Seb lacked the balls for that kind of confrontation.

'Then we'll roll out the red carpet for him. Or I'll put the kettle on. Guess when I get home I can tell guys I've been working as your butler.'

She wished Brandon wouldn't keep talking about going home. When he left, as she knew he must, she'd have to find some way to cope in the chill and isolated darkness, knowing that he wasn't within shouting distance and if she needed help he wouldn't be able to come to her aid. Maybe he'd stay a little longer, at least until the police investigation was complete. She wrenched open the door. 'Seb. What brings you up here like a crow looking for carrion?' She smiled.

One of life's pleasures was keeping people on their toes, and this wasn't the kind of welcome he'd expected. His eyes widened slightly.

'It's okay.' The smile was genuine. Cody's dealings with Seb Mulholland had never brought her anything more sensual than the peculiar and unique pleasure that came from finding something new. His reality was trapped between the pages of old books and, though most of what it revealed was barely even humdrum there were gems to be had and he knew where to look. Her heart skipped at the thought.

'Just black humour. British humour, I thought, but likely I got that wrong?' She stood aside to let him in. 'Come on in and tell me all about whatever you've come to talk about. Brandon's going to make us a lovely cup of tea. I don't think you've met Brandon. He's my brother. Brandon, this is Seb.'

'Hello, Brandon. Delighted to meet you. I'm sure we've met. St Andrews? No? Edinburgh? New York?'

Balanced in the hallway, feet braced apart like a cowboy ready to draw, Brandon was looking the newcomer up and down with suspicion, as the two of them rumbled through two unconnected lists of places where they hadn't met. Jealousy, totally unjustifiable, bubbled out of his every pore, heightening her delight at seeing Seb so that she almost giggled.

'Seb. Darling. Come through to the sitting room.' Seb was anything but her darling, and Brandon must know that, but there was something about him that made her suspect he regarded her as an eccentric, and she played up to it. It never did you any harm in life for your closest associates, as well as your enemies, to be just a little bit wary of your unpredictability.

'I won't stop long.' This was unusual. Seb was normally gregarious to the point of being unshiftable and she'd become skilled at manoeuvring him off her territory. 'It'll have to be a quick cuppa. I'm on my way to London. But I was passing and I called in. I have something you might be interested in.'

She'd hoped it was that. Her heart gave a little kick, the same sort of excitement she'd felt the last time she'd given herself to Lynx to have the wickedest of wicked ways with her. The memory of his death dampened her enthusiasm, but only for a moment. 'Of course I'm interested. Come in.

Sit down. You're lucky to find us here. Someone died in the lane outside and the police had us out of here last night.'

'Someone died?' Seb handed his coat to Brandon and plucked nervously at his scarlet silk tie, a warning light that promised danger where none existed. 'Oh my.'

'Yes. Some poor girl killed with a rock. A jealous boyfriend, I expect.' She was being ridiculous. If Seb had seen the news he'd know what had happened, but she couldn't seem to stop herself prattling on, her voice pitched higher than usual, her speech more rapid. 'We were allowed back into the cottage this morning. I was surprised it was so quick, but they seem to be getting good at going over a crime scene. I should write to whoever their chief is and tell him he's got at least one satisfied customer.'

Even she thought her laughter was a little bit forced. Under Brandon's warning gaze, she wrestled back control. 'Sit down. Seb likes his coffee with sugar, Brandon. And bring the last of those chocolates. Now, Seb, tell me what you've got. Did you get lucky again?'

He sat and placed his bag on the sofa next to him, looking hurt. 'It's not luck. I remember everything. It's a question of finding the right information at the right time and tracking things down.'

'Maybe the police could use you.' Cody shivered. Jude Satterthwaite and his team might be good at getting a crime scene cleared but they seemed less than efficient at catching a killer.

'Maybe I should offer.' It was the closest she'd ever heard him come to a joke. Without looking at her, he undid the clip on his bag and took out a brown A4 envelope.

She wasn't the only one with a wicked sense of humour,

a need to exert her power. He held the envelope on his lap between the finger and thumb of each hand, and smiled.

Cody cracked. 'May I?' She held out a hand.

He slipped a hand inside the envelope and withdrew a second packet, wrapped in acid-free paper – letters, tied with a faded red ribbon. 'I don't know, and it's subject to verification. But I believe these are Dorothy's letters to Mary.'

The missing half of the correspondence that would tell a perfect story. For a moment, he held a hand over the letters in the same way she'd seen Raven hold them over her tarot cards, before extracting the top one from the slim packet and handing it to her.

The scent of old paper filled her nostrils and the powdered skeletons of two and a half centuries of dust mites clung to her fingertips. The writing was thin, the paper crazed with age, the ink fading, so that even Cody, skilled in the interpretation of Dorothy's script, struggled to see it, but she could read enough. *My dearest, my darling, my own love...your William and I miss you so much...* Her pulse raced. 'Seb. How did you find these?'

'A little bit of detective work.' Returning the other letters to the envelope he sat back, folding his hands over them with a self-satisfied smile. 'I remembered a property prospectus I saw when I was looking for a little place in the country a few years ago. It mentioned that it had been the country retreat of William Knight – the academic who had the previous letters,' he added, for Brandon's benefit. 'I visited it at the time and there was a study full of his books and papers that had been there for years.'

'You have an extraordinary memory.'

'It's served me well in the past. Hopefully it'll serve me

well in the future. I went back hoping against hope that the study hadn't been emptied. It had, but the contents were in boxes in the garage.'

'And you bought it all?'

'Yes. I had to pay a little more than I did last time. My reputation preceded me.'

'Maybe someone else remembers everything they read in the newspapers, too.' Cody's heart had stilled a little, enough for her to remember that you achieved more by playing it cool. Dealing with Seb was like playing saloon bar poker with a plumply smug devil. 'How much?'

'I paid five thousand. I'll be looking for a substantial profit.'

The letter she held in her hand contained nothing more than a few endearments, but he'd have chosen it as the least exciting one, the teaser. What did the rest hold? 'You've read the others. Are they worth my while?'

'That's something for you to decide, but having read them I'm prepared to offer you a fair deal.' He tilted his head to one side. 'I'm looking for fifty thousand.'

She wanted those letters, wanted them so much, but not enough to make a complete fool of herself. 'Fifty thousand? Are you mad?'

'Aren't they worth that to you?'

'The principle isn't worth it. Why should you make ten times what you paid for them?'

'Because I can sell them to someone else. More, possibly, if it goes to auction and you find yourself bidding against a collector.'

'They're Dorothy's letters, not William's. He has the market value.'

'Shall we test that?' His wit was as dry as his heart. 'You can afford it. I know how much you made from the first half of the correspondence.'

'No doubt you read about that in a newspaper, too.'

'I read an article estimating how much money you've made from your research into the Wordsworths, yes. And your colourful friend down in the field seemed to know a lot about it, too.'

'Oh, so you've been talking to people about me?' Desperate as she was for the letters, she wouldn't humiliate herself for them. She'd spent her childhood and her adolescence being bullied by a man and she'd vowed when she escaped him that no one would bully her again. People had tried. Owen, fatally, had tried. Even Lynx, whose bullying was welcome in its own, delicious, way, had overstepped a mark, but she'd never expected anything of the sort from Seb. 'I know you're trying to rip me off because you think I'm a weak and feeble woman, Sebastian, but you have a lesson to learn. It won't work.'

'Of course, you can keep that letter. It's the others which are interesting.' He folded down the flap of the envelope, dropped it in the case and clicked it shut.

For a second Cody's blood took control of her rational mind. She could seize the letters. Somehow she and Brandon would persuade the police that they were hers and he'd stolen them. Or if the worst came to the worst—

But the place was crawling with police. She subsided into her chair, her frenzied brain calculating. Were the letters worth the money? Were they worth the humiliation?

'I'm sure we can work something out.' Brandon put a tray of tea things on the table, poured the tea and offered

Seb the box containing the solitary remaining chocolate she'd had from Lynx.

Cody loved marzipan. On another day, irritated with him, she'd have had no qualms about snatching it from under his nose but she controlled herself, watching him lift it out of the box. 'Oh, lovely. Thank you. Handmade.'

She accepted this minor defeat with grace, but on the major battle she still fought. How was she to get the letters without being made to beg for them like the worst kind of addict? This was why she tried never to reveal her weakness. People took advantage of it. The gesture of donating the journals to the Wordsworth Trust might have been designed to deflect from her need to keep Mary's letters, but Seb, who knew about it, had seen through it. 'Obviously I want the letters,' she said, forcing herself to sound casual. 'But not at any price.'

Seb sipped his tea, devoured the chocolate, sipped again. Standing at the window like his sister's bodyguard Brandon maintained that interested smile, but she had no idea whether he understood how important it was to her. Hating herself, she opened her mouth to accept Seb's offer.

'Tell you what,' Brandon suggested, coming and positioning himself between the two of them so that she couldn't see the expression on Seb's face. 'Why don't we take a little time to think it through? When do you have to leave for London?'

'I was going straight there.' Seb got out a crisp white handkerchief and removed a smear of chocolate from his fingers.

The plan was a good one. She knew she could rely on Brandon. With an effort, Cody pretended to consider it for a moment before she agreed. 'Can you give us an hour or so,

Seb? Go down to the village. Have a walk round the lake or another cup of coffee or something. Then we'll see. If decide I'd like to buy I'd need to make a couple of phon calls. About the money.'

'That sounds like a plan.' Seb got up, seizing the briefcas in both hands as if he feared being mugged for it. 'Call m when you've decided. You have my number.' He wriggle into his overcoat without letting go of the bag, obliteratin the scarlet flame of his tie and becoming once more a gre and unthreatening nonentity. 'One other thing, Cody.'

'Oh?'

'I've enjoyed working with you.' He shuffled towards th door. 'But I don't feel it's a workable relationship any more.

Not when you rip me off. 'Oh, really? And where hav you gotten a conscience about working with me? I've alway been honest and open with you.'

'But the people I deal with are very—' He struggled fo the right word. 'Fastidious. I can't afford to be associate with anything questionable. And some of your reputatio inevitably sticks to those you deal with.'

'Right. And if there's any doubt about those letter you're in as much trouble as I am, right?'

'Your reputation will be more damaged than mine i those letters are fake.'

But he'd always said he didn't believe they were fak He must be cutting their relationship short because she' become too toxic for him to know. 'Exactly what are yo implying?'

'Well.' Usually urbane, he looked a little flustered. 'Wha happened to poor Owen, for example. And the gentlema in the field. And if you go back a bit there's—'

She held up a hand before he could turn his knowledge into a threat. 'Stop right there. Don't ever suggest—'

Brandon overran her fury, stepping past her and urging Seb out of the door and onto the path as if he were flicking dust out through the kitchen door. 'See you in an hour or so, Seb.'

'He won't get away with this.' Her blood throbbed in her ears as she watched him bouncing his way down the path. 'I'll kill him. I swear I will.'

'Cody. Stay calm. Lashing out won't help anyone.'

'But he's going to tell. It doesn't have to be the truth. He'll say anything. If we don't pay up, he'll ruin my reputation. I have too many enemies.' And too many secrets. And if they came out and she was ruined someone else would get the letters and build upon her years of research to snatch the glory. That was what she couldn't bear.

'We'll think of something, honey.' Brandon seized her hands and held them between his, looked into her eyes. Her breathing slowed. It would be all right. He'd take control. 'Don't worry. We'll think of something.'

'Okay.' Jude had managed to catch Doddsy before the inspector headed back down to Grasmere. 'Let's take a few moments to run through this. We've got as much information about two murders as I think we're going to get. Now we have to start putting it together.'

'Do you want anyone else to sit in on this?' Doddsy took a quick look around the incident room. 'Tammy might have something to add.'

'I think I've got all the information she can give me. You could round up Chris. He usually has something to contribute.' Ashleigh had headed down to the village – a pity, because he could have done with her intuitive thinking at that point, but although Chris wasn't a man to think out of the box his thoroughness left nothing to be desired.

While Doddsy threaded his way through the desks of the others working away on the backgrounds, the contacts and the movements of Lynx and Fi Styles, their friends, enemies and associates, and summoned Chris from where he'd had his head down over his laptop, Jude sat back, tapping his pen thoughtfully on his pad. He turned to look at the whiteboard where a picture was building up, piece by piece, a spider's web of conflicting information with Cody at the centre of it. But was she the spider or the fly?

'Busy?' he asked, turning back, alerted to something by Chris's slightly creased brow.

'No more than usual. But I might be onto something.'

'Okay. I'll let you get back to it in a minute, but I value your input. I wanted to bounce some ideas around. We know what happened, we know where, we know when, we know how. I want to think about who might have killed Lynx and Fi Styles and why.'

'I've been thinking about it.' Doddsy scrawled a list on his pad. *Cody. Brandon. The Gordons. Storm. Raven.* 'Where do we start? With the obvious?'

'Yes. Cody. Because as far as I can see she has the best reason and the best opportunity for killing both Lynx and Fi Styles, even though there isn't any compelling evidence to prove it.'

'There's forensic evidence to place her at both sites.'

'Not where Lynx's body was found. The tests only show

she was in his tent, and she's admitted that. There's nothing to link her to the murder weapon.'

'It had been cleaned.'

Jude turned to the board once more, where an image of the broad-bladed knife overlapped a picture of Lynx's sprawled, bloodless body. 'Not well enough to remove all traces of Lynx's blood.'

'Blood's more pervasive than fingerprints. It doesn't clear her.'

'That's right. And while we have no one who saw her there at the time of the murder, it doesn't mean she wasn't there. She claims to have been up at the cottage and her brother confirms that, but what was to stop her nipping down, committing the murder and coming back?' The killer would have been covered in blood. Briefly, Jude wondered whether he could persuade Detective Superintendent Groves to authorise a thorough search of Cody's cottage but he knew in his heart that the grounds were still too weak. He'd been lucky to persuade him to support a request for surveillance. 'Has anyone managed to find where the knife came from?'

Chris shook his head. 'I've got someone looking at that, but it could take a long time. It needn't have been bought locally, and it could have been bought online. Or someone may have had it for a long time, in which case we may never find out.'

'Okay. And let's bring in what we have from Tammy. It's incomplete, because there are plenty of tests still going on, but we know for sure what killed her.' The slab that had shattered the journalist's skull had come from the top of the wall. 'From behind, again, so either she was taken completely unawares or she had no reason to worry about turning her back on whoever she was with.' But the stone troubled him. It was a handy weapon – too handy, and its use pointed at opportunism rather than premeditation, though the latter couldn't be ruled out. Cody, he was sure, was capable of either. 'Unlike Lynx, she was struck from the side rather than above. The back of her head was smashed in. The blow didn't require particular strength. In some ways it might have been a lucky strike. But that's all we know.' He sat back, hands flat on the table.

'I had someone check her phone records.' Doddsy chipped in. 'There are a couple of calls from Cody, presumably to arrange the interview that Ashleigh was at, but there are no calls between them after that. So if Cody did attempt to lure Fi Styles into some sort of a trap, she almost certainly didn't do it by phone. We've been through the B&B where she was staying and there are no notes or anything to suggest a reason why she went there at that time of the morning.'

Jude thought of Fi – naive and ambitious, not getting the information she wanted from Cody. 'An idea of a meeting might have been floated by Fi herself. Cody quite often went for an early walk, I believe. So it might also be that Fi tried to doorstep her, and perhaps threatened her. I don't know what with. Exposure?'

'Not over the Wordsworth letters.' Chris spoke with certainty. 'Aditi followed that one up for me, and as far as I can tell the only people who've suggested they aren't genuine are people who dislike Cody Wilder intensely. Anyone who's in any way impartial accepts them.'

'Fi may not have known that.' Doddsy took his turn. 'My guess would be that she saw that as a way to make a name for herself and was still following it up. If she came up Coffin Lane to try and catch Cody by surprise – as she did to get the interview, if you remember – and bumped into her, then Cody may have lost her temper and hit her with whatever came to hand.' He waved a hand at the photo of the stone. 'As you say, the choice of weapon suggests opportunism. But even if the meeting was arranged it doesn't mean the murder was premeditated.'

That hadn't been the case with Lynx. 'And down at the New Age camp? Lynx was murdered by someone who wanted something. That's why they searched the place.'

'If it was the letters, then it wasn't Cody who did it.' Doddsy, this time. 'She had them. But she said she'd asked him about taking them.'

'Raven and Storm told us Fi Styles had spoken to Lynx.' Chris flicked back through a thick notepad. 'What had he told her? We'll never know, of course. But does that point to Cody after all?'

Most of the evidence did, but evidence often pointed to more than one possible culprit. It was a question of finding enough to prove one of them guilty. 'Or her brother. He strikes me as hard as nails, and we haven't really considered him.' Not for the first time, Jude wished he had the benefit of Ashleigh to offer some insight into Cody's or Brandon's mindset. 'But he has no reason to kill Lynx that I'm aware of.'

Chris ran a hand through his hair. 'Maybe he thought he was protecting his sister. He's that he-man type, isn't he?'

'I'd say she can look after herself. He claims to have been asleep in his bed when she found Fi Styles and she confirms that. She says she saw his bedroom light go on. And Fi was very recently dead. But who else would kill Lynx?'

Chris's face set in a stubborn line. 'I know who I think did it. You don't need to look any further than those Fla Earthers.'

Doddsy, forgetting himself, waved an amused hand in the constable's direction. 'Chris, those guys have had a dozen accusations levelled at them in the past year, and they've never been proven to have done anything wrong.'

'They lied to the police.'

In Chris's eyes, that was almost the ultimate sin. Onc more, Jude allowed himself to see the hippies through thei own eyes rather than through the eyes of others. 'Thei philosophy is to do no harm.'

'Except for lying to us, and stealing the murder weapon and concealing it. And all that nonsense she tried to sell Ashleigh over the tarot cards. We know what all that wa about – pointing the finger at someone else. All that stuf about the non-existent stranger in the woods. It was a lie and for my money that means we can't afford to believ anything else they say.'

Storm and Raven had every reason to lie, thinking they' never be believed if they told the truth, but if there wer untold truths about their relationship with Lynx there wa no apparent reason why either of them might choose to turn their vengeance on Fi Styles. 'I want to know mor about them. I'd like to know more about Lynx, too. How he came to be here and why. Is there any other reason wh they might have something against him?'

'I'll get someone to go back to it.' Chris made a note, thoug Jude knew he'd already covered every possible avenue.

Doddsy had ticked off the names on his list of suspect as Jude had gone through them until only the Gordon were left. 'Next up. Graham and Eliza Gordon. They blame Cody's attitude – they say Cody herself – for the death of her daughter. Cody clearly can't be responsible, but that shows a twisted view of things.'

Twisted enough to allow them to try and wreak revenge on Cody for something she hadn't done? 'And they were the second people on the scene after the deaths of both Lynx and Fi. Coincidence?' Everybody who worked with Jude knew he didn't believe in coincidence.

'I can see that they might have had a swipe at Fi Styles thinking she was Cody,' said Doddsy, thoughtfully. 'But I think they'd have admitted it. Guilt if they hadn't meant to, triumphant if they did. And why kill Lynx? You'd hardly mistake him for Cody. And don't forget. When Lynx was killed the Gordons were out walking their dog at the other end of the village, and we have a witness who spoke to them.'

'No, that's fair enough.'

'We're clear that we think Owen killed himself, aren't we?' Chris stole a guilty look at the incident board, from where Owen's poet's face looked down on them.

'Yes.' Still nominally in charge of this part of the investigation, Doddsy frowned. His tone showed that there was one thing, at least, about which he had no doubt.

And yet, Jude reflected with a sigh, there was something so convenient about Owen's suicide, so neat. He'd spoken to Fi. Who else had he spoken to and what had they said? Or was it possible that they were dealing with three separate causes of death — that Owen's suicide had been followed by Cody killing Lynx for reasons of her own, and that Storm had killed Fi thinking she was Cody, and it was revenge for Lynx's death?

It was possible, but whether it was believable was another matter entirely. 'Okay. We'll leave it there and see what else we can find out.'

'How are you getting on, Tyrone?' Inside the cafe, Ashleigh was running through the questionnaires the door-to-door officers had returned to her, looking for any detail that might shed some light on the mystery of two violent murders. No one had seen anything. That was what happened when you operated in the dark, in the winter, but nevertheless she'd hoped for some crumb of comfort.

'Fine. Or not fine, from your point of view.' He gave her his best smile, the one she'd noticed him bestowing freely on Doddsy, and slipped another sheaf of paper onto the table in front of her. Barely six months into his probation period, he was already organising officers who'd been in the force for years. Some of them wouldn't like it. 'This is the lot from the team up along Easedale Road. Apart from the Gordons, nobody was out along Red Bank Road yesterday morning and nobody saw anything suspicious in the village.'

She sighed, glancing at her watch. It was nearly lunchtime. 'You'd better take a break, then. How many more places do you have to cover?'

'I'll find out and get back to you.' He turned and headed back towards the door.

She watched him go, deep in thought. On the pavement outside, a man in early-middle age was stumbling along the pavement as if he were drunk. Her attention caught, Ashleigh looked more closely, even as Tyrone closed in on the man. There was something familiar about the grey hair and the glasses.

Of course. She knew him from the press coverage of Cody Wilder's lecture. He'd been the master of ceremonies, the man who'd discovered Dorothy Wordsworth's journal in a box of old books in St Andrews. There had been a photo of him in an article, sitting behind Cody as she stood at the lectern.

Strange. She thought he'd left Grasmere as soon as the lecture was over.

The man lurched forwards. Tyrone caught him by the arm and, holding him up, looked to the cafe for help. Seeing panic in the constable's face, she sprang across to open the door. 'Tyrone. What's happened?'

'This gentleman isn't well.'

Holding the door open with her foot, Ashleigh grabbed the man's other arm. Sebastian Mulholland. That was his name. His skin had faded to grey and his body was shaking. 'Let's get him inside.'

Graham Gordon, once again on the spot, leapt to the rescue. 'Is he ill? Shall I call an ambulance?'

'Yes.' And almost before they were inside the cafe, Sebastian Mulholland's legs gave way beneath him. Between them, Ashleigh and Tyrone lowered him to the floor where he twitched and lay still.

18

'Dead by the time the ambulance got here.' Ashleigh was walking up Coffin Lane at Jude's side while behind them Grasmere went once more through the motions of dealing with a major incident – the sirens, the police cars, the blue tape. 'We gave him CPR, but there was nothing we could do.' She shivered. 'I could feel him slipping away. It was awful.'

'The post-mortem report will be interesting on this one.' Jude's expression was grim. It might be natural causes or it might, at a stretch, be accidental death but both Ashleigh and Tyrone had been struck by how quickly the man had been taken ill. 'Sebastian Mulholland. Another contact of Cody Wilder's.' That was why he'd targeted so many resources on what would normally have been treated as routine.

'Yes. Either she's completely lost the plot and is killing everyone around her, or someone's completely incompetent when it comes to killing her.'

Neither of these options presented a particularly comforting option, nor offered any prospect of an easy solution. 'I wish I could lock the woman up, either for her own safety or for everyone else's, but she doesn't seem to care.'

'Do you think she did it?'

Gravel crunched underfoot as they headed up Coffin Lane and mist wreathed around the shoulder of Silver How above them. 'Do you?'

She hesitated. 'No.'

'Any reason?'

They were almost at the cottage, just at the spot where Fi had met her brutal and untimely end, and they paused here. Overnight rain had sluiced away the last of her blood. She's scared and she's nervous.'

'Not that scared and nervous.'

'Oh, but she is. Can't you see? She'll always come out ighting but she's scared. She's always looking over your houlder when you're talking, as if she's afraid of something.'

'You need to ask the tarot cards.' He was rewarded by her smile, the recognition that it was a joke.

She dug him in the ribs. 'It isn't the cards I asked about his. It was my own eyes. It's obvious.'

Jude was sceptical but not closed-minded and her hobby amused him more now that it had done when he first came cross it. Now at least, he was beginning to grasp that she didn't let it guide her. 'I've been reading up. Cody would make a fine High Priestess.'

'Ha!' She shook her head at him. 'I'll make a fortune teller of you yet.'

'I prefer to keep to scientific evidence.' Ashleigh had begun to shuffle her way up to the cottage but he stayed out. 'I disagree with you on Cody. I think she's the clear main suspect.'

'But there's no evidence.'

'Not yet. This isn't public, but I've asked the boss to

authorise audio monitoring of the Wilders' cottage, and he' agreed. Because I think that's going to be the most likel source of information.'

'Is it set up yet?'

'Who knows?' He shrugged. Once the request had bee authorised, it would be the last he'd hear of it until th recordings had made their way back to Groves and he' decided whether the information within them was wort acting on. 'Those intelligence guys don't keep us foo soldiers in the loop.'

'You're so snooty about them,' she said, affectionatel 'You talk about them just the way the uniformed lot tal about us.'

He was smiling as they moved on again, past the spo that Fi's ghost might one day haunt and up the path. Cod arrived on the doorstep just as they arrived, tucking the end of her scarf down into her jacket against the brave breez and flicking her ponytail free of the collar. 'You again, Chie Inspector? You don't seem able to keep away from her And I see there's another furore down in the village. Is ou mad knifeman about his dastardly work again?'

'It may not be significant.' Cody was the one who alway seemed to seek drama, and there was nothing Jude coul do to tone down the blue lights and the increased polic presence. 'Unfortunately, a gentleman was taken ill down i the village and an ambulance was called.'

'Oh, I see. And every time a sparrow falls from a tree yo feel the need to come up and make sure I'm all right You people do like a bit of drama, don't you? I'd hav thought you have better things to spend taxpayers' mone on.' She turned back to the door and called in. 'Brandon! Where are you?'

'I wouldn't normally bother you, but as the person taken ill is someone you know, I thought I'd better check on you. And now I know you're well and safe, I'd like a word with you.'

'Someone I know?' she said over her shoulder. 'Who is it this time? One of those lunatics in the cafe who think I'm to blame for their flabby parenting?'

'No. It's Sebastian Mulholland. And I'm sorry to say he's dead.'

That stopped her. She swung back to face him, squinting into the low winter sun. 'Seb? That's impossible. He was here earlier this morning and he was perfectly fine. Brandon and I were just going down to the village to meet him. He has some letters for me.'

'May we come in?'

She stepped back in, already unbuttoning her coat. As it seemed he always did, Brandon materialised behind her in the hallway, fastened up in a heavy-duty fleece that was too thick even for a Cumbrian winter. 'The police are back. It's Seb. He's dead.'

'Dead?' His face was a mask painted in appropriate measures with shock and respect. 'But that's impossible. He—'

'I'm sorry. He collapsed in the village and the paramedics declared him dead, despite Sergeant O'Halloran's attempts to save him.'

'I'm most grateful to you.' Cody almost snapped at Ashleigh and her voice shook in fury, Jude thought, rather than shock. 'I can't believe that happened. He had some letters. I was going to buy them.'

'I think this is a little more important than letters, don't you?'

She paused for a moment, then raised her eyes to challenge him. 'Of course. You'll have to forgive me. I'm like a rattlesnake. If you poke me with a stick, I'll bite. And now, of course, you want to ask me the same old questions and I'll give you the same old answers. Because I'm not stupid. You think the death is suspicious, or you wouldn't be here.'

'We treat every death as suspicious until it's proved otherwise.' That was what they drummed into you. *If in doubt, think murder.* 'You say you were about to go and see him, and that he'd been to see you. That's what I'd like you to talk me through.'

He could never read Cody Wilder. She always gave the impression that what she presented – bold and brash, like a child's painting in gashes of primary colours – was simple and straightforward. That might be what she wanted him to believe, even what she herself wanted to believe, but the glimpse she'd given him into her soul when she'd talked about her father hinted at something much more complex. Even someone as smart as she unquestionably was could almost reach her forties and still be in denial about what made her tick.

'Come and sit down.' She turned, smartly, and marched into the living room.

Following her, Jude tried not to look too obviously to see where someone might have stowed a listening device, but there was nothing. He'd have to take it on trust that the intelligence team were as smart and efficient as they liked to think they were. 'Mr Wilder. Perhaps you'd join us.'

'Sure.' They sat in the living room and this time neither Cody nor Brandon moved to offer coffee.

'Let's get this done, shall we?' Cody tossed her head at them. 'Seb appeared at the door this morning at about ten o'clock. There, Chief Inspector. I'm getting good at statements now, aren't I? We invited him in and Brandon made tea. Seb was on his way to London, though he didn't say what for and I didn't ask. He'd come with a proposition for me.'

She had her hands flat on her lap and the tips of her fingers whitened as she pressed down. 'And?' Jude prompted, as she seemed hesitant to continue.

'He'd found what he thought were letters from Dorothy Wordsworth to her sister-in-law, and he offered to sell them to me. The price he was asking was high, but the documents obviously have a significant value, especially within the context of my work.'

'How much was he asking?'

Another fractional pause. 'Fifty thousand pounds. For half a dozen letters.'

Jude whistled.

'Exactly.' She shot him a hard look. 'I asked for proof and he gave me one letter to look at. I told him I'd think about it and that if he gave me an hour or two, I'd make a decision. After that, he left.'

'And he left you the letter.'

'Yes.' She got up and crossed to the desk, unlocking the drawer and taking out the folded sheet, carefully nurtured between two pieces of paper. 'You'll likely want to take it.' Her voice quivered with doubt.

The paper was frail, so much so that even Jude, so accustomed to handling artefacts with the utmost care, was terrified of damaging it. He handed it to Ashleigh who, with equal care, sealed it into an evidence bag as if it were dynamite. 'Yes.'

'Will I get it back?' She was regarding him with the anxiety of a parent with a sick child. 'He gave me the letter. I was going to go down and offer to negotiate over the price, but if he hadn't budged, I would have paid him what he asked.'

'Yes, if you can prove he gave it to you.'

'I can vouch for that,' chimed in Brandon. 'And everything else my sister has said.'

'You made him tea, Dr Wilder said.' Jude turned his attention away from his fascinated contemplation of Ashleigh as she labelled the bag containing the promise of Cody's heart's desire. 'Anything else? Biscuits?'

'Chocolates,' Cody turned a cold eye on him. 'So maybe someone's trying to poison me. You didn't do much to prevent that, did you?'

What was he supposed to do? Personally taste every morsel of food before she ate it? Disbelieving Cody's profession of victimhood, Jude was still getting his breath back at such effrontery when Ashleigh, looking up from the bag, took over. 'Where did the chocolates come from?'

'Lynx gave them to me, the last time I saw him. He said someone had given them to him, but he'd stopped eating chocolates because he was vegan. So I took them.'

'You ate them?'

'Just one. Brandon had some of them, but I think Seb ook the last one.'

'No. There's one left.' Getting to his feet, Brandon fetched he box of chocolates and laid it on the table. They'd looked andmade, Jude remembered, each sitting in its little paper ase, crammed into a small box. Half a dozen of the vrappers, empty, still floated around in the box and one hocolate remained, hidden beneath them. 'Didn't you offer hem to me?'

'Yes, I did. I've been offering the goddamned things to nyone who came.'

Jude stared at the chocolates, his brain whirring. If omeone had placed the chocolates in Cody's house in he hope of killing her then they'd been putting random trangers, himself included, into a fatal game of Russian oulette which Seb Mulholland had lost. The idea was reposterous. 'Thanks. Obviously we'll take that.'

Brandon handed the box to Ashleigh, who bagged that oo, then followed Jude's lead and got to her feet. 'So now ve need to watch what we freaking eat, do we?'

''I'll make sure there's an officer outside the cottage—'

'No. That's the last thing I need. People thinking I'm cared. Why give them the satisfaction?' Cody looked owards Brandon, as if he were all the assistance she needed.

The chocolates came from the Gordons.'

Jude groaned. So that was why, when he'd tried to ound up Ashleigh and Doddsy for a hastily convened team neeting she'd insisted it wasn't wise to hold it in the cafe and they'd assembled, instead, in the corner of a tea roor looking down on the river. 'Seriously?'

'Yes. They make their own, and they often pass th misshapes on to other people rather than throw them awa Raven was particularly fond of them. And yes, they gav some to Lynx.'

'But surely they couldn't have been intended for Cody. O if they were, that's an astonishing lack of care for anyon else. They can't have known he'd give them to her when h could equally possibly have given them to Raven or Storm

She shrugged. 'I know. And they seemed genuinel appalled at the idea that their chocolates could have cause any harm to anyone. I didn't tell them what happened, c course. I implied he had a nut allergy, but I don't think the were fooled.'

'Can we be reasonably sure it was poison?' Jude looke to Doddsy. 'I know nothing will be certain until after th PM, but there must be some indication.'

'There is. I spoke to the paramedic who treated him an I had a quick word with a specialist in toxins. The paramedi had seen something similar before, in a small child, wh survived. He recognised the symptoms as being those c taxine alkaloid poisoning. You get that from yew trees.'

All three of them looked out across the river to th churchyard, where the traditional assemblage of yew tre in the churchyard overshadowed the graves of Willia Wordsworth, his wife and his sister.

'There's yew up in Coffin Lane, too. I noticed it the fir time we went up.' Ashleigh wrote it down. 'And some in th back garden at the Wilders' cottage. But that needn't mea anything. It's all over the place here. Such a pretty tree. The have it on sale in the garden centre. You can get saplings with berries on. It certainly isn't in short supply.'

'We'll have to wait for the toxicology test results before we can be sure.' Doddsy was in a melancholy mood, and so he should be, on the fourth dead body in little more than a week. 'There may be something else.'

'I can't wait for the results. If someone has a vendetta against Cody, then we're short of time. Not that I think that's the case. She could have done them all except Owen, and it's pretty clear she bullied him to his death.' His phone rang and, looking down at it, he saw Chris's number. 'Chris. What have you got? Anything?'

'I'll say. I think I've got dynamite.' The constable's voice crackled with excitement. 'Total dynamite.'

They were alone in that part of the cafe and the waitress was busy elsewhere, so he flicked the phone on to speaker and laid it in the centre of the table where they could all hear, if they leaned in. 'Go on.'

'I was following up on Lynx, trying to get a sense of what he might have done, what he might have threatened to do. I couldn't find anything. I went through all the stuff I could find about Cody when she was a young academic, every reference. And I found the story of the Wilder family.'

Through the plate glass window, the River Rothay grumbled its way through the village beneath overhanging willows, their leafless twigs dipping into the water. In the churchyard beyond, a regiment of green spikes prepared to burst out as daffodils, heralds of spring. It was hard to imagine anything less like Wyoming. 'And?'

'It's even more Wild West than you think. The mother died. She'd always been frail. A couple of years later the father, Brandon Wilder Jr – a nasty brute by every account – died in a snowstorm and there was a rumour of foul play. The police went out and questioned the kids, but they stuck to the same story. Pa Wilder had gone out in a storm to check on the cattle and not come back. When the storm was over, Brandon went out to look for him and found the truck empty and no sign of him.'

'Okay. And is that necessarily suspicious?' A storm, wolves, bears. In Jude's hazy knowledge of the place, Wyoming wasn't the safest to be out alone.

'I chased up the police department and they sent me the case notes. Here's the thing. Daddy Wilder went off in his truck but when they found it after he was dead the driver's seat had been readjusted.'

'In what way?'

'He was tall but the seat of the truck was pushed forward. I asked them straight out – could one of them have bumped him off?'

'Good thinking.' Jude said it automatically, as if the death of Brandon Wilder Jr was his case. 'I can see how that might have worked. If he'd been out with Brandon and Brandon had left him out there to die, then he and Cody would have had to get the truck back later. It would be a hell of a risk.'

'But the risk would be worth it,' Ashleigh said, 'when you think what he put her through. Wouldn't it? And maybe she'd rather have taken the chance of landing in jail than spending the rest of her life stuck out in the wilds with him. Just him and her and Brandon.'

'I called the guy in the police department.' Chris's voice piped up from the phone in the middle of the table. 'It's frontier country out there. They all knew the man by repute and no one was going to miss him. They chose not to look closely at it. I got the distinct impression that no one was too bothered about catching whoever it was. They have the death penalty out there and they maybe thought if he was murdered no one deserved to be punished for it.'

It was just possible that someone else cared. If that old case were to come alive, Cody's extramural academic career would end even more spectacularly than her stint with the university had done. Jude sat back while the waitress drifted over with top ups for their coffees, eyed them with interest, then drifted away again, her curiosity unsatisfied. 'This is starting to make sense. Lynx was at the university at the time, she said.'

'Yes. He was a couple of years older than her, so he'd have seen the story, the speculation about what happened and the quiet decision to let it go. We know he came here when she came, and maybe it was because of her. And we know he threatened to tell the world about her father.'

Power? A perverted joke? Something else? They hadn't been able to build up enough of a picture of Lynx to understand why he might have done it. 'Lynx had been talking to Fi Styles. She'd been looking around, trying to find some story about Cody that would make her name. We'll never know what he told her, but we can guess what Cody might have thought it was.'

'But did she think it was worth killing for?'

Somehow, despite Doddsy's presence, Jude had taken Ashleigh's hand. She disentangled her fingers from his and tapped them on the table. 'Surely not. The police in Wyoming weren't keen to dig out evidence at the time, and it was twenty years ago. That's a hell of a cold case.'

And it didn't explain Seb Mulholland's death. Jude shook his head. 'The bookseller. What about him?'

'That's the clincher, Jude.' He'd almost forgotten about Chris. 'As soon as I heard he'd died I got on to searching for him. It didn't take long. He worked for three years in Wyoming at the university library, as an archivist. In the second of those three years, the Wilder story was in the papers. In the third, Cody came to the university. They almost certainly met.'

There was only one person to benefit from those three deaths and Chris's discovery had confirmed that Cody's uncompromising support for violence in self-defence was rooted in her father's death. If not a killer herself, she was almost certainly an accomplice. And if then, why not now? 'Okay.'

'That's incredible work, Chris.' Ashleigh was trying to make up for Jude's apparent lack of enthusiasm, but it wasn't that he underrated the contribution. Far from it. It was just that there was one thing that didn't quite make sense. The letters. Cody wouldn't hurt Seb Mulholland if it risked her losing the letters.

Or would she? Maybe the balance of risk was too great and what he knew was too much of a threat. She might be gambling on buying the letters from his estate. The pieces of Doddsy's mixed puzzles fell into place in front of him and made a triptych of murder. 'Here's what I think could have happened. Cody turns up here with Owen, and the two of them fall out. But before he decides he can't take any more, he sets out to make mischief. He tells Fi Styles something – probably that the letters are fake. It appears that isn't true, but that doesn't matter. What matters is that

Cody fears exposure. As soon as Fi let slip that she knew something, she was marked down.' Because Cody, with some justification, could have turned into the most ruthless protector of herself and her reputation. 'Then she spoke to Lynx. Storm heard Lynx threatening to reveal something about her father. I assumed it was the abuse – but maybe it wasn't. Maybe Lynx knew the story.'

'Right.' Doddsy was seeing it, too. 'And so she had to kill Lynx. She throws the knife – wherever she got it from – in the water, tears his place apart to make to look like a robbery. Then she lures Fi Styles up to the house on some pretext or other and brains her with a slate. And that's fine. Owen can't tell. Lynx can't tell. Fi can't tell. Her secret is safe.'

'Yes. And then Seb Mulholland turns up with some more letters and asks an extortionate amount of money for them. And if she doesn't pay? Maybe he also threatens to reveal what he knows. And when he appears, she has a chance to poison him. One chance. A couple of crushed seeds from a yew berry and he's a dead man within an hour.' It all remained to be proved, of course, but time would solve that. 'I bet there's some in the garden.'

'She knows yew is poisonous.' Ashleigh's sympathy for Cody was still there, he could tell, but for once it wasn't over-riding her judgement. 'Tyrone saw her shouting at some poor woman with a toddler about not letting the kid play with the berries.'

The pieces were coming together. Now he had to think about the next step. 'Thanks, Chris. That's good work.' He closed off the call and pocketed his phone.

'How unlucky.' But Ashleigh was speaking ironically, not with any sympathy. 'Just when she reaches the height of her career, someone comes back to bite her. And you can see th deal. It wasn't even what they knew, but what she thougl they knew, what she was afraid of. Even Cody Wilder has conscience, it appears.'

It couldn't be much of a conscience if the guilt of on killing that no one would hold against her was gre enough to drive one person to suicide and kill three other If Owen's death was suicide. Jude still harboured doub about that.

'Lovely theory,' said Doddsy, with a sigh. 'One I wish I' come up with myself. But what we need now is somethin we can offer up as sufficient evidence to arrest her. And w don't have that. Unless there's something up at the cottag Do you reckon we've got enough to apply for a searc warrant?'

There was the audio monitoring. That was the most likel source of information. The relationship between Cody an Brandon was so close that whatever she'd done, he woul surely know about. 'We'll leave it for a day or so, shall we They won't be going anywhere.' And there was surely n one left for Cody to kill.

19

'At least we got through that without any more dead bodies.' Cody slammed the door on the cold wind and the outside world, most of all on the police activity that was still too obvious in the village. The morning walk on which she'd dragged them both hadn't helped to charm her conscience. She dropped to her knees in front of the fire and touched a match to the kindling that Brandon had laid before they left, watching for a moment as the warm, welcoming flames licked around moss and twigs, crept over the edges of the logs and took hold with a satisfying smell of pine resin. She got up.

'We sure did.' Brandon tossed his jacket onto the back of the sofa and strode across to stand beside her in front of the fireplace, thumbs tucked into his leather belt. Looking at him, Cody was reminded with a shiver of their father, and how he'd cracked the buckle of his belt on the kitchen table to bring silence whenever he wanted to speak. The terror had lasted until Brandon had become a man and brought their nightmare to an end but today the image of the devil, the clearest she'd seen him since the day of his death, flashed across her consciousness. Despite herself, she backed away.

She passed a hand across her forehead. You always had

to look forward, but if she could do one thing differently, it would have been to safeguard her sanity by keeping a lifetime of silence about the brutality of the relationship she'd had with her father. The man who should have supported and protected her had almost become her destroyer and if it wasn't for Brandon's wickedness she'd have gone under. Evil had conquered evil and she'd always be grateful. 'What is it?'

'I've been speaking to Laura. She reckons it's time for me to go home.'

The clock showed that it was one o'clock. The police had cleared out of the village but Jude Satterthwaite must know more than he'd let on, and had left a uniformed officer sitting in a patrol car on the edge of the village where she could see him. No doubt they'd claim he was there for her reassurance but she interpreted it as a deliberate power play from a man who thought he was smarter than she. 'Oh, you can try, I suppose. But they won't let either of us leave until they've found out who it is.' And that was a good thing. She'd have the benefit of his company and when he went, he'd surely miss her more than he thought he would. There was no relationship as strong as theirs, forged in the heat of interdependency and mutual self-defence.

'I know that. But they'll pick the dude up soon and then we can go.'

'Since you're so smart, you might want to tell me who it is.'

He shrugged. 'Must have been one of those wild guys down by the water. Or those crazies in the shop.'

Cody thought of the Gordons. She knew what went on in the mind of a killer and what she saw when she looked at them was stupidity, naivety and uncharacteristic hatred but she didn't see murder. 'The police won't let you go for a while, I imagine. Even if they do, it would be nice if you stayed. You should get Laura over. We could meet, be friends.' For the first time in a while there was something to be enthusiastic about. She could check out Brandon's intended and if she thought the woman was a snowflake she'd warn her off. Brandon needed a strong partner. 'A short break in the Lakes. Since she works so hard. Though not as hard as she'll have to work on the ranch. Is she ready for that?'

'We ain't gonna stay there. I've got a buyer for the place. And Laura doesn't need the money. We're going to live in LA.' A pause, during which something about the tone of his voice caught at her and caused her to look up before the blow. 'That's why I maybe won't be able to come over any more.'

'What do you mean?' She understood she might have to share Brandon but she couldn't survive without him. 'Then I'll come over and see you.'

'No, honey. I'm afraid not.'

'Why not? I'm your sister. Think of everything we've been through together.' *Think of the violence and the desperation and the death. Think of that night in the snowstorm. Think of what only we know.* 'I need you.'

A slight curl in his lip hinted at coming rejection. 'And Laura needs me more. Her job comes first.'

'Her job? You mean it's about money?' At his shrug of dismissal, their father's instant and irrational fury erupted in her veins. 'Are you bored of living alone on that ranch with no one but the wolves and the coyotes for company? I can understand that. But going to be a gigolo for an heiress?

You should be ashamed of yourself.' Her breath came sharp and a wail of desolation shivered inside her, but the anger overrode it. Appalled by it, she was nevertheless unable to hold it back. 'I know you only care about me.' Just as she only cared about him, as Dorothy had only cared about William. 'If it's money you want, I'll give it to you.'

A muscle in his face twitched at the insult. 'This isn't about dollars. One day you'll fall in love with someone. I hope you do. Then you'll understand. You have to sacrifice things for them. And I can't live in that place on my own.'

'Oh, it's your conscience.' She controlled herself, knowing she was in a battle with an enemy whose powers she didn't know. A wrong word and she could lose him. 'You're going to LA,' she pursued, hoping she'd misunderstood the finality of his tone. 'I can come and see you in there and you can come and see me in New York. Bring your wife. It'll be swell.' Because she wasn't going to let him go.

He fidgeted, picking his phone out of his pocket, looking down at it, turning it over in his hand. 'No, honey. I don't think so.'

'Why not? Doesn't your new girl approve of me?'

His silence answered the question.

'Are you a yellow-livered coward?' she challenged him. His betrayal was bad enough, but the fact that he was pandering to the misjudgement of some woman who'd never met her hurt more. 'Really? You're cutting me off because some girl who's never met me has decided the media are telling the truth about me?' But the media probably were telling the truth. Controversy was one thing, and courting it was supping with the devil, so in the end she had no grounds r complaint but for all that, Brandon had no right to walk way. 'Why didn't you tell her what I'm really like?'

'It ain't like that.'

'Then what is it like?'

'She's got plans. Big plans. She's a smart girl and she ants to change the world.'

'You mean she wants to go into politics?'

'Cody. Honey. You gotta understand.'

'Understand what? That I'm not good enough for her?' ut she did understand. No one would support a candidate hose political ambitions would be sunk the moment meone set to looking over her sister-in-law's Twitter feed. hat you've chosen someone so small-minded she can't ear someone who has a different opinion?'

Silence.

'Brandon Wilder. You've shacked yourself up with a leeding heart liberal and you're doing what she tells you? nd giving me up, after all we've been through?'

'Quit me the political lecturing, Cody.' He thrust the hone deep in his pocket and stood there, scowling and nmovable, daring her to come closer. 'You won't change y mind.'

'We've been through too much together for you to walk way.' Her heart jumped up to her throat in fear at the ought of isolation, of bearing their secret alone. 'We stood y one another. I was always there for you. You were there r me. I need you now and I'll need you again. And you've st your head over some stupid little rich girl—'

'She isn't a stupid kid. She's a smart, tough cookie, like u. She's president of MarCo. A tech firm in Silicon Valley.

That's why I'm moving to her. She's got prospects and have a ranch. You can sell that.'

Had he taken leave of his senses? She laughed out lou 'It's the only life you've ever known. Have you ever eve been to LA? You're a cowboy, a real one. The city wi drive you mad. What if there are kids? Will you be the or staying at home wiping their butts and cleaning their snott noses? Will you be the dude with the plastic smile, thr steps behind her? Is that your ambition? To hold the Bib at your wife's inauguration?'

'Guess it is,' he said, through thin lips, 'if that's what sui us best.'

She stared. 'Not so much the wild man, eh? Not s independent after all. When a woman whistles—'

'I always came when you whistled.'

Until then. She walked over and stood as close to him a she dared, toe to toe so they almost touched and his breat was hot on her forehead. When she looked up at him h eyes were as hard as the diamonds that were rumoured t lie under the ranch. What they'd done in the bleak Wyomir midwinter lay between them like a sword in a stone, waitir for one of them to draw it and strike. He knew as well as sl did that neither of them could survive the truth unscathe 'Then listen to me now. No one tells me what to do. I dor stay away when any man tells me to, any more than I con running when they call.'

'I'm not telling you what to do. I'm telling you what I' going to do.'

Love made people soft, or so she'd always thought, b Brandon was different. Love had tempered his roughne and steeled his resolve. 'You've got to choose. Take a risk on your wife's political career. Let her make a sacrifice for you.'

'Honey,' he said, pretending to sigh. 'I know you're stressed. I know it's a shock. I can forgive you the overreaction. But I'm in love with Laura. Do you begrudge me that?'

'If you're that much in love with her, why are you here?' More silence, threatening her. 'In your own interests, obviously.'

'In our interests,' he corrected her. 'I didn't want to cut you off. I didn't want to make a big deal. I want us to part as friends. But there wasn't a right moment.'

There never would be. She drew in a long deep breath, waiting for the sting in this scene that she knew would come. He was as ruthless as she and once he ceased to be her only ally, he'd quickly become her deadly enemy. 'What do you want from me?'

'I want you to destroy your letters.'

'My letters?' She stared at him in stupefaction. 'Jeez, Brandon. Those letters are all I have left.'

'You're hiding them. You told me so. But hiding them isn't good enough. I want you to destroy them.'

When the shock passed and misunderstanding turned to clarity, Cody burst out laughing. Stepping away from him, she crossed to the bureau and, taking her keys from her pocket she opened the drawer and took them out. 'Here.' The packet was reassuring between her fingers, but it came with a twinge of anger. She should have given Seb the money and taken the rest of Dorothy's letters. He'd still have died but she'd have had a legal claim on them and now they belonged to someone else.

Resisting the temptation to fan them out and wave them in front of him, she treated them with appropriate care, sliding them out of the packet. 'See for yourself. There's nothing in here of interest to you. Pretty damning evidence for the whole Wordsworth family, perhaps, but nothing you need to worry about.'

He took them but didn't look at them, and as he did so she realised he'd already seen them, that the person who'd disturbed them in the drawer of the bureau was no intruder but Brandon himself. 'Where are the others? The ones I wrote you when you went to Laramie.'

'The ones you wrote me and boasted about what you did to Daddy?' The emphasis on the last word was sick with mockery. 'Those ones?'

'I couldn't find them in New York. Tell me where you put them, and if you don't burn them, I will. Because if those ever come out—'

He'd been to her apartment? Wheedling his way in through the concierge, no doubt. She snatched three sharp breaths like a boxer throwing a series of punches, and regrouped. 'Oh God. You thought I was talking about those? No, it was Dorothy's letters I care about.'

'Give me the Laramie letters.'

He clenched a fist, just like their father had done, until what was left of Cody's courage curdled in her heart but she dared to stand up to Brandon in a way she'd never done to an older enemy. 'Why? Because you think your sweet little liberal will throw you over in favour of her career, huh? Doesn't she love you for what you are, Brandon? Is this all about what you're pretending to be? If she knew the truth about what you are, you'd be finished.'

His eyes narrowed, lips folded together, and in his cold anger the resemblance to their father was complete. 'Yes. And so will you. You think you'll survive in that shark pool you call academia when you've given all the people who hate you a reason to destroy you? We're in this together, Cody. Give me my letters and I'll destroy them. It's best for both of us.'

Her heart hammered in her chest. He was like his father in another way, too. He was a fool. 'You're a simple soul, aren't you? Don't you know me better than that? I got rid of them.'

'What?' When he clenched his fist again the memory weakened her, and she stepped back out of his reach.

'Why would I keep them? You're right. They'd have damned us both.' The speculation had been bad enough, and it was only the community's fear and hatred of their father that had saved them from too close an investigation. 'Do you think I could risk someone finding them?'

'Why didn't you tell me?'

'Why should I?' It had been the obvious thing to do.

'Because then I wouldn't have—' His face was white, beads of sweat standing out on his brow. 'I wouldn't have worried about you.'

He should have branded the word LIAR on his forehead with one of his own cattle irons. 'You wouldn't have come to see me, either.' Now she understood that her triumph had been irrelevant to him and he'd had no intention of coming to her talk. His only care was for himself. 'You'd have slunk off to California and I'd never have seen you again. But you won't get away with it.'

'You're a bitch.' His voice rose. Even the intonation was an echo from the mountains of hell.

'And you,' she cursed him in defiant reply, 'are just like your daddy. Go back to your pretty little Democrat. But always look over your shoulder, baby. Because one day I might get angry with you and then… I'll tell the world what we did and we'll go down together.'

She had the satisfaction of seeing a light go out in his eyes, an acknowledgement of the power she'd always have over him, but his fist clenched around Dorothy's letters. 'Be careful with those! They're precious!'

His eyes met hers for a second, then he laughed. 'All's fair, Cody. You won't tell. You've got too much to lose. But I'll teach you never to threaten me.'

'No!' She was too slow. Instinct, and an understanding of how his vengeful mind worked, how he could be faithful to only one person at a time, showed her what he was going to do but Brandon the cowboy was as swift as a snake and as strong as a steer. Her snatch for the Wordsworth letters connected only with thin air. With his right arm, he blocked her way and with the left he thrust the papers into the fire.

'Stop it!' She struggled against him, but he held her back, dragging her away from the hearth leaving a trailing boot poking the letters into the heart of the blaze. Flames licked around the edges of the paper, gobbled them up. 'No!' Her moan, another echo from the past, cried out against her own impotence, and just as she had done then, she closed her eyes in submission. Brandon's strong hands clung to her wrists like unbreakable chains while the fire hissed and sighed and crackled, and then it was done.

He released her with a laugh of contempt and, ignoring him, she stepped past him to the fire. Reaching for the poker, she tried to pull the last of the letters out, in vain. Mary

Vordsworth's signature disintegrated into flakes of ash and ie evidence of an incestuous relationship went with it.

Still clutching the poker, she turned to face him. One wipe and she could hurt him, but the damage he'd inflicted pon her with that rash, angry action deserved so much iore than pain. Her brain was already calculating her evenge. 'Get out.'

'Gladly.' Backing away from her without taking his eyes ff her, he reached behind him for his coat, flung over the ack of a chair.

'And don't come back. If you do, I'll kill you. I swear it.'

'You'll keep your mouth shut, Cody Wilder, or I'll kill ou.'

'You'll regret choosing her.'

'I regret standing by you. I should have let the old man o what he wanted. I should have let him finish teaching ou the lesson he started. Because you're a bitch and you eed to be broken.'

Lifting the poker, she moved towards him, but he read o menace in it. He turned his back on her as he left, as if show the extent of his contempt, and the temptation to nash it down and split his skull threatened to overwhelm er, but she resisted it. 'You didn't come here to see me at l, did you? You came to make sure your secret was safe.'

He carried on putting on his coat.

'You came because I told you Owen was threatening ie. You thought he'd found out about Pop, didn't you? nd you killed Lynx because you thought he had those tters. And Fi, because she knew.' Seb, too, because he ad the misfortune to have a connection with that past, a iotographic memory that might be triggered by the wrong thing. 'But you were wrong! The letters I was talking abo were the Wordsworth letters, not the freaking Laram ones!'

He stalked towards the hall.

'And Owen.' She ran after him as he flung open the do and disappeared down the path. 'I don't understand. Ho did you manage to kill Owen?' But his tall figure disappeare down the path and out of sight down Coffin Lane.

Numb, Cody turned back to the hearth. The fragi notepaper had survived for over two hundred years a dusty box of books, but it had no chance against t chemistry of fire and air. The last gasp of the Wordswor letters disappeared up the chimney, final victim of Brandon villainous acts of self-defence.

She'd made so many mistakes, either trusting Brand too much, or not trusting him enough, keeping tho treasured letters with her as a talisman instead of leavi them somewhere where they would have been safe.

Violence bred violence, one betrayal only led to anoth Whatever it cost her, Brandon would pay.

Jude was thinking about heading down to the cante for a sandwich, and then going to his car to retrieve t box of cakes he'd picked up on the way in and releasi them to the hungry hordes in celebration of his birthd Ashleigh, at least, had remembered and shuffled a ca among the papers on his desk. He paused to smile acro the room to her and saw she was taking a call and looki particularly interested in whatever she was hearing. Alwa alert to that kind of thing, he waited until she flicked c the phone and crossed the incident room towards him. 'That was Tyrone.'

'Any update?' He frowned. Since the previous meeting he couldn't quite rid himself of the frustration that came with his certainty. If Cody was the killer, he wanted her arrested, but if he couldn't justify it to himself with the evidence, there was no way he could justify it to someone else.

'Not exactly. But it appears there's been some sort of domestic fallout up at Coffin Lane.'

Jude groaned.

'It's all right.' She was quick to reassure him. 'No one's hurt. But apparently Brandon stormed out of the cottage in some kind of huff and Cody was standing on the doorstep shouting at him.'

With an eye for the importance of the smallest thing, Tyrone was going to be an excellent policeman one day. Jude sat back and chewed the end of his pen. 'Any idea what she was shouting?'

'Something about Owen.'

Jude stayed still for just a moment longer. Getting the audio monitoring looked to be a good call. The only pity was that he'd have to go through so many hoops to find out what had been said. 'Bear with me a moment.' He pushed back his chair and strode out of the office and along the corridor to Detective Superintendent Groves's office, rehearsing what he would say. Groves was increasingly tetchy with his male colleagues these days, almost as if he had to compensate for being particularly careful in what he said to his female ones, and Jude, who he'd never particularly liked, was accustomed to being on the sharp end of his superior officer's tongue.

The door to the office was closed. He stood there for a moment in perplexity. For all Groves's faults, he was available whenever he was required and punctilious about letting anyone who wanted to know where he might be. Jude turned back and headed into the office again.

Something had happened in the moment of his absence. There was an air of anticipation about the room and a quick glance showed him that Aditi Desai was looking as if all her Christmases had come at once. He crossed over to where Doddsy and Ashleigh, heads together, were looking at best taken aback. 'Have I missed something?'

'I'll say.' Doddsy gestured towards his desk. 'Check your emails.'

Jude sat down, flipped up the screen.

Notification re D/Supt Groves.

He opened it up.

For information. D/Supt Damon Groves has taken leave for an indefinite period. All inquiries will be directed to…

Jude stopped reading. He could quite see why the incident room was rippling with merriment, because he'd seen for himself, once he'd started to look, just what kind of a negative influence the man had had on those he worked with, but it left him with a major headache. Without Groves's authorisation, he had no way of accessing the audio recordings from Cody Wilder's cottage. 'Great.' He managed a smile for Doddsy, who had been so quietly hard done by, and he had no sympathy for Groves, but it didn't solve his problem. Questioning Cody would have to wait, after all.

Ashleigh drifted over and perched on the edge of his desk in a familiar, Friday-evening kind of way. 'Yeah, the place will be a whole lot nicer to work in.'

'I imagine so.'

'But?' She could sense there was something wrong.

'Nothing.' Intelligence was intelligence, and it had to be controlled. He had no idea whether anyone was listening in live to the goings on at Coffin Lane, or whether they'd just skim through the audio later for anything interesting. It was the mention of Owen that bothered him, something that sounded as if it might be the tail-end of a conversation that had ended in acrimony and accusations.

But accusations of what?

'Jude.' Ashleigh had been speaking to him and he hadn't been listening. 'I'm going down to the canteen. Come down with me and get something to eat. It's way after two o'clock.'

He pushed back his chair. 'Sorry. I'm just trying to get my head around something. About what Cody might have said about Owen. As far as I know, Brandon didn't even know Owen, and he couldn't have killed him.'

She pulled a face. 'I know. It's weird. I remember when Raven was telling the cards for me, and she was so determined to point out the strange man who'd travelled a long way. I wonder if she tried that trick on Cody, too.'

'Hardly. She'll be even more sceptical than I am. And anyway, Brandon wasn't there when Cody died.'

'No. But do you know something? I don't think everything Raven told us was a lie.'

Jude sat still for a moment, like a cat outside a mouse

hole, trying to sort out the truth from the lies. He was as bad as Ashleigh when he'd criticised her so heavily for her intuition and now had fallen victim to it himself. No matter how obviously the evidence contradicted him, he couldn't believe Owen Armitstead had committed suicide, but neither Cody nor Brandon, the obvious candidates, could have killed him.

Or was it possible? Could Cody have accused Brandon of murder?

He reached for the list of internal phone numbers that lurked in his desk drawer and dialled the Intelligence Unit. 'Jude Satterthwaite here. DCI.' He rolled his eyes at Ashleigh. The Intelligence Unit were the butt of every joke but they got their own back. They controlled information. 'I need your help.'

'Oh, hey Jude.' Someone laughed. 'Let me know what we can do for you.' The voice echoed, as though whoever had answered had flicked him onto speaker and introduced him to the rest of the team for some light entertainment.

'You're monitoring a residential property for me in Coffin Lane in Grasmere. I need to know what happened there this afternoon.'

There was a pause, a flutter of laughter. Was it possible they had so little to do on a Friday afternoon that they had time to mess him around? 'I can't give out classified information. I don't have your name down.'

'Detective Superintendent Groves put the application in, at my request.'

'Fine. Get him to give us a call and we'll pass on what we know.'

'He's off on leave.' Jude was shaking his head. 'I can't get old of him. I need your input. I need to know what's going n in that cottage, and in particular I need to know what ind of a conversation went on there this morning.'

'Matter of life and death, is it?'

'It might be.'

'Right. Then I'm prepared to talk to your Super, if you an get hold of him. But I can't let you know without his uthorisation. More than my job's worth. Sorry, mate.' And ie call ended, to general laughter.

They were right, that was the worst of it. It was Groves ho was authorised to request surveillance and only roves who could take control of the information it roduced. Now he was out of the game. Finding someone se sufficiently senior to access the recordings would take me and time wasn't on Jude's side.

So he'd have to change his tactics. He pushed back his iair and walked over to Chris's desk. 'I need your help.'

'Sure.'

'Yes. Find out if it was foggy in Chicago last week. And id out if any flights were cancelled or diverted.'

He walked back to the desk where Doddsy had abandoned hat he was doing and come to join Ashleigh. They were oth looking at him as if they sensed a crisis.

'I need to know what Cody and Brandon talked about is morning.' He addressed them directly. 'I'm not getting iything form those so-called intelligence guys. So I think I'm oing to take a flyer and go down and haul the Wilders in.'

'But the evidence...' Doddsy shrugged.

'I know. But I'm pretty sure now that I know what happened. wasn't Cody. She didn't know. That's why she's gone to eces. But now we know what happened in Wyoming. We

know the two of them are probably guilty as hell of killin
their father. We know she wants it kept quiet. But what if h
wants it kept quiet too, but he thinks she'll tell?'

'He certainly wouldn't get the sympathy vote that sh
might, if it came to a trial.' Ashleigh shook her head.

'No. And I'm prepared to bet Owen knew, too. Carele
talk from Cody, but it happens. Don't forget – they we
lovers.'

Chris crossed the room at a rapid walk. 'Weather repor
from Chicago for the past week. Good weather for th
time of year. Good visibility. Clear, frosty. No delays o
cancellations.'

'Okay,' Ashleigh said, her voice full of doubt. 'Then ho
is it possible? He says he was delayed by fog—'

'Yes. So the next thing I want you to do, Chris, is chec
flights from UK airports – Manchester is the most like
one – to Chicago on the day that Owen died and the da
after. I'm prepared to bet that Brandon Wilder was o
one.' He turned to Doddsy and Ashleigh. 'Let's get down
Grasmere.'

From the window, Cody could see the police car. All she ha
to do was call the man in and tell him everything, but wh
would be the price? They'd think she was the killer. She w
too tired, and she couldn't face the police, couldn't bear t
prospect of having to relive those years of abuse again, fi
in an interview room and then in a court. She sat down o
the sofa and stared at the ashes.

For his betrayal of her trust and the destruction
Dorothy's letters, as much as the deaths that lay at his do

Brandon deserved the worst she could do to him and the only thing she could think of was to pay him back in his own currency, debased though it might be. He spoke the language of hate and revenge and a Pyrrhic victory over him, just like that she'd achieved over her father, was the best she could hope for. She'd leave him regretting the day he'd turned on her.

And he'd come after her, and then what would happen?

It was after half two and the light was already fading, but it would be early in the working day in Los Angeles. Reaching for her phone, she ran a quick Google search and dialled. 'Can I speak to Ms Maracado? No, it's a personal call. My name's Wilder. Cody Wilder.'

On the other side of the world, strangers passed her in silence through a series of screenings. 'Laura Maracado speaking.'

'Hi.' Cody managed to stop herself calling her future sister-in-law 'honey'. It wouldn't do to patronise her when there was a chance she might be at least as formidable as Cody herself. 'I've been chatting with Brandon and he told me your news. Congratulations.'

'Why, thank you, Cody.' There was definitely reservation in the voice. It had taken the saintly, virtue-signalling Laura a long time to decide to speak to her.

'It'll be cool to meet you but I'm afraid I'm not going to be on the west coast for a while. So I thought I'd call and introduce myself.'

'How kind.' The woman gave nothing away, fencing Cody's charm aside. How much had Brandon told her about the killings in Grasmere? Anything?

'Brandon and I have always been close.' Cody made

herself comfortable, stockinged feet stretched out to warm herself against the last embers of the Wordsworth letters. The bigger the betrayal the sweeter the revenge, and the hush of the hissing flames reminded her of a fundamental truth. Cold? No, the hotter you served your revenge the better. 'I'm so delighted he's found someone who deserves him. Someone who will benefit from his fierce loyalty.'

'I'm sure we—'

'I've been thinking a lot, recently, about our childhood. Such good memories. Just Brandon and me, Mom and Dad. We saw no one for months at a time. When there was no one else, he was there for me. Imagine how that was for two young impressionable teenagers just learning about themselves.'

There was silence from the other end of the line. So the woman was still listening. Now was the moment to press home the advantage. 'Of course he'll have told you everything. You're his soulmate. And of course you'll have forgiven him.'

'Forgiven him?'

'Yes.' Reckless in the dark, Cody tugged at her ponytail and careered towards disaster. 'In such isolation, it was inevitable that we were closer than we should have been. What choice did we have?' Pulling a strand of hair free and twining it around her finger, she snatched a moment to reflect. How far should she go? The question wasn't how much she wanted Brandon to pay for his vandalism, the destruction of the letters, but how much she was prepared to suffer to enable it. 'I knew he'd have explained it, and I knew you'd understand. It took me a long time, but I've forgiven him for the way he took advantage of me, and I know you will, too.'

The silence from LA stretched into half a minute, during which Cody tried to envisage the expression on her future sister-in-law's face. The picture on the company website had shown a steely brunette with fake smile and a taste for good cosmetic surgery. 'Life was hard, and you know how it is. You have to do hard things to survive, things that you wouldn't do in other circumstances. The world won't always excuse that, and I know that's true for some of the things Brandon did. But you will.'

'What things?' There was a sharp edge to Laura's voice.

Oh, this would test her love. 'You can't blame Brandon. Our daddy was a violent man. It wasn't strictly self-defence, of course, but under the circumstances you can't blame him. If Brandon hadn't killed him, he'd sure as hell have killed Brandon. So when they were out on the ranch one day and a storm was coming, Brandon drove away and left him.'

'This is an outrageous allegation.' So, Laura Maracado was a fighter. Cody smiled. 'How dare you try and poison my mind against my fiancé? He warned me what you're like.'

'It's the truth, honey. I know, because I helped him. When he came back without Daddy, we covered it up. I drove the jeep somewhere else and he followed and brought me back. So I'm sure you'll be fine about it, huh? As long as you keep on the right side of him. Because you'll find out he's a mean man when he's crossed.' As Fi and Lynx and Seb, and maybe even Owen, had discovered.

A soft click on the line, followed by the long bleep of a closed-down conversation. Laying the phone down, Cody stared into the fire. It was too late to change anything, now. Brandon had turned his back on her and he'd regret it for the rest of his life.

There would be a price to pay. She knew how he lashed out at those who crossed him. Their father's death had been understandable, justifiable, even, taking a life to save them both, but a man who had slaughtered so many people in the slenderest suspicions that they might endanger his interests wouldn't hesitate to kill the sister who cost him his fiancée.

And yet, and yet. She got to her feet and crossed to the window, staring out at the soft grey-green of Grasmere in its winter clothing. Smoke from the New Agers' campfires, from the chimneys of the village. A dragon's breath of mist from the surface of the lake.

What had she done? As her father's fury had alienated her, she'd learned the lesson of her upbringing, that only violence defeated violence. Hate and terror had taught her well, but if only he'd cared for her the way a father should have done, how different it would have been.

If she'd learned to trust people, she wouldn't be more devastated by the loss of half a dozen sheets of paper than she had been by the loss of Lynx, the one man who genuinely seemed to care for her. She wouldn't have been driven by that fatal impulse and lashed out at Brandon. Her father's wickedness had followed her after all, and Brandon too, a shadow from which neither of them could ever escape. Even William had no words for that.

As she sank into a chair by the ashes of Dorothy's letters and waited for the breaking storm of Brandon's retaliation, she thought of too many lost lives, of Lynx, of Owen and Seb and Fi, and grieved for them all. In the gathering darkness she understood at last just how great her tragedy was and, leaning forward in the chair, she buried her head in hands and gave way to tears.

20

That's Chris.' Jude looked down at the message on his phone as Ashleigh turned the car off the road through rasmere and up towards Coffin Lane through the growing ırkness. 'Do you want to get out and see what Charlie and yrone have to say, and I'll give him a call?'

'Sure.' She pulled the Mercedes up, too sharply, choking to a stalled stop so that he winced. The two uniformed ficers had driven up to the cottage and were standing ıtside, waiting for instructions. In the headlights Jude ould read Tyrone's impatience and guessed that Charlie Fry, ith his wise head and years of experience, had struggled to ep the youngster back while they waited for instructions.

A third car, with Doddsy at the wheel, joined the backlog ogging the lane. Another vehicle was on its way to help ıd Brandon. Was that enough? Watching as Doddsy and shleigh engaged in earnest conversation with the two ıiformed policemen, Jude dialled Chris's number. 'Okay. hat bad news do you have for me this time?'

'You were right.'

'About what, exactly?'

'Brandon. He flew into Chicago from Manchester ernight on Wednesday and got the next flight back again.

And when I took the search a bit further back, I discovere he'd flown into Manchester from Denver on the Tuesday. S it's pretty clear what happened now, isn't it?'

'Yes. Looks like it. You might want to see if you can tra his movements while he was here. Taxi firms are a goo place to start, but he may have got the train to Oxenholm or Penrith and then a taxi.' If Brandon had flown in Manchester to kill Owen and then back again to establis an alibi, it shouldn't be hard to discover his whereabout 'Thanks. I'll speak to you later.' He ended the call, but still stayed for a moment, in thought.

Outside in the darkness, Ashleigh and Doddsy engage in intense conversation. Jude opened the car door and g out, the cold wind catching at him. Cody was ashamed nothing and if she hid things it was from spite. Her ta of abuse at the hands of her father might make her figurehead of a certain section of the feminist moveme and, if she played it right, would enhance rather tha damage her reputation. If the Grasmere murders were hide the Wyoming killing, she might have had a hand them, but he'd seen for himself how much it traumatis her. Surely it wasn't something worth killing again for?

'Cottage is empty,' Charlie was saying. 'I never saw I Wilder leave, but she must have gone out through the bac The back door was open.'

Jude's breath shortened. 'Where's her brother?'

'I lost him down in the village,' Tyrone was saying, h voice urgent, his breath crystallising on the cold air. I didn want to seem too obvious, so I wasn't right on his heels. H must have stepped off the path somewhere. Down by t river, I think. Charlie told me not to get too close.'

'Quite right,' Ashleigh said, intervening to soothe a disagreement before it brewed any more. 'It looks as though he's dangerous and he may be armed.'

Charlie folded his arms over his broad chest. 'He didn't come back to the cottage that I saw. But that doesn't mean he isn't around.'

'So she isn't in the cottage. Any signs of violence?'

'None. But she left in a hell of a hurry. No coat, no bag. Even left her phone.'

'We need more support, then. We need to find her.' Doddsy's anxiety was evident.

'And him.' Of the two of them, Brandon was the more immediate problem, the one who might kill again. 'Get onto that, Doddsy, would you? I'm going to take a look at the cottage.'

Leaving the others behind, Jude picked his way with care around the side of the building. Charlie was too smart to have touched anything but he'd switched the light on. Brushing his way past the overhanging branch of a yew tree, Jude stepped into the kitchen. Cody's waxed jacket hung on the back of a chair. He made his way into the living room where the last embers of the fire glowed red and flakes of ash spread on the rug in front of it. Paper, and very old paper, too.

He recalled the way she'd held those letters, how much they'd meant to her. It was beyond belief that she'd destroyed them herself. Staring with a frown, he was distracted by the pinging of the phone she'd left on the arm of her chair. When he picked it up the screen sprang into life, a notification of a text. Brandon.

Why don't you answer me, you bitch? I'm coming for you.

Pocketing the phone, Jude walked swiftly back round to the front of the house.

Cody couldn't think straight. Brandon had tipped her over the edge and she was out of control, so that her body shook and she stuffed a clenched fist into her mouth to stop herself whimpering like an animal. She'd known he was capable of killing but their father's death, done at a distance, had seemed remote enough to be a sin of omission rather than commission. The violent murders of Lynx, Fi and Seb, who hadn't threatened him directly, were different, the product of her own obsession so that they lay as much at her door as his and she could see no way of atoning. If she challenged Brandon, he'd kill her, and she would deserve it. *I'm so sorry*, she mouthed to the ghosts of the dead, *so sorry*!

The long shadow of their father, stretching out from the canyon where the wolves and coyotes must have picked his body clean, snuffed out reason. If she called the police they might not be there in time. She didn't know where Brandon was, only that the fear of him was in every shadow that surrounded her. Scrambling through the hedge into the woodland at the back of the cottage garden, she picked an uncertain way down towards the road, keeping close to the trunks of the leafless trees, moving as swiftly as she dared to do between them. Beneath her feet the fallen branches snapped like her father's sun-bleached bones.

The lights of two cars, in one of which she recognised Jude Satterthwaite, moved through the village and crawled up Coffin Lane. Unbidden, Wordsworth came into her head as she rolled his lines around her brain in search of help. *My apprehensions come in crowds; I dread the rustling of the grass; the very shadows of the clouds, Have power to shake me as they pass.*

The shadow that moved in the woods ahead of her was no cloud and no ghost. It was retribution, in jeans and cowboy boots.

Brandon would love to think he had her on the run. She dropped to her knees, crawled through the mud and the wet leaf mould, resisting the panic that curled in her gut, the kaleidoscope of images in her brain that made sudden appalling sense. She could only just have missed seeing him kill Fi. He must have lured the woman up to the cottage, killed her and got in through the window of his room while Cody was in the kitchen, pretending to be sound asleep when she'd left the cottage. If she'd been a few minutes earlier, she'd have caught him in the act and then she'd have been dead too.

Crawling in the mud in humiliation was no more that she deserved. Her mouth dry, with that old, remembered terror, she fought to regain some kind of perspective. *A timely utterance gave that thought relief, And I again am strong*. She was a clever woman. She didn't panic. Out in the blood-chilling isolation of Wyoming she'd been far more vulnerable, much further from safety than here.

But the police, so close, might as well be a million miles away if Brandon was closer, knowing it didn't matter to him what the consequences were of his actions. She hadn't thought of that as she'd deliberately doomed his hopes for the future with that call to Laura, and sent their lives spiralling from one act of revenge to the next.

At the bottom of the hill the wall marked the edge of

Red Bank Road. She didn't dare climb over it, but kept crawling. Icy mud oozed through her fingers and a wet branch snagged her jumper. Rhododendrons. Someone's garden. She shivered.

A dog barked.

Despite her desperation, despite her need for silence, she couldn't suppress a whimper of fear. The rhododendrons gave way to a lawn and a driveway that wound to a house, out of sight. Five yards away the drive opened onto the road.

She ran, launching herself up like a sprinter from the blocks, over the road and over the wall, throwing herself to the soft ground without regard to bumps and bruises. Now she was a hundred yards from the police car at the top of Coffin Lane, probably a hundred more from the blue lights that flashed outside the garden centre.

That close.

She crawled along the wall, followed as it turned towards the lake, and scrambled over it and into the New Agers' field.

'No sign of either of them?' Jude had left Ashleigh struggling to turn the Mercedes in the narrow and crowded lane, and was calling in to the police officers in the village as he and Doddsy set off down towards the village. Charlie Fry was reversing the police car down the lane ahead of her.

'Not in the village. They may be in the woods.'

'Keep looking. I've got more support coming. The male suspect is dangerous and may be armed.' Jude closed off e call. 'It's Cody I'm most worried about. She could be ıywhere.'

'She's done a runner,' Doddsy said, his tone fringed with dgement. 'That must be what it is. So maybe she did kill em after all.'

'I don't buy that.'

'There's a police car sitting in the village. She can see it. ıe's meant to see it. Why the hell wouldn't she think to go ɔwn and ask for help?'

Jude thought back to the text, the sheer vindictiveness of e ashes in the grate. 'She's terrified of her brother.'

'She must be, if she doesn't think we can be trusted to ːlp her when she needs it.'

Ignoring him, Jude carried on down the lane. The police r came behind them and stopped and Tyrone got out. Vant me to go and join in the search?'

'Jude!'

Jude spun round. A figure burst out through the gate into e New Agers' field, one he recognised immediately. Storm. something up?'

'Your woman from up the hill.' Storm tossed a savage ok in the direction of the cottage. 'She's down in our mp, claiming her brother wants to kill her. Not that I ame him.'

'Where is he? Did she say?'

'In the woods somewhere. She swears he's following her, ıt the woman's in such a state I wouldn't believe her. I ɔn't care. Just come and take her away before she brings any more trouble than she already has.'

'Stay here.' Jude took a couple of steps down the lane.

'No.' Storm scowled at him. 'I don't give a damn abo Cody Wilder but I've got Raven to think about.'

'Whatever.' There wasn't time to argue. Jude turned the two policemen still in the car. 'Get down into the villa and see if you can find him. Doddsy. Tyrone. You cor down with me. We'll get to Cody and make sure she's saf

'I'll come too.' Ashleigh had parked the car at the botto of the lane. 'You might need me.'

His instinct was to send her away, to make sure she ke safe, but he couldn't do that. 'Yes.' Cody or Raven mig welcome Ashleigh's input.

He sprinted the last few yards down to the field, wi Storm beside him and the others in his wake. 'It's ok Dr Wilder. Jude Satterthwaite here.' The mud squelch beneath his feet as he slowed to cross the field. 'I'm going take you somewhere safe.'

'Safe? That bitch isn't safe!'

Raven screamed. A dark figure vaulted the low wall fro the woods and ran across the field into the dancing lig cast by the campfire.

Brandon. 'Where the hell is she? Who's hiding her?' I kicked at the campfire and it flared up. 'Where is she? here?' Bending to snatch up a branch, he touched it Raven's weaving tent. 'Burn, Cody Wilder. Burn!'

Jude had begun running again but the tent flared into l ahead of him, forcing him around it. From behind it, fro the depths of Lynx's tent, Cody's voice burst out into t night. She might be scared but she faced her fear. 'I'm ov here. What's the matter, Brandon? Can't you understa how life works? If you destroy someone's life, they'll destr yours. It's karma. Take me on if you want. If you dare!'

'Police!' Jude shouted at him. 'Brandon Wilder, stop where you are!'

He didn't, snatching up a second burning branch from the campfire, holding one in each hand like a fire eater paused to perform. 'You bitch! After everything I did to protect you! All the things you made me do! The people I killed to keep your secret!'

He lunged forward, touched one of the flaming sticks to the tent. The canvas flared up. Screaming as she emerged from its depths Cody jumped aside, the only place that was left to her – away from Brandon and away from Jude and Doddsy.

'No one come nearer!' Brandon's voice cracked in the smoke as he headed after her. 'No one comes near me until I've burned you on earth like you're going to burn in hell!'

Jude kept running but Doddsy, with a surprising turn of speed, got to Brandon first, shoulder to shoulder with the American and barging him away from his sister. The burning branches fell from Brandon's hand as they sprawled to the ground but Brandon shook himself free, scrambled up to his feet, and turned once more to his sister.

Smoke, flames, shadows and screams wove together. The brazier tipped over, spilling burning coals over the grass between Jude and Doddsy. 'I'll get her!' Doddsy shouted, and dived to reach Cody even as Brandon turned and broke for it.

Jude took him down, a bruising collision that sent the two of them rolling on the wet ground. Ashleigh appeared beside him as he pinned Brandon to the ground and Tyrone closed in, too. The handcuffs closed on Brandon's wrists and Jude, sitting back on his knees, turned to look for Cody and saw flame.

Time ran past him at two speeds. His own movements, pushing himself to his feet as fast as he could, were aeons slower than the split-second flaring of the burning brand that had somehow brushed his friend's jacket as he fell. 'Doddsy! Your coat! You're on fire!' And even as he hurdled the burning slick from the upturned brazier that lay in front of him, the flames took hold and Doddsy disappeared behind a sheet of orange.

21

'All right.' Jude was weary beyond endurance. It had been a long night, a long week, and duty had obliged him to carry on with the task of arresting and questioning Brandon and dealing with Cody when his mind was very much on other things. 'Dr Wilder, I realise you've had a traumatic day. Maybe we'll take a break.' The clock in the interview room in the police headquarters – surely wrong – showed it was half past eleven in the evening but when he checked his watch, he saw that it was right. Time had played tricks on him and the night had run away.

Cody, her face expressionless, shrugged. Somewhere behind those eyes he was sure she was fighting a battle with herself, with her caustic, outspoken nature. 'Do I go back to the cottage?'

'Probably a hotel would be better for the night. You could try the George.'

'Then perhaps you can get someone to sort me a taxi.' She stood up and picked up her jacket, standing for a second with it suspended from her forefinger. 'Chief Inspector. It does no good to say I'm sorry, though I am. But you have to believe me. I had no idea what Brandon did. No idea.'

She must have assured him of it a dozen times and he did

believe her, but he still struggled to sympathise. Having been dealt a hard hand in life wasn't, in his view, an excuse for making life hard for others. In the initial interview Brandon had confessed, and the detail of what he'd done and how he'd done it would come in the morning. He could have done without Cody's insistence on unloading her guilty soul and cursed himself for giving in to her. He checked his phone, for the twentieth time. 'Let's leave it until tomorrow, shall we? I still have other things to see to.'

Belatedly, Cody seemed to realise what they might be. She stopped in the middle of picking up her bag. 'Is Inspector Dodd all right?'

'I don't know.' If it was very bad news he'd have heard. He clung to that, turning away so that she didn't see the expression on his face. 'Let's resume tomorrow. It may not be me who speaks to you. It will probably be Sergeant O'Halloran.'

'You'll be speaking to my brother again?'

'Yes.' He'd take a positive delight in taking on Brandon, black as sin from the crown of his cowboy hat to the sunless depths of his soul.

'You'll have to tell me how he killed Owen. I can't work it out.' She paused to stare across the car park towards the town, deep in thought. 'For what it's worth I didn't play any part in killing my father, either, though I was glad he died. It was entirely Brandon's doing. I was complicit in hiding the evidence. No more.' She paused for a moment. 'No. I'll be honest. I'd likely have killed him, eventually. If he'd lived he would have destroyed me.'

There would be no proof of what had happened in the Wyoming storm, just one sibling speaking against the other d that was for someone else to sort out, on the other side the world. 'Tomorrow,' he said, like a sleepwalker.

'And one more thing. Despite what I told Laura aracado, I never slept with Brandon. It wasn't that sort relationship.'

He really didn't care. What Cody did, how she squared r conscience and her morality with the things she'd done d said, were no concern of his. All he was interested in as the extent to which she'd been involved in the deaths of ur innocent people, and it looked to him as if she was in e clear. 'As I say. We'll deal with it tomorrow.'

He held the door open for her and followed her down to ception, where Ashleigh was sitting waiting for him. She mped up when he came in and waited while he called a xi, furnished Cody with the number for a hotel and signed r out of the building that was officially closed. Only then d he dare ask. 'Any news?'

'You haven't heard? It's not good, Jude, but it's not bad her. He's badly burned but he's going to make it.'

'I'll need to go and see him. I'll need—'

'Not at this time of night.' Regardless of the setting, she t her arms round him.

He held onto her, pressing his cheek against her hair. 'd lost sight of her in the chaos of the evening, but she ıst have been picking up the slack. 'You didn't have to ait for me, but thanks.'

'I did have to.' She turned her face up to his and kissed n, quickly. 'I have your car. But I'd have waited anyway.'

'I'll run you home.' They'd had plans for dinner out and evening in, but those were left in the smoking embers of campsite.

'Thanks. We'll have an early start tomorrow.'

'You'll have to deal with Cody for me. She won't be a trouble. She'll be too busy making excuses and proving th she couldn't have done it.'

'I feel sorry for her. What a god-awful childhood s must have had. It's no wonder she can't handle people. W she any help?'

'Oh yes. She couldn't tell me enough.' He led the w across the car park to where the Mercedes stood in solita splendour, and took the key from Ashleigh's outstretch hand. 'If I'd had some of this detail a few days ago might never have been in this situation. She'd heard t washing machine early in the morning on the day Lynx w killed. Brandon had told her he couldn't sleep because was jetlagged, but my guess is he was washing the blo from his clothes. She thought she'd heard him movi around when Fi was killed, but she decided it was part a nightmare so she tried to forget about it. And he was t one who gave the chocolates to Seb. There were two le but he only offered one in the box. To make sure he g the right person, I imagine.' He'd never seen anyone distar themselves from someone they claimed to care about quite clinically as Cody had gone about cutting herself free fr Brandon. 'He confessed to her. It'll be on the tapes, if ever get to hear them.'

'And Owen?'

'Owen had threatened to ruin Cody a couple of tin and she'd told Brandon about it. I've no doubt he turned intending to silence the poor kid, and was lucky with opportunity to make it look like a suicide.' He start the car.

'He must have thought that was enough. And then he realised he had to kill again.'

'And again.'

They fell into silence. The smoke from the campfire lingered in Jude's nostrils as he drove back to Penrith, hands balanced still on the steering wheel, contemplating the evening as if at a distance. Light, shadows, screams would echo in his head when he slept. Doddsy hadn't screamed, only twisted in fear as he tried to shake off his flaming jacket. It was Storm who'd saved him, beating the flames down with his hands until the others had reached him.

He broke the silence. 'Is Storm all right?'

'Yes. He wouldn't go to hospital but I did manage to persuade him to see a doctor. The Gordons have taken the two of them in again. They're lovely people. So kind.'

Jude pulled the car up at the kerb outside the house she shared with Lisa. 'I thought they might have ditched this stupidity about modern medicine after that nonsense over the knife. He doesn't know how close he came to being charged with perverting the course of justice.'

'I did try and talk to Raven, and see if I could persuade her to go and see a doctor. She says she doesn't know how. But I tipped off Eliza Gordon, so maybe she can do something to help.' She unclipped her seatbelt but made no move to get out.

'Let's hope so.' He shared her reluctance to part. Ashleigh understood him, knew the strains of fighting other people's demons as well as your own.

'Tyrone was really upset about it, too.'

He nodded, watching her fingers playing on her lap. 'I'll talk to him tomorrow.'

'Jude. Why don't you come in?'

It was tempting, so tempting. 'We've a lot to do. It'll be an early start.'

'Yes, and it's been a bugger of a day. And your birthday, too. Don't tell me you want to go home alone.'

He rested his fingers on the steering wheel. His own company was the last thing he wanted but there was too great a risk in depending on other people. 'Thanks for the offer, but I still have things I need to do. I'll see you tomorrow.'

'Make sure you get something to eat,' she cautioned him, as if she were his mother.

'I've got two dozen cream cakes in the boot.' He managed a wry smile at the direction his birthday had taken.

'Oh, Jude.' She leaned towards him for a kiss that would have led them somewhere else on a better day, then opened the car door and got out. 'Call me if you need me. Any time.'

When he'd watched her safely into the house, he turned the car and drove back down the hill into Penrith. The mention of food reminded him how long it had been since he'd eaten and the cakes held no appeal, and he was reluctant to go back to his house because he knew what he'd find there. For the past few years, on his birthday, the postman had delivered an anonymous packet containing thirty chocolate coins in silver foil. He drove along Middlegate and up through the square, slotting the car into a space in Great Dockray.

There was a queue. Rather than join it, he paused outside to check the message that popped up just as he parked. Chris.

Update on Doddsy. Serious but stable. Expected to make it. Call for further update tomorrow am.

Already regretting having turned down the offer of company he tossed the phone from hand to hand, infuriated by his own powerlessness, and distracted himself by calling Tammy. Though it was nearly midnight, he knew she'd answer. She was a night owl, and even if she was back from the crime scene at Grasmere, she'd still be awake. 'Hi, Tammy. I'm just checking in.'

'Oh, hi Chief. Another quiet night for all of us, eh?'

'I'll say. Are you home?'

'I just got in. I'll be back up there tomorrow.'

'You'll want to look for blood in the washing machine or in Brandon's clothes. And yew berries in the garden or in the bin. Seeds removed.' Brandon was an opportunist and, until the end, he'd been a lucky one. Jude passed a hand over his forehead. It would wait. 'That's not why I called. I wanted to make sure Tyrone's okay.'

He stiffened. Becca, close but not too close to Adam Fleetwood, her head bent towards him in conversation, came along down the path from Angel Lane into Great Dockray. He stepped back into the shade and hoped they'd go on past.

'I know he's seen a few grim things already, but this shook him up. He'll get over it. He'll see a lot worse before he gets his pension.'

In all probability there wasn't much worse than seeing someone you cared for going up in flames like a human torch and if Jude wasn't mistaken Tyrone had quickly become as fond of Doddsy as he was himself, though in a very different way. Maybe Tammy hadn't worked that out, or maybe she was using her robust common sense as a shield against so many of the grim things she herself had seen. 'It wasn't great.'

'I hear Doddsy's going to be okay, though.'

'So they tell me.'

Becca and Adam came closer. Jude's voice must have given him away, because Adam turned and flicked a very obvious glance towards him. 'Well, well,' he said to Becca in a voice that was meant to be heard. 'Look who it is.'

'See you later,' Jude said to Tammy.

'You look after yourself, Chief.'

He ended the call and stuck the phone and both hands deep into his pockets, before turning towards Becca and Adam to show exactly how mature he was and exactly how little he cared. 'Evening.'

Becca flicked a quick look at him, remembering. 'It's your birthday, isn't it? Happy birthday.'

The two of them had stopped, and she did a little shuffle on the spot, as if she wanted to keep moving. She'd done something to her hair so that it looked blonder than normal even under the streetlight, and she'd puffed it up so that it looked attractively casual. A whiff of scent drifted across to him. So it was a special night out with Adam, and she'd made an effort. Why shouldn't she? 'Thanks.'

'Oh, of course. Happy birthday.' Adam, the obvious, the only candidate for those thirty pieces of silver, was pretending to forget. For a moment Jude regretted a lost friendship – a decade of birthday drinks, a long night out in Berlin during a shared Interrail trip, a wild camp on elvellyn to watch a midsummer sunrise. Change had come on them too soon. 'Friends all busy, are they? Or don't u have any anymore?'

After a few drinks he'd always been a braggart, the big an playing to the gallery. Prison, it appeared, hadn't done ything to change that, but now there was no audience for m but Becca because Jude wasn't going to join in. 'I was orking late. I expect I'll go out for a few pints tomorrow.' e flicked a look to Becca, who avoided it. If there had been opportunity, he might still have sought a sympathetic ear om her. She knew Doddsy and was fond of him. *I nearly st my best friend tonight*, he might have said to her, and e'd have listened.

Adam took a step forward, his body tense with a dden shot of aggression, and it was left to Becca to avert nfrontation, reaching out a hand to his, fingers just uching as if she held him on an invisible silken leash. ome on, Adam. Let's go.'

'I'll see you about.' Foregoing the fish and chips, Jude ted for discretion, sliding back into the car and picking his phone. He'd made a mistake. 'Ash. Sorry. I wasn't in great mood earlier. Can I change my mind?' She'd been ht and he couldn't bear being alone.

'Of course.' She sounded as though she was expecting his ll. 'Come on over. Or would you rather I came to your ace?'

His house would be cold and that damning package ould be waiting for him on the mat. 'I'll come to you, if u don't mind.'

'I'm about to order pizza. Shall I get some for you?'

Relief washed over him. 'Ham and mushroom. Large.'

'I'll see you.'

He flicked off the phone, tossed it onto the front seat a headed the short distance to Ashleigh's house. At the end Great Dockray he passed Becca and Adam, their touchi fingers now a firm hold of hands.

It would have been easy to talk to Becca but she'd mad clear to him that he didn't deserve her goodwill any long and now she'd found a replacement. He hoped, genuin he thought, that she'd be happy without him.

ACKNOWLEDGEMENTS

There are many people to thank for their help. First up, like so many authors I've benefited hugely from the support of the online community in terms of advice, answers to research questions and general moral support. Perhaps bizarrely, I have to thank the Romantic Novelists' Association, from whose members I learned a lot about writing in general, and about persistence in particular. Thanks also to the CWA and other Facebook groups for sage advice.

If I listed everyone who's helped me I'd have an acknowledgements section as long as the book itself, but as usual special thanks go to my online friends the Beta Buddies. Without their constant encouragement, virtual hugs and constructive criticism I would have given up long ago.

I must give a special shout out to Liz Taylorson, who advised me on all things Wordsworth, wrote Cody's academic biography for me and came up with the title of her book.

And, of course, I must apologise to anyone who may have stumbled over my browsing history…

Once my book had reached the "completed" stage I

couldn't have progressed without the help I got from my agent, Anne Williams, and from the team at Aria Fiction. (Shoutout to Hannah Smith and her colleagues!)

Lastly, of course, I have to thank my family... who put up with a lot.

About the Author

Jo Allen was born in Wolverhampton and is a graduate of Edinburgh, Strathclyde and the Open University. After a career in economic consultancy she took up writing and was first published under the name Jennifer Young in genres of short stories, romance and romantic suspense. In 2017 she took the plunge and began writing the genre she most likes to read – crime. Now living in Edinburgh, she spends as much time as possible in the English Lakes. In common with all her favourite characters, she loves football (she's a season ticket holder with her beloved Wolverhampton Wanderers) and cats.

Hello from Aria

We hope you enjoyed this book! If you did let us know, we'd love to hear from you.

We are Aria, a dynamic digital-first fiction imprint from award-winning independent publishers Head of Zeus. At heart, we're committed to publishing fantastic commercial fiction – from romance and sagas to crime, thrillers and historical fiction. Visit us online and discover a community of like-minded fiction fans!

We're also on the look out for tomorrow's superstar authors. So, if you're a budding writer looking for a publisher, we'd love to hear from you. You can submit your book online at ariafiction.com/we-want-read-your-book

You can find us at:
Email: aria@headofzeus.com
Website: www.ariafiction.com
Submissions: www.ariafiction.com/we-want-read-your-book

@ariafiction
@Aria_Fiction
@ariafiction

Printed in Great Britain
by Amazon

51095634R00178